# TEASING THE PRINCESS

### NANA MALONE

## COPYRIGHT

This is a work of fiction. Names, characters, places, and incidents either are the product of the author's imagination or are used fictitiously, and any resemblance to actual persons living or dead, business establishments, events, or locales, is entirely coincidental.

Teasing the Princess

Cover Art by Amy Daws

Photography by Wander Aguilar

Edited by Angie Ramey

Published in the United States of America

# ONE

*Ariel*

Something was very wrong.

From the mounted cameras in Jessa's apartment, I couldn't see the princess. She wasn't in her apartment, and she wasn't scheduled to be out. Roone was on duty and hadn't reported in that she was leaving.

I angled the cameras, turning them just so, and then I could see it.

*A body.*

Judging by the size, it was a male.

Giving zero shits about someone seeing me with a gun, I shoved mine into my holster and bolted across the hall.

This was supposed to be bloody easy. Roone was supposed to go over there and tell her the truth. Simple. Sure, I had expected yelling. I had expected screaming. I hadn't expected a vanishing act.

I found the door slightly ajar and pulled my gun from my hoslter.

The good news was I knew where the hell Roone was. The bad news was the man on the floor.

"Fuck. Oh God! Roone. Wake up!"

What was wrong with him? I checked his pulse, and it was slow but steady. I checked him over for injuries, but I didn't see any blood. Shit, what the hell was wrong with him? Had his dick atrophied or something? Could you die from that? What was that thing that happened when you had a hard on for longer than four hours? Could that kill you?

Then I saw it. In the hollow between his shoulder and neck... a tranquilizer dart. *Fuck.*

Someone shot him with a tranq gun. Where was the fucking princess?

My heart hammered against my ribs, pounding irregularly. I sucked in short, jagged breaths. *Focus dammit, focus.*

I couldn't freak out. I had a team to run. I tugged my phone out of my back pocket and sent a broadcast out to my crew. "Alert. Alert. No eyes on the princess. No eyes. I repeat, no eyes."

Immediately I started getting responses. "On alert. Searching." If there was any trace of her, they'd find her. I needed to stay here with Roone. *What the fuck had happened?*

He was supposed to tell her the truth, and they'd fight, kiss, and make up, and we'd all go home. My stomach knotted. I wrapped my fingers around the dart in Roone's neck and tugged, wincing as I did so. God, what drug was in the dart? How much had he been given?

*Focus on the task at hand. Find the princess, wake his ass up.*

Calling the police was going to be a problem because they'd want to know who the fuck had access to a dart gun like that. And if it was the princess, I didn't want anyone asking those kinds of questions or alerting anyone else to her whereabouts. Well, anyone other than us.

Going back to my training, I shifted my position to his head, squatted behind him and slid my arms under his shoulders, and then I hauled. Jesus Christ, he was big. If he was awake, he'd probably chuckle and say, *That's what she said.*

"Come on, you stupid giant. I don't know what she gave you, but I need you to wake up. You are my partner. You do not get to die on me. Not today."

I hauled and pulled and bent and twisted and prayed. *Come on, Roone. Come on.* It took me a good fifteen minutes, but I was finally able to move him to the couch. First, I had to squat and use my legs to get his top half up on the couch, and then I bent down to move his legs.

I took his shoes off before I ran to the bathroom for wash-cloths. Cool ones. I wet them and placed them on his forehead and the back of his neck. If she tranqued him, then it wasn't like he'd taken something. I hesitated to give him any drugs to wake him up. *Do you have time for that?*

God, did I? I didn't think I did. But I had to make sure he was safe. I knew what the king would want in that respect.

I ran my hands through my hair. *Think. Think. Think.* I didn't know what she'd given him, so waking him up with any kind of counteragent could cost his life. But if I didn't wake him up soon, then the Princess would be further out of our grasp. How would we find her?

*The recordings, you have them all.* Hell yeah, I did. I ran back across the hall, unplugged the laptop, then hauled the wires and all the other extra equipment with me as I ran back to Jessa's flat.

I did a quick and dirty connection and pulled up the feed over the last hour and a half since I'd last spoken to Roone, and then I hit Play. Jessa had come back. She looked ill. Clutching her stomach, pausing every now and again to take deep breaths.

Was she sick? Had she just simply gone to the doctor? No, she wouldn't have left Roone here.

*And hello, someone tranqued his ass.*

Had someone tranqued her as well and taken her?

I tapped my foot anxiously as I watched. I lifted my brow when Jessa moved her book case, aimed her elbow, and slammed it into the dry wall.

*Holy shit.*

And then she reached in and pulled out a bag.

That was tradecraft. Who the fuck taught her tradecraft?

It occurred to me then that not only had I underestimated her, but we had grossly overlooked something. Had her father taught her this? But how would her father have known?

On the video, she grabbed a few other things and shoved them in the bag. Then she turned her head quickly as if listening for something. Maybe a knock at the door.

I glanced over at Roone. "Was that you?"

Jessa continued packing and then sat in her bedroom for a few moments. Finally, Roone gave up and just barged in. They spoke for a moment. Then Jessa reached in the bag for—oh God, was that a gun?

I tried one of the recorded videos from another camera angle.

It was certainly shaped like a gun. I couldn't see that well, so I tried another camera angle. Oh yeah, that was the one. The two of them exchanged words. Roone had his hands up trying to talk to her, and then she fired. So that was confirmation that she'd run instead of being taken. That only made me feel slightly better.

After tranquilizing Roone, Jessa shoved the weapon back in her bag and was out the door in seconds. So, we had a runaway princess on our hands. Given her father's surprising skillset at hiding her over the years, it might be even harder to find her now.

---

*Jessa*

MY HANDS SHOOK.

*Holy shit!* I'd shot him. I'd shot Roone.

*You didn't shoot him. You tranqued him. It's different.*

Yes, that was true. At first, I hadn't known what the hell a tranq gun was doing in there. I'd assumed maybe it was for dogs or wild animals or something, but it ended up coming in very handy. *Unless, of course, whatever was in there kills him.*

That started the worry and panic all over again.

*Stop. He is working for them, the people who've come after you.*

Hell, I was sounding as nutters as my father. Who were those people? Now that I was on the train with really only one destination in mind, I started to think through what I knew. Unfortunately, that was next to nothing. What I knew was that Roone knew both the man who was supposedly my biological father and his son. That was all the information I had.

*Of course, just like your old man, you panicked and fled.* But it wasn't exactly a panic and call the police situation... especially considering the fact I'd used a tranq gun on my boyfriend. Guns were illegal in the UK. I was the one headed for the nick if I went to the police.

I'd panicked. He had been banging on the door right after I had just found out the truth. My mind raced to all the times we'd been together, all the times where he'd had opportunities to hurt me but hadn't.

*But he lied.*

Okay, he didn't exactly lie, but it was definitely an omission. He knew those people, the prince and the king. He'd been in a lot of pictures, and from the looks of it, he *more* than knew them. So what the hell was he doing *here*? And he certainly hadn't come clean with the whole picture of why he was in my life.

That was the truth. He had been lying about everything from who he was to what was he doing in London with me. What I needed to find out was how dangerous they were to me. How dangerous *he* was to me.

I didn't have very many places to go for answers, so I went to the only source I had. The only person who would have information.

I got off the train at King's Cross, and then I followed the directions I had and strode down the road to Phillip's office. I checked the university website for his office hours, hoping I might to be able to speak to him further.

I'd texted him to ask if he had time to see me when I'd run out of my flat, but he hadn't texted back. But given that I really had nowhere else to go, he was my first logical stop.

I asked the receptionist where I would find his office, and she directed me up the stairs to the right. The tread was well worn. I could see the obvious traffic pattern of students going to and from over the years from the scuffs on the wood to the dirt on the banisters.

The walls looked freshly painted, as if it had been done within the last year or so. Announcements were tacked along next to the windows for tutoring, and flatmates, and cars. When I reached his office, I knocked.

"Come in." When I opened the door and poked my head in, his eyes went wide. "Jessa. Did we make an appointment?"

I shook my head. "I'm so sorry to just pop in on you like this. I—" My voice wavered, and I stopped myself, clasping my hands together to keep them from shaking. I continued, "I just need more information and I—"

He stood abruptly. "Of course. Have a seat."

I was grateful for it because my legs were just about to give out on me. I'd already fainted once today. I really didn't want a repeat.

"The paramedics said that you would be okay."

"Yeah, I just—I wasn't really okay. And then I started to think and realized you are the only one with answers for me. I'm so sorry, I should have called." I shifted on my feet, feeling self-conscious.

He picked up his phone. "From the looks of it, you did. But I was busy, you know, papers."

"Of course. Again, I'm so sorry."

He held up his hands. "No don't worry about it. We can talk all you want. And if you like, I can drive you home when we're done chatting. I don't want you taking the train. Not after earlier."

"No!" *Okay, way too forceful.* "I mean, I, um probably won't be staying at my place for a bit. You know, boyfriend issues, so I think maybe it's best to just get a hotel or something."

He frowned. "Has something happened?"

I shook my head. "No. If you could just tell me more about my father and the file you gave me, I—"

He sighed. "I was afraid it would be too much of a shock. I'll tell you what I know. Most of it is historical knowledge."

I could see the light at the end of the tunnel dimming, and I couldn't let that hope vanish. "Anything. Please. I will take any information you have."

"Okay, well, the Winston Isles is an island nation in the Caribbean, but I know that they have a British military agreement. If Britain goes to war, then Winston Isles provides its servicemembers. If Winston Isles should ever need troops,

British Isles will send some. They're not exactly part of the Commonwealth, but they have that agreement. Although, I don't think their royals are connected or related to ours here. From what I understand, their first king became monarch after an uprising."

"Th-they had a war?"

He waved his hands again. "Oh gosh, not recently. If I remember my history correctly, it was the 18th Century or so. Their first monarch was victorious in winning separation from England, and the people made him king. King Jackson."

I licked my lips. "Do you have any books? I would love those books."

He nodded. "Sure. There's nothing a man of my profession loves more than books. When your father's delusions started, as I believed them to be at the time, I tried to learn as much about them as much as possible."

He pulled an ancient-looking volume from his bookshelf then brought it over to me as he dusted it off. "I was curious about the place your father was so fixated on, so I researched. I think this book has the history, at least the more recent history going back two hundred years or so. From what I remember of that, there were two generations of succession scandal. The one that pertains the most to the situation is the scandal about King Rhyse, your grandfather, being named the king out of turn. There are people who believe that King Rhyse's uncle, Angelus, was supposed to be king."

I frowned. "I don't understand. My grandfather wasn't supposed to be king?"

"No. He was *named* King. As he was not yet twenty-five when his father Cyrus died, Angelus, Cyrus's brother was supposed to be named regent. The law at the time stated that if the crown prince was under twenty-five years of age at the time of the prior king's death, the regent is supposed to sit on the throne until the crown prince is thirty. At that point, it was the duty of the Regent's Council to determine if the prince should be deposed or if he is fit to lead. But King Cyrus forced a change to the constitution right before his death to put Rhyse on the throne. There are some factions that did not accept the change. Angelus would likely have been named the king if Rhyse was found unfit at thirty. He was a bit of a wastrel in his youth, but keep in mind that in those days, anything could have been made up to make him seem unfit." He shrugged. "There is nothing some won't do to hold on to power."

"So in the minds some faction somewhere, I'm not royalty."

Phillip's smile was soft. "That's correct. They call themselves the Heirs of Angelus. According to them Angelus's descendants would be in line. And keep in mind that's separate of the scandal when King Roland, Rhyse's eldest son, abdicated and his brother, your father, Cassius was named king. At the time, Roland didn't have any children, so Cassius was the legitimate choice. But there are those who think that Roland's heirs should be on the throne. And if they could find a way to depose the current monarch, then Roland's heirs would be in line."

I chewed my bottom lip. "But the second scandal isn't really a scandal because Roland made the choice to abdicate and didn't have any children at the time."

He nodded. "You're right. But when it comes to wealth and power, people will do anything to gain it and hold on."

"But in truth, Angelus's heirs weren't really the rightful heirs anyway if he was going to force a council vote in his favor. He was making his own power grab."

Phillip shrugged. "That is the way of kings and kingdoms. If history books are to be believed, and if all had gone according to plan, then Angelus's descendent should be on the throne. I think you would still be a princess, though a minor one. And you know, worthy of all trappings, I suppose, but no, not the in-line-to-the-throne kind of Princess."

I shook my head. "Jesus Christ. This is such a trip."

"Well yes, of course. It's not every day one finds out one is royalty."

"But I'm not. I'm just *me*."

He nodded. "I understand. Maybe not as well as you do, but I get the idea. From what I understand, the current prince, what is his name again?" He frowned as he tried to remember. "Yes, Lucas."

"Lucas? The name doesn't sound very regal."

He shrugged. "Well, that's because it's not. He wasn't a prince until just recently. I saw something on it in *Hello!* or some other magazine."

"You read *Hello!*?"

He grinned. "I have to keep up with my students, don't I? Anyway, he was a regular bloke, and then the new king went on a hunt for him. He's an illegitimate child of the previous king, like you."

"Wow, I guess so when you put it like that."

Phillip shook his head. "Honestly, I wouldn't get too in your head about it. Your father loved you, that's all that matters."

"Yeah, but which father?"

He frowned. "Well, your father Andrew, the man who raised you and tried to protect you. If he was afraid of these people, there must have been a reason."

I shook my head. "I know. It only makes sense that there would have been a reason, but if they went looking for Lucas and made him a prince when they found him, why would they be looking for me to hurt me?"

"I don't know. Obviously, I'm not a royal. But with your father's illness as a factor, maybe they thought he was influenced by others. You know how these things go. History is littered with stories of entanglements and spats. It could be anything."

"I have to find out."

He frowned. "I think you need to be careful. What if they *are* trying to hurt you?"

*He has a point there.* "I feel like I owe it to myself. I need to find out. I need to understand who these people are, if any of this is even true. We have to consider the source. My father, after all... I mean, honestly."

Phillip sat on the edge of his desk. "Jessa, I'm afraid for you. Because if your father was right and you were actually in danger, then these people should be dealt with warily. I don't think you waltzing in and saying 'Hi, I'm your sister' is the safest approach."

"Well, I'm not suggesting that I would walk up to them and do such a thing. I'm just thinking that I should find out more about them. Maybe there's no danger. Maybe my father was just a very sick man. Maybe I spent my life hiding for nothing. Maybe these other people from this Heirs of Angelus faction are really the ones who want to hurt me."

He swallowed as he nodded slowly. "And maybe you spent your life hiding for a very good reason. I would just tread lightly. I feel very protective of you. I wouldn't want any harm to come to you."

"I think that's a risk I need to take. I have been hiding my whole life, and it's time to stop doing that. I don't want to hide anymore."

"I just want you to be careful and aware of what you're doing."

"I am." At least, I thought I was.

*Then how do you explain the tranq gun in your bag?*

"Good. From what I understand of the previous king, Cassius, he made a lot of enemies. And your father was very afraid. I just wouldn't want you thinking that this is the instant family you've been looking for."

"I'm not looking to run away from or toward anything. I loved my father. But I owe it to myself to find out the whole truth. And maybe these people can give it to me."

"Maybe. But read that book first. It paints a picture of people who would do anything to stay in power. And if you're going to walk right into their lives and give them access to the one thing they have been wanting all these years—you—a certain risk comes with that."

He had a point. What if they were really dangerous? What if they were going to make me marry some horrible ally? What if this was some kind of princess job?

*You have an overly active imagination.*

"I appreciate everything you've told me. You've been so helpful. I think I know what I need to do."

"Let me guess. What you need involves going to the Winston Isles?"

"Yeah, it does. I need to know what I'm dealing with, *who* I'm dealing with. I'll be careful. They won't even know I'm there. I will go as quietly as possible. No one knows who I am." Except they'd sent someone to watch me. It couldn't be a coincidence that Roone lived across the corridor and worked with me. But I needed some answers, and the only way I was going to get them was to go to the Winston Isles.

# TWO

*Roone*

My mouth tasted like someone had packed it with alcohol-soaked cotton. What the hell? I tried to lift my head, but very large, very heavy elephants stormed through, determined that I should keep it down. I tried again though, and as soon as I did, a wave of nausea and dizziness hit me. My stomach cramped, and oh shit, something was coming up, and it was going to be a rocky road.

*Breathe. Easy does it. Fight the urge.*

I tried to talk, but any movement just made me more nauseous. Someone or something strong was attempting to roll me over. Just in time too, because I wretched. Oh, and lucky me, there was a bucket.

I was pretty certain I was going to die. But fucking aye, this was going to be a shitty way to die. And today was not a good day to die.

I had to do something. I tried to force my brain to focus and function, but something was stopping it. Oh yeah, what was that?

"Easy there, killer. Let it out. Let it all out of your system."

I knew that voice. "Who?" God, talking was such an effort. "What... happened?"

The voice was female and *tsked* at me. "Well, it seems like the princess shot you full of some ketamine cocktail. I called the doctor. Don't move your arm too much. You have an IV in it. It's flushing your system."

An IV? Who was talking? An American? The voice was familiar. Not grating, but I wanted to be irritated at it. I peeled my lids open and then shut them quickly. "God, that hurts."

"Yeah, it's going to hurt," the voice muttered. And then something was sliding over my face. I blinked again. Suddenly the piercing light was gone. Shades? "Thank you."

"Yeah, I never thought you'd actually say those words to me."

"Who drugged me?"

"The princess, Jessa. She shot you with a tranq gun."

I frowned, trying to sort the words out. *Princess.* Oh God, the princess. *Princess.* I needed to find the princess. I forced myself to a sitting position, and the room spun.

"Nope, you're not going anywhere. And don't move your fucking arm. As big as you are, apparently you have little tiny veins. It took forever to get the IV in your arm."

"IV?" I peeled my eyes open again and stared at my arm. Shit. That *was* an IV. I swung my head up looking for the beeps and bleeps of hospital monitors, but there weren't any. Instead I saw bookshelves, sparse walls... *Jessa. Jessa's apartment.*

Slowly it started to click. I'd come to find Jessa, to talk to her, to tell her the truth. But why was I here? And then she'd been angry. She wouldn't listen. Then she'd shot me. Tranq gun. Which meant that the voice... I blinked again. *Ariel.*

"You need to find Jessa."

"Do you think I don't know that? I'm already on it. The

whole team is out. It's just you and me here. I brought the coms in here, as well as the monitor. The team is out looking for her, trying to track her movements. She hasn't used her cards. Not even her Oyster card. She's probably using cash, which leaves us nowhere. But we're hitting up anyone that she may know. I've got men sitting at Chloe's place."

My tongue felt like it wanted to stick permanently to the roof of my mouth. "I feel bad."

"Yeah, you're going to feel it. She gave you enough to fell a horse. And even though you're as big as one, you're not going to feel too peachy for a while. But the IV solution I gave you should make it all go away faster."

"I feel like shite."

"Yeah, that's normal."

I tried again to push myself up, and Ariel swore at me as she helped me to a sitting position. The room spun less this time. Okay, so the IV was working, getting rid of whatever the fuck was in that tranq.

"Everything went bad."

"Yeah, I see the hole in the wall. I don't know how much money she's got on her, but it could be enough to stay hidden for a while."

"I fucked up."

"No, *you* didn't fuck up. *We all* fucked up. We were behind the curve from the moment we got here. We need to catch up. There's something else going on. Something we're missing, because there's no reason she should have run. She's fucking in love with you."

I tried to shake my head. "She doesn't love me." Hard truths. Also, I should not have shaken my head because it just made the room spin.

"You know nothing about women, do you? I see the way she looks at you. What made her run? I watched that tape backward and forward, and you didn't do a thing, surprisingly."

"Arsehole."

"I told you, I'm a bitch, not an asshole."

"Call home."

"Yeah, I've already called. They're supposed to call me back at ten."

"Huh, where is she?"

"You relax. There's nothing you can do anyway. You're fucked up. Until this shit leaves your system, you're grounded."

I tried to shake my head again, having forgotten the lesson I had just learned. I stopped abruptly. "No. Find Jessa. Need her... understand."

"Yeah, I get you, but I need you at your best to find her, and that's going to take time."

After a few minutes, Ariel brought me tea with too much sugar in it. I groaned and tried not to drink it, but she insisted. "You need the sugar. It's also going to help you process all that shit inside you. Come on."

The more I sipped the cup, the better I felt. I hated it when she was right. Then she tried to shove food inside me. The last thing on earth I wanted was to eat, but the fucking crumpets were goddamn delicious. I was able to wash them down with tea, and the moment they hit my stomach, I first thought it would cramp and reject, but then it felt like sweet nectar. *How long have I been lying here?* "Long, out..."

"You were out for three fucking hours. I think I got to you not long after she left though, so I've had everyone looking for her that long."

A phone rang. I turned my head toward it, and Ariel put it on speaker. "What the fuck happened?" Sebastian asked.

Ariel sighed. "The princess, it seems, had a go bag. Something spooked her. She took off. She tranqued Roone on her way out."

Sebastian swore. "What the fuck? Why did she have a go bag? And is Roone okay?"

Ariel shifted a glance to me. "Yeah, I had a doctor bring over an IV. Another hour or two and most of it should be out of his system. But he's out of commission for the moment."

Sebastian gave a series of colorful curses.

Penny's voice came on the line. "Okay, any idea how long she had before you found Roone?"

Ariel shrugged. "I'm not sure, and Roone obviously has no way of knowing. But from the tape, it looked like minutes. I'll watch again and fully assess, but it wasn't long. The problem is she paid cash for a taxi. Then she could have taken a train to anywhere in the city. It will take longer to find her. I've already got programmers working on getting access to the CCTV cameras. Then I'll be able to access them and track the taxi. I'll find her."

Sebastian's voice was firm. "Stay there. Find her. If you can't find her in a couple of days, come home. We need to regroup."

I frowned and tried to shake my head. "Not going home. Jessa needs me."

Sebastian's voice went into his *I mean business* register. "That is an order. You have forty-eight hours."

I groaned as I tried to shift. "I'm finding her. It's my responsibility."

"Ariel, give him an order. Forty-eight hours. If nothing turns up, the mission is cancelled. Come home."

Sebastian and Penny hung up.

Ariel's voice was soft. "Look, I get it. You care about her. You're blaming yourself right now. But that won't help. And you can't antagonize Sebastian."

"I'm not afraid of him. I vowed that I would bring his sister home, and that's what I'm going to do."

"And if you get killed in the process?"

I shrugged. "At least I've kept my word."

———

*Jessa*

THE MOTEL WAS NOT EXACTLY where I would normally want to stay. But I needed someplace that would accept cash, so the Travel Lodge it was.

I held my phone in my hand, knowing what I needed to do, but not able to do it yet. Hell, at that point Roone would have been an easier call to make. But I couldn't call Roone and make him explain. Phillip had a point. I didn't know him. I didn't know any of these people. But this other call I couldn't avoid.

If they were in on a plot to hurt me, I wasn't going to let it stop me. I needed to do this. I needed to figure all of this out, understand who I was dealing with, and then decide on a plan. But I couldn't make that plan if I was worried about what was going to happen for the rest of my life. So I pressed one and made the call. Evan answered on the first ring. "Jessa. Is everything all right?"

I never called on the weekends, so of course, he was worried.

"Yes. I'm fine." God, I was the worst liar. "Um, I just wanted to say that I'll be taking some of my holiday."

There was a bit of silence. "Excuse me?"

"Yes, you know I have some vacation time banked. I... I need to take some of it."

"Is there something wrong?"

"No. I just... you know, it's been a while since I've had a break, and honestly I'm exhausted. I really am. So I think it's best if I just take some time and relax, have some fun, you know, that sort of thing."

I could tell his brain was trying to process. "So, just like that?"

"I'm so sorry. I know this probably puts us in a bit of a bind, but I just... you know, I'm tired, exhausted."

Again, more silence from him. "Well, I mean, if you need a few days..."

"I'll be taking a week." I said it definitively.

"A week? We're in the middle of the entire revamp with London Lords. You can't take a week."

"Well, I need at least a week. It's been two years since I've even taken a day off, Evan. I'm sorry."

"You're not giving me any advance notice?"

"No, I'm not. I don't feel well. I've been getting sick. It's time. I'm sorry. But Chloe is up to date on everything, and if there are any last-minute questions, I will be available by phone. I promise. But I would really rather nobody called, because like I said, I need a vacation."

"If there's something you need that we could do differently, we could."

"No, there's nothing I need done differently. I just need a break. And I'll be available by phone. I've never asked for anything. Maybe this time you could just not ask a ton of questions?"

He sighed. "Well, okay. I'll come by your flat and we can discuss this further. I'm worried about you."

Why did he want to stop by my flat? That was not the kind of relationship we had. "I'm not home. I've headed out of town to clear my head."

"What? Jessa this is very untoward. You should have discussed all of this with me."

"I know Evan, and I am so sorry. I just can't do this right now."

"And what am I supposed to tell Rick?"

"Well, I called you because I was hoping you would understand. You were my mentor. You know I don't take time off. You know how hard I've worked for the team."

"Yes. Obviously, yes, you've worked hard. It's just such a short notice."

"I know."

"Fine. As long as Chloe knows the status of everything, we'll manage."

"Thank you so much. I appreciate it."

I sighed, relieved. There was no way I could manage what I'd just learned while also having to work every day. I felt like I was such a prima donna, but it couldn't be helped. There was no way I was going to survive, otherwise.

I hung up with him and ran my hands through my hair. My fingers got stuck in the curls and knots. I needed to shower and deep condition. Some time under a dryer would make me feel more like myself.

I glanced at my ticket to the Winston Isles. I was headed for a place I knew nothing about, to people I didn't know, to see if I could uncover the mystery of where I came from.

Yeah, it sounded like a totally smart thing to do.

# THREE

*Jessa*

I HATED TO SAY IT, but the Winston Isles felt like I belonged.

Everywhere I turned there was the distant sound of calypso music. The fragrant flowers in the air didn't necessarily remind me of a permanent vacation, but they smelled like belonging. The faint, sweet nectar had been a constant since I'd woken up here the day before.

Then there was the water. It was the first place I'd gone after the plane. I'd dropped everything in my room and walked out to the ocean. Hell, I couldn't even swim. But the moment I put my feet in that bath-water-warm ocean, the soft waves lapping at my toes, my body instantly relaxed.

Maybe it was the vacation vibe. Maybe that was all this was. I'd lived a hard several years in a row, and I just needed a break. I was willing to accept that. After all, it made sense. But there was a part of me that felt like I belonged here. I felt like these were my people. Which was exciting, terrifying, worrying. After all, I'd always thought I knew exactly who I was. But I didn't, did I?

But in the short time that I'd been exploring the islands and watching my potential family, I knew I might need more time here.

*Do you need more time, or do you want to stay?*

I didn't think I should *want* to stay. I didn't think I should feel anything. But, sitting in the café atop the White Croft Hotel, watching the pretty blond with the pixie cut hair, and the brunette with the shiny straight locks hanging down her back, I wondered if they could be my family.

*Or were they the enemy?*

They didn't *look* like the enemy. Not like I would even know what the enemy looked like. These women, they looked like me. Like me and Chloe out to lunch. Completely normal.

*Except they sent someone into your midst to spy on you.* Normal people didn't do that. These women, with their lattes and wide smiles, on the outside, they looked like everyone else. On the inside there was something... different.

Out of the corner of my eye, I watched as a man built like an oak silently walked up the stairs. I only noticed him because he reminded me of Roone. My gut clenched with that fleeting thought.

But, as big as he was, he was silent. Shoulders much wider than Roone's. This guy was built for coverage, or for football. American football. Rugby, maybe. But he was also very tall. He smiled at the two women at the table and then took a post at one of the corners. He grabbed a seat and a glass of water. He just sat there, never adjusting his sunglasses, but casually enjoying his day in the sunshine.

As far as I could tell around the sunglasses, his gaze stayed on the women. Yeah, he was worth noting, but only for a similarity to Roone. Other than that, I should have ignored him, except for the second and third men that walked up the stairs, both as tall, neither as broad. But they had that same ease of movement, as if they were well acquainted with exactly how their bodies moved and how to make them most efficient. They were bodyguards. All three of them.

Is that what Roone was? Or was he a killer? Or something else entirely?

But I'd never been in danger with him. At least, none that I felt. But I had no idea who he really was, so what the hell did I know?

After the third man took an opposite corner of the first and the second one sat closer to the women, a pretty black girl jogged up the stairs. There was something about the way she moved too. Her smile was easy, relaxed. But she still moved efficiently. That was until she tripped on one of the stones on the patio and went flying. Bodyguard number two was up out of his chair as if he fully expected this and caught her easily. When he placed her back on her feet, she smoothed her skirt, tucked her blouse back in, and then beamed him a wide grin.

Wow, that smile was full of sunshine and light.

She'd also dropped her purse, so the contents spilled everywhere. The two women at the table jumped down to help her pick them up. One of the tubes of lipstick rolled toward the bar though, and no one noticed it.

The woman wore enormous shades that completely covered her face, but from the looks of it, she was Queen Penelope Winston, my supposed brother's wife. I'd been surprised to learn that there was a brown princess. Well, I supposed England had one now, so it must be good enough for everyone.

And she was beautiful, if not exactly princess-like. Her hair was a wild disarray of curls, and well, there was just something inelegant about her. She was extremely clumsy. Over the course of the last day, I had watched her trip, nearly fall, get her clothes stuck on hooks, and generally need assistance on all manner of things. But she was also strong, not a complete disaster.

A car had backfired the day before, and her bodyguards dove for her, but she had jumped to cover a little boy who had been walking behind her. With zero care for herself, she'd fully covered him, tucked him in her protective arms, and rolled to the ground with him. But it hadn't been whatever kind of threat she'd thought it was, just a backfiring car. When she stood, she'd checked him over to make sure he was okay, and then her guards tucked her under their arms and she fought them the whole way.

I didn't know her, but I liked her already. I knew who the other two were as well; her soon to be sister-in-law Bryna Tressel, and Bryna's best friend, Jinx. It wasn't like I had a full dossier on the women like I did on the men, but a question or two around town and the gossip magazines told me exactly who they were.

I knew I probably wouldn't get straight answers from the king or the prince, not that I'd be able to get anywhere near them, but these three... these three were up for the taking.

I finished my drink, stood up from my seat, walked over to the bar, and picked up the tube of lipstick. Then with a deep breath, I marched over to the girls. "Excuse me, I think you may have dropped this when you dropped your purse."

I had taken off my sunglasses so that she could see my eyes and sense my sincerity in them. The blonde's gaze flickered up, and then she coughed. "Oh my God. I love your skirt."

I had worn a floral, A-line paneled skirt with a petticoat underneath it. I don't know, it sort of felt islandish. I was taken aback by the compliment. "Oh, thank you. Uh, it's vintage."

Bryna smiled widely at me. "My God, your skin is amazing. What do you use?"

"Honestly? Cheap soap and water. Mostly good genes from my mother."

My gaze landed on the princess, or rather, the queen. Her

dark eyes were smiling, and her lips faltered a little but then broke into a wide grin. "Sometimes you've just got to use what works. Thank you for grabbing my lipstick."

She looked like she wanted to say something, but she didn't. And I had no idea what to do at that point.

I was so stupid. Had I thought I'd just walk up to them and invite myself to sit down? I should have had a better plan, and if I didn't do something quick, I was going to blow this opportunity.

Well, how can I turn that table?

As I turned to go, it was Jinx who called out. "Wait, someone with a sense of style that good, I need in my life. As you can see, I could use the help. Do you like fashion?"

Fashion, no. I never really had the time for clothes. I got one of those services that deliver clothes to my door, because well, I'd spent most of my time taking care of my father and working. But I was happy to fake it.

"No. I just sort of wear whatever I like."

Jinx nodded. "Yeah, me too. Except, the things that I like never seem to go together, so I always look a little crazy."

Bryna tapped her arm. "Don't listen to her. She always looks great." There was a bit of silence as if none of them knew what to say, and there I was, awkwardly standing there stalking them. *Ugh, I'm the worst at this.*

It was Jinx who came through again. "Well, um, I accept all the shopping help. I feel like I haven't seen you around town before, and the Winston Isles is so small. You must be a tourist."

"Um, sort of. I'm thinking of moving," I said noncommittally.

Penny beamed at this. "Well, it is a beautiful island. If you would like some tour guides, we got you."

"Yeah, I'd love it. And as payment, I can pick you up something in a boutique," I said to Jinx.

She beamed at me. Bryna watched me carefully, but she was friendly. Her body language was open. She just seemed quieter. Did she know?

She gave no indication that she knew who I was. And she really shouldn't, but I didn't know anything for sure. I needed to tread carefully. "Yeah that seems great."

Finally, Bryna perked up. "Well, if you are here as a tourist, then you need to join us. We're having some drinks and dinner." She reached out her hand and introduced herself. "I'm Bryna."

I hadn't thought this through, I didn't have a fake name to use, so I pulled one out of my ass just in time. "Hi, I'm Jessica."

Penny shook my hand too. "Just call me Penny. Nice to meet you Jessica."

I shook Jinx's hand as well. It looked like I'd made some friends, in theory. I swallowed the bite of unease as I easily lied to them. But if I wanted answers, I needed to get close. They seemed nice. *Stop thinking of them as your friends, because they may be very well be the enemy.*

I didn't normally like to think in those terms, but it was time I started being my father's daughter, and I needed to be more careful.

---

Penny

*HOLY SHIT.*

I could barely keep it together. For weeks, months we had been looking for this girl. And she just strolled up to us and handed me my lipstick?

Everyone, even Jinx, was able to play it cool. And if Ariel were here, she'd be the easiest one of us all. She was a master of effortless nonchalance. Luckily, we'd been able to pull it off.

Hopefully I'd come across as nice and charming and hadn't scared her off.

Hell, we'd even invited her out. The key was to *not* tell my husband.

Easier said than done because Sebastian was far too interested in gossip.

"So, you're really not gonna tell me what happened at lunch?"

"Why is it even interesting?" I typed in my PIN code on the keypad, opening the door to my office. I knew what Sebastian was here for—an afternoon quickie. As if I had no work to do. He might've grounded me from field work, but I was still an intelligence operative, so I actually had work to do not just royal engagements.

It felt good to do charity work, and it felt good to work on programs that connected youth to the joys of the arts. That work was rewarding. It was the endless dinner parties and planning state dinners and deciding which china needed to go with what that bored me to tears. It wasn't me. Sebastian knew it wasn't me. I was just as likely to get paint on the fine china as I was to get some earl or count's name wrong.

I finally just hired someone to do all the planning for me and to work with my mother-in-law. Queen Alexa was more than happy to still be useful. Sometimes she was a bit concerned that she was stepping on my toes, but I assured her nonstop that she was doing me a favor.

I loved being queen. Well, mostly I loved having Sebastian. But there were aspects of the job that I did not love.

And the more royal engagements I did, the less time I had to paint.

And at my core, a painter was still who I was. More often than not, Sebastian would join me in the shower and have to wash some streaks out because I'd been walking around half the day with a streak of white paint on the end of one of my curls and no one told me.

He always kissed my nose and then helped me wash it out. Because he was much happier when I was painting than when I was out in the field.

"Seb, you know I have work to do."

"Uh huh." He closed the door behind us. And then locked it. "I knew what that meant. "Sebastian, we do not have time for this." I giggled even as I said it.

"I can be quick."

"When have you ever been quick?"

His grin was wolfish. "Come on, just a little taste? I don't know. I've been really needing you since this morning."

"Sebastian, we made love twice this morning. I was late to work."

"I know. But just the thought of making a baby, makes me want you all the time. Well, I mean I basically want you all the time anyway. So not much has changed."

I rolled my eyes. "Oh my God, all I said was I was going off birth control. It's going to take some time for the hormones to get out of my system. We're not going to make a baby right away."

"But oh my God, the practice."

"You just want me barefoot and pregnant."

He grinned at that. "Just thinking about that gets me so hot."

"There will be nothing hot about me pregnant."

He shook his head. And then leaned in to nuzzle my neck. "Oh, I beg to differ. Your boobs are going be huge."

I glanced down. "Well, that might be an added benefit to pregnancy." And, a little me and Sebastian. A little boy with his father's eyes. A little too serious, but still full of mischief. A little girl with my smile and wild curls. I could see it now, and there would be a lot more laughter in the palace. Although it worried me with all the danger we'd been through lately. But I knew it was what Sebastian wanted. And I wanted it too. I just wished there was less chaos.

"You are not playing fair. You know how much I like it when you do that."

He nipped at the column of my throat with his teeth. "What? This?" He did it again.

I whimpered. "Not fair."

"Okay, I'll play nice. He backed away a bit. But then he lifted me gently and set me on my desk before he stepped between my thighs and shoved the skirt of my dress up. "Just tell me what you guys talked about today."

"Why does it matter?"

"Well, I want to know if Jinx kicked that guy to the curb or not. Lucas and I have a bet."

"Oh my God, you're ridiculous."

"I know, but still."

"Why are you so nosy? I swear to God, you gossip more than any of us girls do."

"Really, it's Lucas's fault. He bet me a hundred dollars that Jinx keeps that loser of a boyfriend. I said she was too smart."

"You'll have to ask her. Can't the queen have some secrets?"

"As long as her secrets involve whatever puts a smile on her face like that. Tell me, is it me that puts that smile on your lips?"

I giggled. "As if I would have time for anyone else? You are on my ass twenty-four/seven."

His brows lifted. "Well, I don't think that's where it's supposed to go to make a baby, but we can definitely try that."

I groaned. "Oh my God, you're incorrigible."

He grinned. "I mean you're the one who said I need practice, so I need to practice *all* the things to get this whole baby-making thing right. I'm bound to get it wrong once or twice."

He went to nuzzling my neck, and then kissing, and then his

hands slid up my thighs until his thumbs traced the edges of my panties. "Sebastian."

"Yes, my queen."

"You know that queen shit gets me hot."

He chuckled low. "Oh, I know. Your panties are already wet. Is that because I called you my queen? It's just a statement of fact."

I hated to admit it, but something pulled low in my belly whenever he said it. But I think it had less to do with the word than the way he said it. Reverently, like to him, I was everything. Having the total focus of someone like that, someone like Sebastian, on me was its own aphrodisiac. I figured at this rate, I'd be pregnant in a week. "You know what you're doing to me."

His lips grazed mine gently as his thumb stroked over my clit. "Absolutely. And I plan to keep doing it."

"Sebastian, neither one of us has time for this right now."

"Oh, I know." The *zik, zik, zik* sound of the zipper of his jeans tugging down mingled with the sound of my moans. He had my number. He knew how to make me hum in seconds.

And I knew how to make him happy.

I just hoped I'd be able to bring him the one thing I knew would make him happier than anything else in the world. And I wasn't talking about the baby.

---

*Ariel*

I'D FUCKED UP. I'd fucked up big.

What was it about my father that made me ever believe anything he said?

With my teams occupied trying to locate Jessa, I was hard at work trying to locate my father. If anyone could shed some light on what the fuck was going on it would be him.

His passport didn't have any hits, but he had enough friends that he could have easily made it off the islands. He could have chartered a flight from any of the smaller islands in the Caribbean, or even chartered a boat. He could be anywhere.

The father I'd known would have had some trouble with forging a passport, but who knew the kind of people he ran with these days? After all, he'd managed to bypass my security protocols.

Someone had made another attempt to access Jessa's internal files. But this time the security protocols had been changed. Whoever it was clearly didn't know we'd detected the first breach.

Of course, I hadn't wanted to believe that my own father was capable of that, because in terms of his own skill set, he wasn't. He wasn't one for computers, never seeing any benefit of them. But if he was working with someone, then I'd basically opened the gate and invited the wolf into the hen house.

*Relax. Calm down. Think it through. Start systematically.*

I still had a team to manage, so from my work station at Roone's flat, I'd start at the beginning, the date my father had asked me if he could stay with me.

I checked my exit and entrance logs, and all looked normal. He had left and returned about the ordinary time required for employment. How bad was it that I didn't even know what my father did for money these days?

*You probably don't want to know.*

None of that seemed untoward, so I moved on to camera footage. I had some footage of Dad headed the wrong way to the palace. But when I checked security footage, I hadn't seen him anywhere *inside* the palace, so maybe he just walked the exterior of the building. Cameras were spotty through the grounds, so it was entirely possible that he just wanted to take a walk, even though he'd promised he would stay far away from the palace.

Before, I'd reviewed the tapes as someone with mild concern. Now, I reviewed the footage with the eye of someone who was being security conscious and not someone who was pissed off at her father. Again, I watched the video playback, laser focused and paying attention to his movements. He went to the left toward the Rose Garden, but thenAriel nothing.

I fast forwarded. I didn't see him come back around, nor did I see him on the new path. Where the fuck had he gone?

For two days, everything had been fine. He'd followed the same path, left toward the Rose Garden and then... disappearance. It was on the third day that I had spoken to Penny. I'd asked her to look out for him. So, a couple of clicks of my mouse, shuffling some screens, and several tabs later, and I was looking at the footage of day three. Again, left. Again, toward the Rose Garden. Then disappearance.

The Rose and Tower gardens were connected, but someone would legitimately have to walk through the massive hedges to get from one to the other. And then that someone would also have to know where all the cameras were hidden to avoid being seen. And even with that, it was almost impossible to completely hide from the cameras. At some point along the walk to the gardens, you'd be seen. So how had he done it?

I put a pin in that one and checked the paths that had been accessed. My paranoia had made me put a little alarm on Jessa's file in particular, her whereabouts, just to alert someone if anybody went looking. Everything about her case was so confidential. The files on her whereabouts had been accessed, but I couldn't tell by whom or how, because that server room was down in the tunnels where it was nice and cool and unmonitored. I'd overseen that whole project.

So it meant someone knew to go down there and access them because they knew that they wouldn't be able to access Jessa's files from anywhere else. That told me it was an insider, because no one outside of the immediate group knew that Jessa was alive or where she was. The only problem was that I still couldn't tell *who* had accessed them because for all intents and purposes, the file logs said *I* had accessed them.

*Me?* But I hadn't. I wasn't even home when it happened. And the firewalls I had built, with a little assistance from Matthias Weller of Blake Security, were inaccessible from where I was. So how did this happen? And how had it not tripped a single alarm?

I knew what I had to do, but I really didn't *want* to do it. Doing it would mean that I'd failed. Doing it would mean that I wasn't as good as everyone thought I was.

*Doing it also means that you're protecting the princess, which is currently your job.*

That thought alone was enough to get me moving. I picked up my phone and scrolled through my contacts. I made a call to the one person who would know what to do next.

He answered on the first ring. "Ariel. I didn't expect to hear from you."

"Hey, Weller."

"If you're calling me, it means there's a problem."

"I would love to say that there isn't, but I do need your help."

"What's up?"

"Okay, I'm on an assignment abroad."

"It's a secure line, Ariel. I know you're on Jessa duty."

"Wow, okay. It makes it easier to speak plainly. I don't know how much you know, but someone accessed Jessa's files, particularly those on her recent whereabouts. I'm not sure exactly what they were looking for, but here's the kicker... it says *I* accessed the files."

There was a silent pause. "What?"

"Exactly."

"If you're overseas, you couldn't have accessed the files."

"I know. Exactly. Which is why I'm calling you. I'm hoping you can dig a little deeper?"

"Yeah, I'll see what I can do. It might not be something I can handle from here. I might have to come to Winston Isles."

It was my turn to pause. I needed to tell him everything. But I also didn't need him telling the king. "Well, it's a little complicated."

"Isn't it always with you lot?"

"Look, I know you're on the Winston Isles payroll, and you know that I would never let anything jeopardize the mission to protect the princess, but I need help, and I don't know how to get myself out of this jam."

Something changed in his voice then. It went softer, but somehow more determined. I knew Matthias had a huge hero complex. All those Blake Security guys did. If someone said they needed help, those guys went into overdrive. I hated manipulating him, but it wasn't really a manipulation. After all, I *did* need help and I *was* in a lot of trouble. Trouble I wasn't quite sure how to get out of.

"You could have called Penny."

"I could, but there's no way I'm going to take advantage of my friendship with the queen. I need to first find a solution and *then* take it to Penny and Sebastian."

"Okay, shoot. What do you need?"

"A couple of weeks ago, my father called. He needed a place to stay."

"Okay."

"Well, we don't exactly have a close relationship because he is a gambler, a petty criminal, nothing major. No felonies, nothing like that, and nothing violent, obviously."

"Go on." His voice was clipped but not angry. I didn't think so, anyway.

"I know I should have said no, but parental guilt and all that. Anyway, I said yes and gave him strict instructions to stay at my place. He wasn't to go near the palace. But checking the surveillance, I could see he went silent. About three days after he arrived, I couldn't find him. He stopped answering his phone. I asked Penny to look in on him, just in case. We didn't talk often, but he was still my dad. But he seemed to have gone dark. I was no longer seeing him going in and out of my flat. I started to worry. It's not unusual for him to just vanish, but around the same day he vanished, those files were accessed the first time. And now someone has tried again."

Another big silence. Okay, if he wasn't going to say anything else, I was going to continue. "Anyway, Jessa pulled a Houdini the other day. We're here in London for another couple days, and then it's back to the island. I just don't understand what anybody was hoping to gain from her file. We know precious little about her past. And we were already here watching her, so if anything bad started to happen, we would have stopped it. But the fact that it says *I* accessed those files, worries me, and I can't see any further than that. Someone has set me up. I need to know who. For that, I need someone who's really good. Someone like you."

"You don't need to flatter me."

"Oh, don't worry, I wouldn't. But then, you already know how good you are."

I could practically see him shrugging. He was so nonchalant. When I first met Matthias, I'd quietly hacked his system and had almost been caught more than once. For the purpose of the meeting, my hack had helped, but any longer than that few minutes, and he would have discovered me and shut me down quick. He was that good.

"Okay, I'm going to ask the obvious. Why haven't you told Penny and Sebastian?"

"Well, I would rather fix my mess first and find out if there is a reason to panic and worry before I tell the king."

"Okay, that makes sense. But Penny is your best friend, so maybe the faster you come clean, the better. I'll help you either way, but I'm just saying you don't have to lie. Take it from someone who knows."

"I appreciate it. But I need to be clear with what the hell is going on with the old man. If he's been compromised in any way, I need some proof."

"Okay, I'll help you. But just know... you might not like how this pans out."

I sighed. "Yeah, I think I'm prepared for that."

# FOUR

*Roone*

"WHAT THE FUCK do you mean come home?"

"Roone, this isn't a fucking suggestion, come home. It's been seventy-two hours, and you don't have her."

"If you give us more time, we would have her."

Ariel paced the living room of my flat. She was shaking her hand. "Sebastian, Your Majesty, we can leave a partial team here to keep looking for her, but I'll be perfectly honest, the trail has gone cold. She's not using her cards. Yesterday, it looks like she bought several plane tickets, one each to Madrid, Paris, Toronto, Vancouver, Los Angeles, and one to Miami, but I don't know which flight she got on. She checked in for all the flights. So right now, anyone's guess is as good as mine. And from whichever destination she chose, she could have gone anywhere. If she has multiple passports, we can't find her that way."

Sebastian swore. "Even more reason why you need to come home. Pull back the guards."

Ariel frowned. "With all due respect, Your Majesty, I feel

like we need to leave at least a guard or two on her friend Chloe. Just in case someone tries to make a point with her."

I voiced my opinion about that idea. "Our job isn't to guard Chloe. Our job is to guard Jessa, and she's in the wind."

Ariel shut her mouth and ground her teeth together. I could practically hear them gnashing.

This was fucking bullshit. "Okay, well, you can call Ariel home, but I'm not coming."

There was a bit of silence on the line, and I could tell Sebastian was frustrated with me. But I really didn't give a shit. "Roone, I get it. You want to do your best, but there's nothing to be done there. It's time to come back. We'll regroup as a team."

"I'm not abandoning her. If I have to go to each of those destinations and poke around, check in with contacts, then I will."

"Roone, this is a direct order."

"Oh, is it?" It was rare that he ever gave me one of those. "Well then, you're going to need to wait. I have some time off coming. Maybe it's time I took it."

"What the fuck is wrong with you?"

That was a good question. I'd fucked up. Jessa was running around without protection because I hadn't just ignored the order and told her who I was. But how had she found out? At the end of the day, it didn't matter. She'd been scared, and she'd chosen to shoot me with a tranquilizer instead of bullets, for which I was very appreciative.

But, I couldn't go back, not without finishing the job. I would get Ariel to run one of her fancy-schmancy predictive algorithms on where Jessa might have gone, and then I'd start there.

"Honestly, if the order is come home, then I'm going on vacation."

" This is the time to choose to go on vacation?"

"You know I've always wanted to check out Rome. Toronto too."

"Roone, stop being a dick."

"*You* stop being a dick."

When we fought, we tended to deteriorate into our secondary school versions of ourselves.

"You did your best."

"I beg to differ. If I'd done my best, she would be here, safe. Even better, she'd be back in the islands with the full guard around her. Instead, she's somewhere in the world completely alone. And that's on me."

Ariel shook her head. "No, I take responsibility. I was leading the team."

I knew what Ariel was doing. She was trying to deflect, take the heat off of me. But I knew what I'd done. "No, it's my fuck up. I have to fix it. One way or another, I'm not coming home yet."

Sebastian sighed. "Roone, she isn't your responsibility. She's mine."

"If you say so, Your Majesty. But I'm taking a vacation."

Sebastian cursed under his breath. "Take me off speaker."

I took the phone off speaker and put it up to my ear. When he spoke, his voice was low. "Stop blaming yourself."

"I'm not." Ariel left the room, presumably to give us privacy. "Look, give me a few days. I'll chase down the leads, see what I can come up with. If I come up with nothing, then I'll do as you ask and come home. But I have to try, Sebastian. I feel responsible."

He sighed. "This is Lucas all over again."

"No, it's not."

"Yes, it is. You were obsessed with finding him too."

Yeah, I had been obsessed with finding Lucas, but the difference was I hadn't fucking fallen for Lucas. But I wasn't going to tell Sebastian that. "This just goes to show it seems I can't always do my job right."

"I know you're going to take on this responsibility, but it's not yours to bear. Just do what you need to do and come home."

"Roger that. And I'm not coming home without her."

"For all our sakes, I hope you do find her."

---

*JESSA...*

A girls' night... with my sister-in-law... the queen. And my future sister-in-law. Oh, just NBD.

For the most part, I'd had few friends, enough for a girls' night, but no real crowd. But after just a few days on the island, I had a group. One where I felt like I belonged.

Minor detail... they had no idea who I really was. And yes, I knew that just because Roone had done it to me didn't mean that I should do it back to them. It was dishonest and cruel.

But I was having fun. Honest to goodness fun. And if everything went right, they would never know.

We'd had drinks at Jinx and Bryna's followed by a limo ride. I peered out of the window. "Where are we going?"

Penny laughed. "We're going to go enjoy the movie theater at the palace."

*Shit.* My mouth hung open. "What?"

"Yeah. After a variety of incidents, I am no longer *allowed* to go to a movie theater like a normal person, so I have to see them in the palace. If these guys want to see a movie with me, off to the palace we go."

I glanced around. "You guys realize that's weird, right?"

Bryna laughed. "Yeah, it's weird. But the theater at the palace is amazing. Once you go private butler, there is no going back."

Jinx grinned. "Also, it's free. And I can have as much popcorn as I want."

Penny shrugged. "There are some perks. The least of which is that I will be able to sit in my comfy pajamas and watch the latest rom com. I'm for it."

I swallowed hard. What were the odds I'd be able to make it out of there with no one the wiser? Yes, I wanted to scope out the royals, but not like this... not where I could be caught and shoved in a dungeon.

"Well, I guess off to the palace we go then." Internally, I was shooting myself. Oh sure, I knew enough to laugh and smile with the others. Tonight had been fun and illuminating. I found out more about Penny than I ever thought I would need or want to know.

It turned out she was an artist, actually a decent one, too. But as a queen now, it wasn't like she could really sell her art. She was also a Royal Guard, and that story had me fascinated. Because how did one go from artist to Royal Guard, and how in the world did that work with being queen? From what she'd said, it had been a challenge.

My brother apparently didn't want her to be a Royal Guard. But they'd worked out some kind of arrangement where she wasn't supposed to go out in the field any longer. Although from the sounds of it, I thought a part of her missed it.

"I had no idea when I brought over your lipstick that I would be rubbing shoulders with royalty. I didn't know that was a thing that could happen."

Penny laughed. "Well, welcome. It's not that glamorous, honestly. Just an old building."

"Well, it's glamorous to me," I muttered. The car pulled up to a gate that automatically opened and then drove up the winding drive toward the palace. It grew dark inside the limo, and finally, the car came to a stop and opened up in what looked like actual tunnels.

"Are you guys leading me to slaughter in the dungeon something? Because I have to tell you I did not sign up for that."

Bryna laughed. "Oh relax. There are no dungeons, *supposedly*. I've never gotten a straight answer on that."

I blinked. "Wow, you are just filling me with confidence."

Jinx laughed. "How do you think I feel? I live with her. And any number of days, I have random men in my house."

Bryna whacked her on the shoulder. "Jinx. That makes it sound so dirty."

"Well, it's true. You have a guard detail now. So, it's not like you have the same guy over and over."

"Yes, but you might want to explain that before you suggest that I just have random dudes in my house all the time."

Jinx giggled. "Well okay, good point."

The doors were opened for us, and we all shuffled in. I tried to take in every little thing. I expected ornate tapestries and marble floors, but it looked like the lobby of a hotel, honestly. Marble floors, yes, polished to a high shine, but no tapestries. There were chandeliers, but they were dim and muted, until we went to a hallway on the left. Ah, there was a tapestry, and an angel scene was painted in rich colors on the ceiling. A white polished marble floor and gilded posts between the arches completed the look. It was absolutely incredible.

I was so busy looking around that I paid zero attention to which way we were going. I would need an escort back out.

*Are you sure you want an escort out of here? You could stay forever. You could meet the king.*

Penny led the way and pushed open a set of double doors that led to the biggest media room I'd ever seen. It actually looked like a theater, which made it all the more incredible. "Holy shit."

Penny turned and smiled at me. "I know, right? I think that was my response exactly. I grew up here for the most part, but I never came here for movies or anything."

I frowned. "You grew up in the palace?"

"My father's been head of security for the family for a long time. So, I grew up in a bungalow a quarter of a mile away on the palace grounds."

That was fascinating. Sebastian's and her lives were so intertwined before they ever fell in love. "That must have been incredible. And I'm guessing lonely too."

"Lonely. There was a lot of that. But growing up in and around the palace was kind of fun. I had a great time. There are all these tunnels with secret nooks and crannies, and it was pretty great sometimes."

We all picked a seat, and Penny made a call for popcorn. Jinx made a request for her kettle corn mix, and we settled in. When the door opened, we all turned. I'd assumed it would be the concessions, but instead, it was the one person I didn't expect to see.

*My brother.*

His gaze landed on Penny first, and while they were engrossed in each other, I watched him.

*Is he everything you imagined?*

I guess so. More, maybe? He was tall. Lean. There was no softness to him though. I didn't imagine he sat behind the desk all day. There was something about him, something self-assured. Like he was well aware of what he looked like and how he carried himself, a natural-born leader who exuded confidence like he'd grown up with it and never questioned his place in the world. He had dark brown hair, and the curls slightly framed his face. His eyes were maybe hazel. I couldn't tell for sure, not in the dim lighting.

But, that smile. The way he looked at Penny made my gut

clench. He loved her. It was apparent on his face and the way his eyes lit up as if she hung the moon and the stars.

*Wow.* I didn't know anything about him, but I could have just seen that one look and it would have told me *everything* about him. He was capable of great love.

*Yeah, but will that love extend to you?*

He dipped his head to kiss Penny, and immediately Bryna and Jinx protested.

"Eeww..."

"Oh my God, you two, get a room."

I giggled, wondering what could be so bad about Sebastian kissing Penny. And then I understood as that one kiss turn into a second that lingered. And then Sebastian dipped his hand into her hair and looked like he wanted to stay there a while.

Wow, okay yeah. That was a little too gooey.

And then he looked up, kissed her on the nose, and then flipped off Bryna and Jinx, who only laughed.

"Don't worry, I'm leaving. I just came to kiss my wife. That's all."

When he turned our gazes locked. I knew logically there was no way we should have known each other, no reason why I should feel like he could see into me. Nonetheless, I could feel it. I *knew* him.

I refused to look away. I refused to speak first either.

*But what if he has no idea who you are?*

He smiled hesitantly, and then turned his attention back to Penny, who shrugged. When his gaze returned to mine, he started to speak and then cleared his throat and tried it again. "What are you doing here?"

"I—" I frowned, glancing around at Bryna and Jinx. I couldn't see Penny because he was blocking her. "Uh, Bryna and Jinx invited me to hang out?"

His gaze darted back to them then back to me. He stepped forward then hesitated.

Penny stood then and stepped around him. "I'm so sorry Jessa. I hope you'll forgive our mild deception, but I got the impression you wanted to meet your brother. And I didn't tell him you were coming, so you'll have to forgive his current state."

My gaze darted to her. "You knew?"

Jinx stood then. "Yeah, we recognized you right away."

*Could I run? Would I make it back to the limo? And if I did, then what? Ask Jeeves to fire it up so I could make my escape? Are they going to kill me?*

"You guys are as bad as Roone."

Sebastian's brows lifted. "Roone. You knew?"

"A little too late."

Before I could say anything else, the door to the theater opened again.

*Brother number two.*

Lucas had a big grin for everyone. "I heard my fiancée, my future baby mama, was here."

Bryna just shook her head. "Not now, Lucas."

"What do you mean not—" He froze when he saw me. "Holy shit."

I didn't know what else to do at that point, so I waved. "Hey, I'm Jessa. Is this the part where you guys shove me into the dungeon? Or are you going to do the whole murder thing right here, because I feel like this is not a good day to die."

Sebastian frowned. "Why the hell would we murder you?"

"You sent a traitor into my midst to watch me. I've been led to believe that it was to bring harm to me. My father was afraid of you people his whole life."

Sebastian scowled then. "That man was not your father."

"*Yes*, he was. He was the father I knew. Unlike the father who abandoned me."

Lucas winced. "Oh, burn. But maybe, just maybe we can all have a conversation before this gets crazy. I feel like we have a lot to talk about."

Sebastian nodded. "Since you're here Jessa, I assume it means you want to find out the truth. So, what do you say? Will you allow us to explain? This is your show. You entered into the belly of the beast. Now you're here. What's your next move?"

I swallowed. He had a point. I was here. Now what? "Like you said. We have a lot to talk about."

Sebastian's nod was slight. "Then by all means. We should probably do this in private. Follow me."

# FIVE

*Jessa*

FOLLOW ME, he said. And like the idiot lamb to the slaughter, I followed. Now I was alone with my brothers.

I may or may not have miscalculated.

*You're the one who showed up with no plan.*

Okay fine, I'd grossly miscalculated. And now I was in a room with two men who possibly wanted me dead.

As I glanced back and forth between my brothers, my mind raced trying to think about all the ways to start this conversation. 'Hey, I'm your long-lost sister. Nice to meet you. I know this seems awkward, but I didn't really mean to sneak my way into the palace just to get closer to you.'

*Maybe they actually want to get to know you.*

In the end, all I could muster was, "I have no idea what to say right now."

Sebastian ran his hands through his hair. "That makes three of us, I think."

"Maybe I should just go?"

Lucas's brow popped. "What? No. You have to stay. Seb, make her stay."

Sebastian groaned. "Lucas, despite the rumors you keep perpetuating, we don't actually have dungeons here. If she wants to go, she can go. I can't stop her."

Well, that was a relief. No dungeons.

"I'm sorry I snuck in here, I guess. Please don't be mad at the girls, I wanted to know about you, and I thought I could just observe. I didn't think about what would happen after."

Sebastian and Lucas exchanged a glance, and Sebastian said, "If you want to know something, all you have to do is ask."

"I guess I just... I mean you wanted to know about me. Did *you* ask?"

Lucas snorted. "She has a point there."

Sebastian sighed. "Okay, yes, I deserve that. I didn't give you a chance. And while I had my reasons for intruding on your life without your knowledge, I didn't really take into account how you would feel."

"You told Roone not to tell me?"

He nodded. "Yes. I sent him to protect you. And given how you'd grown up, I didn't want you to run. The way you'd grown up with your father, I didn't know if or how much you hated us." The way he said 'father,' like he was deliberately using measured words, irked me. "My understanding was that he did his best to keep you safe and protected, but I also understand he was quite ill. All I wanted was to keep you safe and minimize any upheaval in your everyday life."

"You realize how intrusive that was, right?"

He nodded slowly. "Yes. And I would love to tell you that I wouldn't do it again, but that's a lie. Because I would. From the moment I found out about you and Lucas, my only goal has been to keep the two of you safe. Like our father would have wanted."

I narrowed my gaze. "You see, you use that word, *father,* but he's not *my* father. I didn't know him. And my whole life, I've been told to fear everyone. Question everything. Trust no one. And it's impossible for me to stand here and just believe that you mean me no harm."

"It's the truth. Just think it through yourself. All the times Roone had access to hurt you, did he? And now you're here, in the palace. Have we made any attempt to hurt you?"

I swallowed. There was still time for all the dungeon torture. "No. You haven't." Someone knocked on the door and brought in scones and tea. My traitorous stomach grumbled. The popcorn hadn't been enough.

Sebastian gestured toward the tea. "Have a seat. If you like, I'll have Lucas—"

Lucas didn't even wait, just piled clotted cream onto a scone and tucked in. Then he poured tea for all of us. He took several sips, then wiped his mouth with the back of his hand. "See, not poisoned. Also, Seb, don't think I didn't notice how you volunteered me as tribute."

Sebastian only shrugged. "Well I know how you've grown to love Chef's scones. Be careful or you'll lose that six pack you love parading around."

"Eight pack, big brother. Eight pack."

Big brother. I sat tentatively as they spoke. The scone did look good. "So, I guess that answers the question of which of you is older."

Lucas rolled his eyes. "As if there was any question. I'm still spry and young. Is that a line I see on your forehead, Seb?"

Sebastian scowled. "Fucking one premature gray hair. I swear, nothing is sacred."

Lucas grinned. "To be fair, I was in the bathroom when Penny and Bryna were discussing your freakout over it. It gave me life, man."

I stared at the two of them. At most, they both looked like they were in their mid-twenties. And neither of them had to worry about their looks in the least. It was intimidating as hell. Had I gotten the dud genes? I knew I was perfectly fine, but I had no illusions about me being some show-stopping model.

"I'm glad the vanity gene skipped one of us."

Lucas grinned. "But I see the trash-talking gene didn't." His gaze flickered to Sebastian. "I like her. Can we keep her?"

Sebastian rolled his eyes. "When you love something, you have to be willing to let it go. If it stays, then it was meant to be yours."

These men, despite their insane good looks, were, for the most part, normal. Maybe I wouldn't know what danger looked like exactly, but I couldn't feel it with the girls or with these two. I was safe here.

So what, exactly, had I been afraid of all these years?

Sebastian cleared his throat. "I know this is a lot. But I'd like you to stay at the palace a couple of days. Get to know us. If you want to go, you can go. But no one's going to hurt you here. Unless of course you still think our nefarious plan is to murder you with scones."

"When you use rational words, I feel like I'm the crazy person. You have to understand, my whole life, there was a boogeyman. Real or imagined. And up until now, I didn't actually believe he existed. Come to find out, there's this whole other world and a royal conspiracy. It means my father wasn't completely insane."

He and Lucas exchanged a glance. "There are some very real dangers, even if they don't come from us. There is a group. They call themselves Heirs of Angelus. We don't know a lot about them, but we believe that they were the ones that killed our father. There's been this whole shadow faction that believes that you, Lucas, and I are not the rightful heirs.

There was a time when I would have welcomed that. A time where all I wanted was a simple life. But our father died because he believed in the throne and all it stands for. They killed him in a grab for power. There were some people who didn't believe that you and Lucas should have legitimate claims on the monarchy, but it was what Dad wanted, so I made it happen."

I eyed him carefully. "How do you feel about it? Can't we challenge your seat on the throne now?"

He shrugged. "Sure. And honestly, part of me would welcome that. It's exhausting. It would give me time to knock up my wife and be a little normal. But this is about legacy."

I ran my hands through my hair. "Is it all worth it?"

"Even if I could step down, I wouldn't. They tried to kill my wife. Then they tried to kill Lucas."

My throat went dry. "Shit." God, my brain hurt. My whole childhood came screaming back into focus. "My father talked about this boogeyman. I dragged him from doctor to doctor, trying to get meds that would work correctly. And all along, he wasn't completely out of his mind. You understand it's a lot to take in."

Lucas nodded and pushed away from the table he sat on. "Look, I get it. I was in your boat. I had a totally normal life once."

Sebastian scoffed at that. "You were a thief, Lucas. Hardly normal."

Lucas granted. "Hey, I was a world-renowned thief."

Sebastian rolled his eyes. "Conman."

Lucas grunted. "Pussy."

I stared at them. "You guys, focus."

Lucas flashed a grin at me. "Look, my point is that I get how you're feeling. You didn't ask for any of this. But we're stronger together."

"I have to think this through. How would they even track me down?"

Lucas sighed. "Well, current theories are that there are people with access to the royal family who are working with them. Like Roone's former partner."

I frowned. "What do you mean his *former* partner?"

Sebastian sighed. "A former guard. He was assigned to Lucas's watch. Our best guess is that they want the three of us together. And considering my father had already set into motion the events to make you and Lucas legitimate, they didn't dare risk leaving one of us unharmed."

"Jesus Christ. They want all three of us dead?"

Sebastian shrugged. "Believe me now? You're in the safest place you can be. This place is a fortress."

"Or, you know, they can walk in the front door like I did."

Sebastian rubbed the back of his neck. "We're working on it. Now, that all three of us are together, whoever's after us is going to have to make a bold move. Whatever it is, we'll deal with it together. And your knowledge will help us."

"I don't know much. My father was convinced I was in danger for years. No one believed him."

Sebastian nodded. "I can't imagine how difficult it was growing up with him, not knowing what to believe or who to trust. Being afraid."

I swallowed hard. "Yes, but what's worse is that he might have been right about all of it."

"Look, whatever happens, we're together now. The three of us will work it out. The hard work your father put in to protect you... we won't take it for granted. We will keep you safe."

"Just how do you plan on doing that?"

As my new brothers exchanged glances, I wasn't sure this was the best idea I'd ever had.

*Roone*

I WAS WRECK TIRED. I'd been in Toronto following up on leads when I'd gotten the call.

Jessa, my little lost princess, had fooled us all and gone home to the Winston Isles. She'd basically walked up to the girls, introduced herself, and made friends. I didn't even know what to say to that. Who did that?

*She does.* Always playing by her own rules. She was someone who wanted to make a statement.

*Is that what she's doing?*

As soon as I heard, I took the first flight back. I hadn't slept in two days, and basically, I was shit for brains. But straight off of the landing strip, I went to the palace and pushed the door open into the conference room where I'd been instructed to meet Sebastian.

It was actually part conference room, part game room. Sebastian had always said people were more comfortable in laid-back environments. I didn't know if that was the truth, because I did not feel comfortable, and I was sure the hell pissed off.

Sebastian looked me up and down. "Mate, you look like shit."

"Yeah, you think? You're telling me I've been running around from hell to breakfast and she's fucking here?"

Sebastian held up his hands. "Relax. Yeah, she turned up on her own."

I ran my hands through my hair. "Who the fuck told her? I didn't break cover. There's no way she should have known."

Sebastian held up his hands. "From the sounds of it, it seems someone was giving her father information, or maybe he was able to piece it together on his own. Either way, he made her a whole folder, on me, Lucas, Dad... And unfortunately, there was a picture of me and you. So that's how she found out that you weren't exactly who you said you were."

"Motherfucker. I told you." I pointed an accusatory finger at him while I paced and talked. "I told you we needed to tell her. It would have saved us a hell of a lot of time because she found out anyway. And you put me off telling her. Anything could have happened to her in the last few days. *Anything*. If only you'd have let me tell her."

He ran his hands through his hair. "I know. I thought I was doing the best thing for her, but maybe not. We had no way of knowing. At the end of the day, I was wrong. But she's here now, so we need a game plan. I need my right-hand man. Are you up for this?"

"Up for *what*? I've been trying to hold this shit together. And you—"

There was a sound at the other end of the meeting room. Someone had come in. The hairs on the nape of my neck stood at attention, and my back went rigid. I snapped my head up. I knew that feeling, that acute sensation.

*Jessa.*

I knew what I was supposed to do. Act nonchalant. Be the soldier. But I was so fucking relieved to see her.

I left my best friend standing where he was and ran to her. Like an idiot, I had my hands all over her. Checking her for injuries or wounds. She was safe. She was here. She was mine.

*No, dumbass, she's not yours.*

She opened her mouth as if to say something, and her gaze searched mine. But then she closed her eyes as if steeling herself. I watched her shutter her expression, and it broke my heart.

I'd done this. I'd ruined it all. I had crossed the line, and there was no coming back from that now because I had completely fallen for her and she would never trust me again. Not that she should have. Because I was a liar. Falling for her made everything far too complicated. The soldier wasn't allowed to love the princess.

---

*Jessa*

I SHOULD HAVE KNOWN. I should have known that he would come and I would have to face him. That I would eventually have to deal with the hollow pit in my stomach. But I wasn't prepared.

I had no way of preparing for this. As much as I craved his touch, needed it as a balm to soothe all of my aches and ease my pain and anxiety, there would be no balm today. Because no matter how I felt about him, the betrayal felt worse.

I could have a calm rational conversation with Sebastian and Lucas. The things that they'd said made sense. But there was a lot to unpack, a lot to think through. This man had protected me. *Lied to you.* Cared for me. *Forced his way into your life.*

My hands shook.

I wanted to run to him and hold him. I wanted to kiss him. I wanted to say I was sorry for the tranq dart. I also wanted to say I'd grabbed the wrong gun by mistake and I'd really wanted to actually shoot him. I'd wanted to hurt him the same way that he'd hurt me, and I wanted him to feel pain.

*No you don't. You love him.*

I did *not.* I wanted him to hurt as badly as I'd been hurt. I wanted him to feel that realization of betrayal to his core. I wanted him to bleed like my heart was bleeding.

Sebastian was staring at him. Roone was staring at me, and I, well I was frozen, rooted to the spot near the large sitting area, complete with plush looking couches, coffee tables, and a massive big screen TV.

There was a pool table across the way, and I could tell that the room was probably used as a game room more often than not. My favorite feature of the room were the shelves of books lining two walls. All kinds of books. I'd spent hours in there the previous day looking for something to calm my mind down. I'd settled on Jane Austin. Of course that didn't help at all because romance made me want to stab things.

"Jessa, you're safe. I'm so sorry, I just—"

I don't know what made me do it. I wasn't violent by nature. *Liar. Sometimes you are.*

My right hand twitched, and I couldn't stop myself. It flew out, wanting to make contact with his cheek, but his reflexes were too quick. He caught my wrist in his fingers then twisted my arm behind my back with enough force to tell me that he meant it, but still gently enough to not hurt me.

All that did was piss me off even more, and I figured I might as well give it a go with my left. Same result. Roone dragged me to him. "Stop. I don't want to hurt you. I'm so sorry." He dropped his forehead to mine. "I'm sorry. I'm sorry. I'm sorry."

I fought his hold. "I hate you."

"I don't hate you."

"I wish I'd shot you."

"A part of me wished you'd shot me too. All I ever wanted was to keep you safe."

I wasn't sure how long we stood there. Roone's strong hands on my wrists, my arms behind my back, my body pressed against his, needing him and longing for what we'd had.

Sebastian cleared his throat. "Is there something you guys want to tell me?"

My brother's voice was what broke the spell. I fought Roone's hold again, and then the tears started, hot and wet against my cheek. My body shook with pain and anger. Roone whispered another 'I'm sorry.' Then he released me and stepped back, arms behind his back, shoulders stiff, posture ramrod straight. He didn't look at Sebastian when he spoke. "No, nothing you need to know. I'm just relieved the princess is safe."

His voice was so cold. He wouldn't meet my gaze. It was as if the Roone I had known in London, the one who'd pissed me off, lived across the hall, protected me, and made me insane, didn't exist. Instead he was replaced by this robot? No. That wasn't right. He'd been replaced by a soldier. As my heart broke in two, I wondered if I'd ever really known him at all.

# SIX

### Ariel

MY FIRST STOP OFF the plane was to see Penny. But after we'd caught up a little and she'd told me the utterly ridiculous tale of Jessa dropping into our laps, it was right to the team meeting.

I'd hoped to see Jessa again, but the team briefing didn't include her, even though it was all about her. I considered trying to find her after the meeting, but it was probably best if I kept a low profile. Matthias was still trying to help me locate my father, but so far he had nothing. That needed to be my focus for the time being.

Well, at the moment, my focus was delivering bad news to the team. "So, we have a problem." Ethan handed out copies of the reports as I continued. "There has been a fire at Hope House."

Roone frowned. "Is everyone okay?"

I nodded. "Yeah. No one was harmed. Some residents were taken to the hospital for treatment of smoke inhalation but nothing too serious. The fire was pretty localized to the office, and it was unoccupied at the time."

Roone stirred next to me. I wanted to ask him if he'd seen Jessa. But from the tight set of his jaw, I could tell he wasn't in any kind of mood for those questions. When he spoke, his voice was low. "So, the one place where all the files would be kept goes up in flames."

I shrugged. "There might be another offsite location, I don't know."

Ethan's voice was mellow when he asked. "What about James Morgan, the director, do we have any other information on him?"

I shook my head. God I was such a fuck-up. I was supposed to be in charge of things, but I'd lost the princess on my watch, my father might have used my security protocols to access information on her whereabouts, and I couldn't even manage the simple things like what the fuck was stored at Hope House, if anything. Right bang-up job I was doing.

*You didn't fail. She is safe. Just things didn't go exactly as planned.*

"To our knowledge, he doesn't know anything. Based on the information he gave Jessa, he's not part of this. We're still trying to determine if there is any correlation between the sketches that Jessa sent him and the attempted kidnapping at the gala. We do have one resident who reported seeing someone." I glanced down at my files. "The guy with the tats was described as having a distinctive one with a shield, a snake, and a knife on it. It also had some language he couldn't understand."

Sebastian cursed. "So the fire was no accident."

I shrugged. "Likely not. The tattoo could very well be the anti-Winston Isles crest. The language he didn't understand could have easily been Latin, or it could be pig Latin, for all we know. But, the local police took the statement. I'll get access to it and can tell you if it's the same tattoo or not once I hack their system tonight. I'm hoping this particular department isn't behind on paperwork."

Roone muttered a curse and ran his hands over his face.

Everyone was silent, as if no one wanted to be the one to break the news. "So, let's not all volunteer at once to tell Jessa this news."

Sebastian cracked his neck. "I can tell her." He turned his gaze to Roone. "But maybe she'll take it better from you?"

Roone cursed under his breath again. "Let's keep it official. This should come from you. Or Ethan."

I shifted my gaze to my partner. "Trouble?"

Roone shook his head. "Later."

I had a feeling it was going to be a hell of a story.

---

*Jessa*

THERE WAS a knock at the door. I still didn't know how I should feel about being here, but the view of the ocean from my bedroom balcony was certainly helping me warm up to the idea of it all.

I had a perfect view of the Tower Garden with a direct line of sight to the ocean. Outside my window, hibiscus and bougainvillea grew, filling my room with their sweet perfume. When I heard a knock, I jogged to the door and opened it. Penny stood on the other side. "Hey. I came to see how you were doing."

The queen was checking on me? "Oh, you know... I just found out that I'm a secret princess, so yeah, I'm feeling pretty awesome."

She chuckled low. "Can I come in?"

I stepped back. "Of course."

She immediately removed her shoes, placed them by the door, and let her feet sink into the plush carpeting. "I've always loved this room. It has the best rugs."

"Did you spend a lot of time in here?"

"Um, yeah, sometimes I needed to make an escape. I wasn't always the best Royal Guard. As this is a guest quarters, I could often come and bury my woes with a bottle of wine in this room."

"That's good to know."

She shrugged. "I was a disaster, to be honest."

I laughed.

"So how are you doing? Really?"

"Things are topsy-turvy I guess. It's only been a couple of days, but part of me feels like I belong here. Not necessarily the palace, or anything like that, but I don't know, there's this feeling of... home. My first night, I arrived and dropped my bags off and then ran down to the beach and put my feet in the water. It sort of felt like homecoming, you know?"

Her smile was fleeting. "Yeah, I know. Even when I was in New York, I knew that I wanted to return. It's funny, because I spent my whole life wishing I didn't have to be here."

"How did you know that you belonged here?"

"At the end of the day, it was home. Sebastian was here. It sounds so ridiculous and anti-feminist, but I fell in love with him in New York. And in a way, I also fell in love with the islands again. All of a sudden I became furiously protective of what was mine and what I'd grown up with, you know?"

"Do you still paint?"

She grinned. "Yeah, I was painting this morning. It's weird... I get these cravings, and I end up with paint still on my nails." She held up her hand, and sure enough, there was some light blue paint. "At the same time, it's like this part of me was activated when we were in New York, and I had to take care of

Sebastian. A part I didn't even know existed. That part that was all about me having to be badass. I'd never connected with being a Royal Guard before, until then."

"I'm still super fascinated by that. You protected him, which is amazing."

She laughed and then eased down onto the couch, sitting next to me. "Amazing sometimes, but it was tricky. Difficult. I didn't like lying, but I had a direct order from King Cassius."

I licked my lips. "Was it a direct order for Roone?"

Penny sighed and nodded. "Yes. Once it was decided how we were going to approach, he was forbidden to spill all the beans. He couldn't tell you that you were a princess and that he was there to guard you. You saw Roone. He's such a soldier. And Sebastian was afraid—"

"I might have run."

"Yes, exactly. Which was why Sebastian decided that we were going covert."

"I know he didn't have a choice. I do, I guess. Well, at least now I do. But God, I just... once we started—" I stopped myself. I wasn't sure how much I was supposed to say, or if I was supposed to say anything.

"Once you started hooking up?"

I lifted a brow. "You know?"

Penny laughed. "Oh my God, Roone can't seem to take his eyes off of you."

"Yeah well, he's very pretty to look at. And he can be so sweet."

"Yep, that's Roone. He's insightful and smart, and loyal. He would rather cut off his arm than do anything to hurt Sebastian or Lucas. He will call them on their shit too, which is awesome. Works wonders for me and Bryna. I think, honestly, he's the reason Sebastian finally got over being angry with me. Are you angry with him for lying?"

"Yes. It's complicated."

"But he loves you furiously."

I shook my head. "He doesn't love me."

Penny shrugged. "I wouldn't be so sure about that."

There was another knock at the door, and I stood. "Should I be expecting more visitors?"

She nodded. "There's someone else I think you need to see."

When I opened the door, my heart stopped. "Ariel?"

Ariel gave me a sheepish smile. "Hey, Jessa."

I turned back around to stare at Penny. "You know her?"

Penny smiled. "Yeah, she's my best friend. Apparently, you were starting to replace me in London."

I turned my attention back to Ariel. "Was Meet Cute even real?"

She shrugged. "Real enough. And surprisingly, you and Roone actually did make a good match. The algorithm even said so. If it hadn't matched you guys on its own, I would have paired you for the sake of the mission, but it's legit."

I stepped back to let her in.

She and Penny hugged tightly. I closed the door and slowly walked back into the sitting area. "That whole time, Meet Cute, wine at my place... all an act?" I could feel the bile rising again.

She shook her head. "No, not an act, but absolutely for your protection. We did our jobs."

I rolled my eyes. "Was any of it real? Is Chloe real? The Evans?"

She held up her hands. "Resist the temptation to do that. You will pick apart every interaction trying to worry about what was a lie and what was the truth. Just know that I genuinely like you and Roone has real feelings for you. Just know that and deal accordingly. Otherwise, it gets a bit weird."

"Actually, we do have something to tell you," Penny said.

I glanced between the two of them. "Oh my God, this looks

like bad news. Please tell me Roone is not married with children or something."

Ariel grinned at me. "He wishes that someone would have him."

"I would have him." Yeah, my libido was not allowed to have a vote. New rule.

Ariel started to speak. "Jessa, there was a fire at Hope House."

I sat forward in my chair. "Oh my God, James, Lulu..."

She put up her hands. "They're fine. Everyone was fine actually. There was some smoke inhalation, but everyone is fine."

I held my hand to my chest. "Oh my God. Jesus. What happened? Electrical? Gas?"

She and Penny exchanged glance. "Arson."

I sighed. "Oh my God. Does this have to do with me?"

Ariel inhaled and exhaled slowly. "It's a possibility. One of the residents reported seeing someone with a tattoo. The one you've been chasing. He's given a description of it to the police, and they're keeping an eye out to see if the tattoo comes up on their databases."

I shook my head. "What is that tattoo?"

Penny pulled out her phone. She held up the screen and I saw what looked like a crest. There was that same Latin inscription, a shielded crest by the castle, and what looked like a chain of some sort, a broken chain. But it was faint, and then there was... was that an eagle? "I don't know what I'm looking at."

She explained it to me. "This is the Winston Isles crest. The chain, the broken one, symbolizes when King Jackson set everyone free, and the Phoenix symbolizes an island nation rising from the ashes of British rule. And the Latin inscription says, *No man bows before this King.* King Jackson preferred equality long before it was even a thing to talk about or think about." Then she pulled up another photo. "This is the one with the dagger, the one you recognize."

I nodded. As I looked closer, I saw that that the chain was replaced with a serpent and the dagger was stabbing the phoenix. "That looks worse, now that I know what everything stands for."

She nodded. "Yeah. This is the crest used by a faction who believe that Sebastian and Lucas have no claim to the throne. That's the only information we have so far. We've been trying to piece it together. My dad has some information, but anything that you can tell us would be incredibly helpful."

I shook my head. "All I have is what James gave me, and Phillip."

Penny and Ariel frowned. "Who's Phillip?"

"He was a friend of my father's. He's the one who gave me the file my father put together and showed me the photos of Sebastian and Roone. Who are these people? And what do they have to do with me?"

Penny shook her head. "I don't know, but we will find out. All of our lives depend on it."

# SEVEN

*Ariel*

THERE WAS a difference between thinking something was fucked up and *knowing* something was fucked up. When it was just an idea in the back of my brain, it was easy enough to play devil's advocate to pretend that things might not be as bad as they seemed, to try and rationalize, to work it out, to think of all the possible reasons why my father had vanished. But, when the truth stared me in the face, there was no denying it.

Back in my barely used office, I had a mountain of paperwork waiting for me. Roone and I had been in London for two months, and no one had touched it, save to leave me more work. I wondered how long I'd have access to this place. The Royal Guard had been everything to me.

For years I thought I wanted to escape. I'd thought maybe, just maybe, I should run away from this place. I should hide. But I was glad I had stuck with it. The guard had given me a family. A home the likes of which I'd never really known before except in Penny's house.

In Penny's house, I'd always felt like family. Would I still be her family when she found out?

I saw the email from Matthias just as my phone rang. I picked it up. "How bad is it?"

He sighed. "Bad. Your passcode was definitely used to access the files. Time stamped when you were definitely *not* in the country."

"I knew that, but hearing you say it, just makes it worse somehow."

"There's something else."

"Fabulous. What?"

"The code that was used to access it was no simple password hack. Someone was trying to leave a message."

"There's a fucking message in the code?"

"Yeah. It doesn't mean anything to me, but maybe it does to you."

"What is it?"

"'Everyone must kneel before our king.'"

I cursed under my breath. "It's a bastardization of the Latin slogan on the Winston Isles crest. This is related to the murder of the king."

Matthias cursed under his breath. "Do we need to get the rest of Blake Security on this?"

"I don't know." I ran my hands through my hair, trying to think. "I don't know what this means." Was my father working with them? Had he used me?

*Of course, he used you, you dumb idiot.*

"So then, the next question is where the fuck is my father?"

"Well, I've been looking. I searched all uses of his credit cards and passport and found nothing. But if he is involved with someone tied to this conspiracy, then they would have a million ways to get him out, a million places to hide him. Think, is there anywhere that he always wanted to go? Anywhere he always talked about?"

I couldn't think of anything. "We didn't grow up with much money. And given his antics, he might not have any friends left." Then I thought it through. "Actually, there was one place. He always talked about driving the Amalfi Coast. He was obsessed with the old movies, you know? Um, James Dean and those kinds of things. He always said that before he died he was going to drive down the Amalfi coast."

"Okay, it's not much, but it's something. It's a starting point. But you have to tell team Winston Isles that you have a problem."

I swallowed hard. "I know. I'm just... I don't know, buying time, I guess."

He was silent for a beat. "Like I've said before, it will be easier and faster if you just tell them. Don't try to hide. Let the chips fall where they may. You're an asset to the team. Nothing will happen to you."

"And I wish it was that easy." Because it wouldn't be. Penny, her mom, Ethan, and eventually, Sebastian, Lucas, Roone, Bryna, and Jinx, they'd all become my family. To have to walk in and tell them this thing, that a member of my actual blood family had done this, had stooped to this level of betrayal, meant I would lose my family.

I would lose game-night Wednesdays. I would lose casually strolling into the castle and straight into the queen's quarters. I would lose the ability to talk to my best friend whenever and wherever I wanted. It would all be over.

*But they are family. You have to protect them.*

*He is family too.*

*Fuck.* I hated him sometimes. Even more, I hated the fact that I loved him. How could he do this to me? What would have been worth doing this?

"Look, I know you're hurting, but you're going to have to make a decision. With the princess back, we're going to have to annihilate the threat, so the sooner you deal with this, the better."

"I know. And I will deal with it. I just have to figure out what the hell I'm going to say first."

"Don't wait too long."

"Yeah, I hear you."

"Oh, the other matter you emailed me about…"

I perked up. "Winchester. Do you know what happened to him?"

"No. Phillip Winchester is in the wind. No hits on his credit cards. University says he's on sabbatical. Has been for six months."

"You're sure? I'm certain Jessa said he was teaching."

"Don't know. He's certainly not this term."

I had a bad feeling. Something had happened to that man. And he was one person we needed to talk to. He might actually be able to shed some light. "Okay. And Weller…"

"Yeah?"

"Thanks."

"Anytime. Let me know if you need me again."

"I got it from here."

What was I going to do, choose my father? Or choose the family I'd made from the time I was six?

*Roone*

"SO, you went and fell in love with my sister, huh?"

I glowered at Lucas then turned my attention back to the azure blue of the Caribbean laid out in front of me. I was seated at the Drive Café. It was one of my favorite views of the best surfing beach.

The Drive had been our hang out spot. In the evenings, sometimes there would be live music. Bands would come, and mostly, the women would be dressed in next to nothing. It was ideal. But at the moment, I felt mainly nostalgic.

I had gotten a couple of looks when I walked in, but nothing I was interested in pursuing. The woman I wanted was back up at the castle and currently not speaking to me.

"I'm not in love."

"Yeah, dumbass, you are. I know the look. Despondent. Lonely. Sad. Not quite sure how you ended up here. Yup, been there, done that."

I hated that I was so easy to read. Why couldn't Lucas just stay out of my business?

"Just leave me alone, mate. I really don't want to talk about it."

"How did it happen?"

He wasn't going to stop. "You're being a dick."

Lucas grinned. "I believe the appropriate phrase is 'a wanker.' I had this friend once, he was British and kind of a wanker himself. He taught me all these fabulous British phrases, like wanker. And twat. And cunt face."

Despite myself, I chuckled. He really was annoyingly persistent. "I'm not in love." *Liar.*

"Are you sure? Because Sebastian rolled into my room and said, 'The man has got it bad.' So I'm just trying to get the real deal. You took my advice. You played the hide-the-salami angle, and it's not working out for you?"

I groaned. "I did not hide the salami."

"Technically, yes you did. But that's neither here nor there. I don't understand what your problem is."

"She's a princess. She's your flipping sister. She should marry a prince, or some billionaire financier, or like a knight or something."

"Well, I've known the girl about five minutes. So far, what I can tell you is she knows more curse words than Bryna does, she has Penny beat on epic side-eye, and no idiot financier would have made her happy. It's one thing if you don't want to be with her. But if you do want to be with her, don't be a dick. I can make you a knight if you want."

I frowned. Did he not know that he couldn't do that? "No, you actually can't. Only the Regents Council can. Have you paid zero attention in your history class? And in case you missed it, mate, I wasn't being a dick. I was forced to be one. I wanted to be forthright and honest and tell her who I was, but I wasn't allowed to. And then when I was about to, she found out another way. So rightfully, she felt betrayed. Lied to. Like I said, I had to deceive her, so I get why she's mad. I never expected her to understand, and she doesn't, so that's that."

"I swear to God, how is such a smart guy so obtuse when it comes to this shit? You're the one who talked me and Sebastian off the stupid ledges. You're fresh out of wise wisdom when it's you on the other end?"

"Do you have a point?"

"Yeah, I have a point. My point is if you want something, fight for it. You might lose, but oh what a battle it will be. You can't stand on the sidelines your whole life, playing soldier, never letting people get close. You think I don't notice? Women are talking about you like you're some kind of legend. And they've seen *me*. These women used to be like, 'Oh my God, Roone! Roone Ainsley. Roone Ainsley.' You're like this unattainable super car for them because you never really peel that layer back and let anyone actually see you. But it looks like my sister got to see it, and for some reason she decided she liked it. Honestly, I don't see the appeal. I'm not really into gingers."

I glowered at him.

He laughed. "But, if she's willing to fuck you once knowing

that, she must be discerning as fuck herself. Fight for her if you want her. Don't let some bullshit get in your way. So, you're not a prince, and? If she'd turned up here with some twat of a prince on her arm, wanting the good life, I'd be concerned. But she turned up here completely normal, trying to do her own version of bad undercover, wanting to get to know us and so in love with someone, she was willing to hide it, or at least try. I want to work with her on not telegraphing her intentions. We're going to fix it, don't worry. Her next attack be better coordinated."

"Trust me, she wasn't trying to hurt me. She's better trained than you think."

He studied me carefully then. "You know what you need? It's a little pizzaz in your life. I'm convinced she can give it to you. All you have to do is convince yourself that you're worthy. You can't let that bullshit with your dad get to you. Sebastian told me a little about his new family, total turds. The fact that they wouldn't give you that inheritance you deserve is bullshit. And as a result, you couldn't take care of your mom, which is even more bullshit. But you know what? They're the twats. That's not on you, that's on them. So don't let that shit carry on into your chance to actually have a real relationship. Not some bullshit chick who's going to be gone in the matter of a week, but a *real* relationship. If you want Jessa, be persistent. Find a way to show her how much you care about her every day until she's willing to listen, until she's willing to hear. My friend Roone, he's a persistent bastard. He never gives up on shit. Maybe if you see him, you can tell him that. Because the only person he ever had to prove he was worthy too was himself. Sebastian and I are already on that train."

I shifted uncomfortably in my chair. Likely, that was the longest Lucas had ever gone without talking about himself. "Careful, there was a compliment in there somewhere."

Lucas took a long pull of his beer. "Now, if we're done with the mushy shit, can we go surfing?"

"Your Highness, you're terrible on a surf board. My job is still currently to keep you alive."

"No, your job is to keep my *sister* alive. What I choose to do with *my* own time is *that* guy's problem."

Lucas pointed at Trevor Knox, one of the newer members of the Royal Guard who was standing behind him. Poor kid looked like he'd been having a hell of a day. If I knew Lucas, he was running him rough shod. "How many guards have you been through since I've been gone?"

Lucas grinned. "Not *that* many. I'll have you know good help is hard to find. It's hard for these guys to keep up with me. I'm a growing boy and I need my best boy back."

"I'm pretty sure you didn't like it when I was your guard. I think the words you used, were 'pain in my ass.'"

"Well, you are a pain in my ass. But you're *my* pain in the ass. You know what? Fuck guarding my sister. She moved home, so you can be *my* guard again. Even better, just be my friend. Wait, if my sister becomes a princess officially, does that mean you're a prince then?"

I laughed. "No, that's not how it works. That's not how any of this works. Haven't you been paying any attention?"

Lucas just laughed. "If you ask me, that's sexist. Bryna is about to become a princess. Penny is a queen. Seems like you should get to be a prince."

I just rolled my eyes. He was being outrageous as usual. But he had said one thing that made a whole hell of a lot of sense. If I wanted her, I was going to have to fight for her. Soldier or not, she was mine. I felt it down to the core of my being. And if Lucas and Sebastian didn't care, then I needed to get over my own inadequacies because I didn't want to lose her.

# EIGHT

*Jessa*

"So, there's like a team Winston Isles weekly meeting?"

Lucas laughed. "We usually call that game night, and laugh all you want, but Ariel is a card shark. I wouldn't trust her."

I had been kidding, but clearly, Lucas wasn't. "Oh, well glad to be invited, I guess."

Inside his office, Sebastian sat behind the desk. There was an older gentleman I didn't know with him. His skin was tan. He was tall and slightly austere, with salt and pepper at the temples. I would say he was good looking though. He looked slightly familiar, but I couldn't place him.

When everyone was in the office, including Bryna and Jinx, we all sat. The older gentleman walked over to me and then he bowed. "Your Highness. I know it's not official, but I would rather refer you in the most respectful manner. Allow me to introduce myself. I'm Ethan. I was a friend to your father."

Sebastian smiled at me. "Ethan was his best friend."

I stood and shook Ethan's hand. He looked confused that I stood. Was I supposed to stay seated? This was weird.

"And I'm also Penny's father."

Penny waved at me. "Yep, that's my dad. He's also in charge of Intelligence."

I nodded. "Well, it's nice to meet you. Now I know why you look familiar."

Sebastian groaned. "Please don't say that."

I suppressed a giggle.

Ethan took his position back next to Sebastian. I looked around. I'd been told that Sebastian's mother was alive, but she'd been away since I'd arrived. "Will the Queen Mother be joining us?"

Sebastian shook his head. "No, I'll fill her in later. She's been looking forward to meeting you though."

"Well, I'm not so sure about that."

Lucas leaned over from his post in a plush suede chair and squeezed my shoulder. "Trust me, she's totally cool. She was honestly more kind to me than my own mother was."

Wow. There was a story there. "Well, I guess that's good?" I glanced around the room. I deliberately did not meet Roone's gaze. I could feel his on me though. Every cell in my body was aware of him. My skin tingled with awareness. I wanted to run over and attach my body to his, like it was supposed to be. But no, we weren't doing that because he'd lied. And I had no idea who he was. "So, if it's not game night, what's the reason for this shindig?"

Sebastian leaned forward. "Well, this would be our planning meeting. We need to decide what to do moving forward. You're here now, so what I would personally like to do is go to the Regents Council and request the vote for coronation. When I first found Lucas, we changed the law to legitimize the previously illegitimate heirs to the throne, you and Lucas, and make you actual prince and princess. It was our father's last wish. That was signed into law over a year ago, and Lucas was officially crowned a few months ago. There's no reason any of them should say nay to your coronation, but if anyone does, I have enough votes to override them. But one way to make sure that doesn't happen is to introduce you to the Council. Honestly, it's just a formality since Lucas has already been crowned."

I shook my head. "You're saying these things like 'crowned' and 'prince' and 'princess,' and I really don't understand. A week ago, I was just sitting in my flat, trying to figure out why my neighbor was so annoying." I still didn't look at him. "And now you're telling me I'm a princess, and I need to be crowned, and there needs to be a vote. I need everyone to slow down for a minute."

Ariel stood and started pacing. "I wish we could slow down, but the truth is someone has tried to kill you more than once. Someone took out your father. Someone tried to take out Sebastian, and Lucas, and Penny." She was most emphatic when she said Penny. "And they are always a step ahead of us. For once, we need to have a plan that does not involve us playing catch up. I want to know what we're going to do and how to we're going to move forward because I need to keep all of you alive."

Ethan stared at her. "Do you have a suggestion?"

Ariel's gaze landed on me, and it felt slightly uncomfortable. "I say put Jessa back in play."

Sebastian glowered at her. "Excuse me?"

She put up her hands. "Listen, just hear me out. Right now, all anyone knows is that Jessa has vanished. She could be on vacation for all they I know."

"Actually, that's what I told my boss, Evan Millston. I told him was taking time off."

Roone asked the next question. "Does anyone know where you are?"

I didn't respond to him. Instead, I kept my gaze on Sebastian. "I only spoke to Phillip Winchester before coming. He is the history professor and my father's friend who helped me. He talked to me about the history of the islands and had some books that he shared with me, so I learned a little bit about King Jackson. He mentioned that there was a faction of the royal court who thought maybe our father shouldn't have been king."

Sebastian nodded. "This much we know. All because Uncle Roland abdicated."

Ethan sighed and ran a hand through his hair as he began to pace. "Actually, this might go even further back, to your grandfather's time. It's an old fight, and honestly, it's more lore and speculation than actual history. Every changing of the guard has been done according to law and without the bloodshed of a coup. But it's been messy as all things pertaining to power are. There's no one even old enough in the Regents Council to remember, really. Maybe a few of us that were close to King Cassius. And those of us with family in the guard would have had the lore passed down."

Sebastian leaned forward. "What do you mean going back to grandad's time?"

I piped up. "I think it's more than lore. At least to these people. Phillip had a book of some sort. He said it was a history book."

Sebastian rubbed at the stubble on his cheek. "You don't by chance have the book, do you?"

I shook my head. "No. In retrospect, I should have asked to borrow it. I mean it seemed old, but what do I know?"

My brother nodded at Ethan to continue. "Okay, King Cyrus, your great grandfather was ill. He knew the custom was that his brother, Angelus, take the throne as regent until Rhyse, your grandfather, came of age and proved himself worthy to the council."

Lucas took out a pad of paper. "I'm going to need to take some notes."

"Should an incoming monarch be under the age of rule, which was set by King Jackson himself, a regent had to be named. And if the Council saw forth that the regent was better fit to rule than the crown prince, the regent would be named king if he was of royal blood. On the off chance that the regent wasn't a listed member of the royal court, he couldn't become king under any circumstances. But if the regent was, say, a king's brother, then he could be named king, if the Council so voted." Ethan kept talking. "But Cyrus and his brother hated each other. The stories tell of some Cain and Able type of rivalry. And Angelus had three sons. Cyrus knew that Angelus would make a play for power and either kill the heir, banish him, or plot to depose him, so Cyrus held a secret meeting with the Council to have the law changed."

Sebastian blinked. "But couldn't that have gone horribly wrong?"

"Oh yes. There was a risk, but it was no greater than actually having Angelus become regent. It came out in Cyrus's favor though. It helped that he was well-loved and Angelus was not. At that meeting, they also stripped Angelus of his voting seat on the council. That part is actually in the history books as a footnote, but no reason is given. Though I suspect it was to make a point."

"I should have made popcorn," Penny muttered.

Her father ignored her. "So, upon Cyrus's death, Rhyse was made king. It was a bit of a scandal because he was so young, but there were some members of the Council who thought he could be easily influenced and controlled. That might have been why they changed the law. Angelus would listen to no one's counsel. King Rhyse proved to be a formidable opponent and a great strategist. Through a loophole, he managed to amass more Council seats in his name when members without heirs passed. Sebastian, as you know, he found a way to pass those voting seats to you, skipping over your father."

"This is some Tudor shite," muttered Roone.

Ethan turned to me and Lucas and gave us a brief explanation. "With every king, his queen, and any children he has, all get an equal voting seat on the Regents Council. Most laws need a majority vote on the Council. The King still gets the ultimate veto, but if he needs something to pass, he must have the votes. Nothing becomes a law that the king doesn't want. But consequently, nothing *can* become a law without the entire Council. So, the Council can't pull a stunt and oust the king because he has veto power. There is one exception... if the king is seen as unfit."

"But that could be anything," I argued. "Can they really depose a king for any reason?"

He nodded. "They need cause, but some can be found. Sebastian, that's why King Rhyse passed all those seats to you. He and Cassius didn't always see eye to eye, and he was afraid of how your father would use the additional seats."

"Jesus Christ, this is complicated," Sebastian said.

Ethan leaned against the book shelf. "Now, when we knew the tattoos were an issue, I did a little digging. There had to be a way Sandstorm was tied into all of this."

"Yeah Dad, that's a good point," Penny said. "He was convinced that he was Prince Roland's son."

"I think it has to do with lineage," Ethan added. "Duchess Maria, Roland's wife, is from Angelus's line. That much is in the history books too. It's why she was such a good match for him, and that was arranged. Angelus had three sons. Each had two children. Maria was the daughter of his oldest."

Sebastian frowned. "But, Sandstorm was Roland's son. Not Maria's."

Ethan shrugged. "You sure about that?"

Everybody stared at him agog.

"With his wild claims, we of course tried to run a blood test against Roland's. But Roland refused."

"He had nothing to fear. He wasn't king anymore. Why refuse?" Sebastian asked.

"He might not have wanted to give Sandstorm's claims credence. It wouldn't have changed anything. He was still going to be a traitor. But my guess is he was trying to protect someone else."

"Who?" I asked.

Lucas ran a hand through his hair. "I think I know this one. Maria, right?"

Ethan gave him a nod of approval. "Well done, my Prince." Lucas preened as Ethan explained. "Maria took a break from court the year Roland abdicated. Her whole life was in shambles. Some say she'd been in love with someone else and had her heart and her dreams broken."

Penny tried to make sense of it all. "Wow. That's a leap."

Ethan nodded. "Yes, it is. I had Robert Sandstorm's blood tested against Sebastian's to see if his claims were true. He was no match to Sebastian, so I knew Roland couldn't be his father. I suspected he might just have been fed lies, but I dug deeper. He'd been absolutely raised by his parents since birth, so where was he getting his theory?"

"I dunno. I'm a touch wanker-town," Roone offered unhelpfully.

Ethan shook his head. "I found hospital records. There was a Jane Doe that delivered in a private suite the same night he was born. She gave the baby up for adoption. That same night, the Sandstorms lost a full-term baby and adopted a motherless child."

Ariel frowned. "This is where you lose me. There would have been paperwork. A trail."

"You would think." Ethan said. "They were closed adoption papers, but I got as far down the rabbit hole as I could. Maria returned to court a month after Robert was born and taken home by the Sandstorms."

Sebastian's voice was low when he asked, "I assume you tested his blood against my cousins?"

"Only recently. I had no other reason to. Once we found Jessa, I started digging further down the rabbit hole. I didn't think I'd actually get a hit. The results came back this week. I thought he was just crazy, but he wasn't. His lineage made him a perfect candidate for the throne. Because he wasn't far off in his claims. He just had the wrong parent."

My head spun. I felt suddenly queasy. "This is incredible. Just to make sure I have it all, this is basically some enormous power play that started when our great-grandfather was named king. And people have used all of the drama to basically try to make a play for the throne."

Ethan nodded. "That sums it up pretty well."

I tried to suck in air. These people were trying to kill me, kill us. Because of a century-old feud. Roone stood and rushed over, kneeling in front of me. His hands were bigger than mine, calloused. Just the way I liked them. It took all my effort not to lean forward and wrap my arms around him and beg him to take care of me. Instead, I met my brother's gaze. "How do we make this stop?"

"That is exactly the question." Ariel said. "I like my plan. I think this will work."

Sebastian and Lucas shook their heads on that one. "No. We're not putting her back in play because there's more at stake here. Based on your reports while you were in London, she's got a legitimate stalker."

I chuckled. "Evan? He's a pain in the ass and kind of a jackass, but he's not a stalker. That's insane."

But as quickly as I was brushing him off, none of them looked at all like they were kidding. Weren't they kidding? "You guys can't be serious."

Ariel nodded. "I do have to agree on this one. He's fixated on someone else before."

"I think I could—" I started, but Roone interrupted me.

"It's not happening. Over my dead body. No one is putting Jessa in danger." His voice was deep. It rolled over me, making my body want things that it shouldn't. But I still couldn't look at him.

Ariel tried to stand him down. "Easy, Cujo, nothing bad is going to happen to her. We'll be watching her like hawks."

I didn't need her to speak up for me. "You guys, this is *my* life."

Sebastian shook his head. "Unfortunately, no it's not. As soon as you became a royal, your life stopped being your own. And right now, there is no way that any of us are going to let you step back into danger."

I chuckled. "You forgot, no one has crowned me yet, so I'm not even a real princess. So when I choose to leave here, and I will, I'll do exactly as I damn well please."

---

*Jessa*

TWO HOURS LATER, I wandered amidst the aroma of bougainvillea and hibiscus, listening as waves crashed on the beach in my new-found paradise.

"Your father used to love this part of the palace grounds too. He always said this was his favorite garden. He used to come down here all the time." I whipped around and saw the most beautiful woman. Her blond hair was down and flowing. The only mark that she maybe was older were the gentle crow's feet around her eyes. Otherwise, she was incredible, and her tanned, supple skin indicated she clearly wasn't afraid of being in the sun.

I didn't know what to do. Should I bow? Should I curtsy? I opted for a curtsy.

She shook her head. "You do not curtsy to me. You're the daughter of my love. Eventually, one day maybe you can just give me a hug."

"You're okay with me being here?"

"I wanted nothing more. If I'd had the opportunity, I would have helped raise you myself."

I stared at her. "So you knew about us? Me and Lucas?"

"Yes, I knew."

"You have to forgive me, but I don't understand how any of this is okay."

"Well, at the time, it wasn't okay. But we were married for convenience, not for love. We fell in love after many years together. You and Lucas were both born before that happened, and Cassius always regretted that he wasn't able to do more for you."

"Well, he could have come to get me at any time."

"You don't think he tried?"

I refused to look her in the eye. "I don't know what to believe anymore."

"He came for you as soon as he found out your mother was pregnant. He tried to set up a trust, wanted you to have every-thing that you would need, including access to him."

"But that's insane. Why would he do that? Most illegitimate children are shunned."

"Well, your father was trying to do things differently. But your mother wanted to talk things out with the other man she'd been involved with, the man you knew as your father. And well, we don't really do divorce here, so it wasn't like Cassius could leave me for her. But he wanted to look after you properly. He was a broken man when he realized that wasn't going to be allowed. I think for most of his life he felt like he failed you and Lucas."

"When my mother died, where was he then?"

"He came for you again, but it was too late. Someone else beat him to it, because you were gone, and he searched for you constantly until the day he died. He searched high and low. Once or twice he thought he was close. And then, three years ago, you turned up all on your own, back in London. The place where it all started. He didn't want to disrupt your life, but he did set into motion your inheritance. He wanted to make sure that you knew that you were always loved, that you'd always have a position here."

"I just don't know what to believe. My whole life I've been taught to be afraid of this mythical boogeyman. As an adult, I found out the mythical boogeyman is actually a real boogeyman who wants, what? To use me against the crown?"

She shrugged. "Something like that."

"I didn't ask for any of this royal intrigue."

"You know, the leaders never do. No one ever asks for anything. I think Lucas was just completely flabbergasted by the whole situation. And now you... What hell must you have gone through?"

"My life was fine." I tipped my chin up, determined not to cry. She didn't know my life. She didn't know what I'd had to endure.

*Stop being stubborn. She's being nice.*

"This is what's really hard. A week ago, I was just a girl with a job who was falling in love with this guy. And now I discover my guy was sent by my newly found big brother to guard me, or something. And I just don't know what to make of all of it. I still want my life to be my own."

"And I think it can be. I think Penny is discovering that. She has implemented a plan of her own so she can be her own kind of person and have to give none of it up."

"What does it mean? Is this all supposed to have some kind of wider meaning? If so, I'm missing it, or not taking full advantage of it, or something. I just... I want it to make sense to me."

"None of it is going to make sense. None of it. I'm still looking for how my love is gone. We had a good life, and he tried to be a good king. He would have been proud that all of you finally met and are now working together for the good of your country."

"I just wish I had gotten to meet him."

She smiled at me then, losing some of the air of regality about her, and showing nothing but the genuine kindness underneath. "I know he would have loved nothing more."

"I don't know how to do this. I feel like I'm failing and haven't even gotten started yet. All of this is so new and so strange and painful. When I came here, I don't know what I thought. Well, I thought all kinds of things, let me just say."

The queen mother laughed then. "Well, I can imagine. Sebastian didn't do well by forcing Roone to keep that lie. He didn't like it when it was done to him, but sometimes we are destined to be our fathers."

"I just want to go back to normal."

"I'm sorry, dear. I'm not sure that's entirely possible. But what I do know is that your brothers will do everything in their power to keep you safe. They will protect you, because whether you knew him or not, your father loved you all very much. And they are committed to finding who killed him, committed to finding out who has put all their lives in danger, and that includes you. You're not going to leave here tomorrow, or the next day, and be looking over your shoulder for the rest of your life. You have an army behind you."

"And you're okay with this?"

"Oh, you better believe it. You may not be a child of my loins, as they say, but because you are his, you are mine. And I protect what's mine. This is our family. Those who have terrorized us will meet an end they haven't ever dreamt of."

I watched her and was equal parts calmed and awed by her. She really was willing to take me in as hers. Phillip had been wrong about these people. Maybe not about the rest, but these people were not my enemy. But there was an enemy out there, an enemy coming for my family. And maybe it was time for my family to fight back.

# NINE

*Jessa*

I WASN'T sure why I was nervous. Nonetheless, I had to wipe the sweat off my palms as I stepped in the room to talk to my brother. "You've got time for me?"

He waved me in, just as he was finishing a call. When I took a seat, he hung up the phone and smiled. "Still feels weird, huh?"

"Totally."

His grin was easy as he rubbed the stubble on his jaw. He was like no king I'd ever seen before. He swore and smiled and laughed and cheated at cards, and that was just what I'd seen so far. "Yeah, I imagine it's weird. I mean, honestly, when I started this whole process, I didn't know what I'd find. I didn't know if you and Lucas would be cool or not, no idea. I just sort of went into it blind."

"So you found out about us, and you just decided that you were going to find us?"

"Basically. I know. Not much of a plan. And I was trying to keep it from the old man. It was a disaster. But surprisingly, I was able to find Lucas pretty easily. You though, you were harder to find."

"Well, I didn't know you were looking. Granted, if I had, likely my father would have made everything a lot more difficult before he passed."

"Yeah, very likely. So, I'm guessing by the nervous rubbing of your hands on your jeans that you have come to a decision?"

I met his gaze. His eyes were hazel, like mine. There was something similar about us around the lips too, I thought. Mine were fuller, but there was something about the shape. Looking at him, I felt like a little part of me was looking at myself. "Yeah, I'm going back. This has been a very pleasant vacation, but there are answers I need, things I need to do. I don't know what this means for the Winston Isles, or who I was supposed to be, but I am glad I came here to find you."

"You want my permission to be bait, don't you?"

I smiled. "I was working my way up to that. You ruined my whole speech."

"There's no speech needed. Your sister-in-law beat you to the punch after the meeting."

"It's still weird for me to hear words like sister-in-law. A week ago, I didn't know any of you existed. Now, I have two older brothers, and I'm about to have a couple of sisters. I know you don't want this, but it's my life, Sebastian."

"I know it's your life, but I at least have to try to keep you safe."

"You don't owe me anything. We just met a few days ago."

"Well, to you we just met, but I've been looking for you forever. When Dad died, all the knowledge of where you were went with him. He never told us where you were, just that he'd found you. He kept it close to the vest. Even Ethan didn't know, and Ethan was privy to everything. All I know is that now we've found you, and I don't want you going back into danger."

"But that's just it. You don't *know* if I'm in danger. Sure, my place was broken into, and someone took Dad's sketches, but that could have been a coincidence."

Sebastian raised a brow. "You cannot believe in coincidence."

"Okay, fair enough. But I'm just saying, it could be anything."

"No, it could *not* be anything. They broke in because they wanted those images, plain and simple. And I messed up. I should have had Roone tell you who you were right away, and then we could have had the conversation and had it done. But I figured you would bolt if you knew. Kind of like I did. The moment I found out about you and Lucas, I didn't take it well."

"You were worried about us usurping you?"

"No, I was mostly looking for Lucas because I was hoping he would just slide into the role of king."

I blinked at him. "You went after Lucas to make him king?"

"Yep. I was running away from my duties. I did *not* want to be a king. But Penny helped me see that I could help so many more people. I was an artist. A photographer, actually. And I still get to do that, but in a different kind of way. I know that all of this is daunting, but I promise you, we'll figure it out. But please God, do not walk into danger before we have a game plan."

"I hear you, and I understand. You're just doing your job, protecting your subjects. The good news is I'm not one of your subjects *yet*."

"I don't like it."

"You try and protect your subjects, your people. *Our* people. Let me do what I can. There's a high likelihood that it's just a stalker, which, I get, is bad enough. But I hate for everyone to go to all this trouble just for me only to find out later that I wasn't in any danger at all. That would be terrible. Just let me go back. I promise, I'll follow your orders. Whatever you want."

My gaze met his, and he was smiling slightly. I, on the other hand, was not. "I'm pretty sure you won't follow a single order."

"Sebastian, this is a courtesy. I'm going home regardless. If you don't want to help, I'll do it myself. So you might as well just give me permission."

He stared at me. "I am going to regret this somehow, aren't I?"

I grinned back. "Yep, probably."

---

### *Roone*

"SO, we're still going to pretend that you and my sister aren't a thing?"

I worked my jaw and stared straight ahead. Sebastian was predictable. Bringing me out to the polo field to talk, it was kind of our thing. Whenever one of us wanted to tell the other one something hard or important, we tended to come out here. "There's nothing going on with us. I was her Royal Guard. Even if I stepped over a line, I guarantee you that I will never make that mistake again."

Sebastian rolled his eyes. "You are still so stubborn."

"Me or you, who's the stubborn one?"

"Remember when I couldn't get my shit right with Penny? I couldn't get around the fact that she lied to me. Despite that she'd taken orders, despite that she was trying to save me, I couldn't get over it, and I was acting like a dick. And you point blank said, I either loved her or I didn't, and that determined everything."

"You're paraphrasing."

"Fine, I'm paraphrasing. But do you remember that conversation?"

"Vaguely."

"Good, because we are about to have the same, or similar type of conversation. You are my best mate. Always have been since we were eleven. I know you have your own set of shit. Everyone does. But you are the one person in the world I trust with everything. With my family, my life, the crown. If I could have made you a prince already, I would have. Instead, I can force the council to knight your ass, if you need me to."

Was he insane?

"You don't need to make me a knight. The Regents Council would never allow it. I'm not a blue blood. And I'm still technically English."

"I don't give a fuck what they say. You forget, I have the votes to do pretty much whatever I damn well please. It's only out of respect that I don't."

"Nor should you. That's a bad precedent, you know that."

"I don't care. That's the point. I sent you in, my best man, to guard my brother *and* my sister. You did what you had to do."

"What I had to do did not include crossing a boundary."

Sebastian just shook his head. "Man, I don't care. All I need is the best person on the job. And that's you. What you do in your own time is not my business, but if I can be best friend Sebastian now, I'd advise you to pull your head out of your ass. She cares about you. She's just reeling from all of this news. A week ago, she showed up in these islands all alone, and soon she'll be leaving with two new brothers, a sister-in-law, a sister-in-law to be, a stepmom of sorts, and she's used to being on her own. She's used to being the one in charge and calling the shots. It can't be easy on her. Remember, *I,* not you, *I,* made everything more difficult on her by not letting you just tell her the truth. Granted, we would have another kind of headache on our hands, but suffice it to say, we did what we thought we had to do, and let's move on from there."

"If you say so."

"Roone?"

I slid my glance over to him as thoroughbreds thundered by. "Yeah?"

"If you love her, like actually love her... then don't be a twat."

For the first time since coming home, I laughed. I truly laughed. I don't know if it was Sebastian with his American accent saying twat or just the effort it took him to be serious with me for a moment. Or hell, maybe I just needed to laugh. I threw my head back and let out all of the tension. Jessa was safe for the moment. Safe. She knew the truth, which was even better. She still hated me, but that was neither here or there. It didn't matter anyway.

She was safe.

Sebastian continued, "I'm not fond of her plan. I don't want to use her as bait, but I might not have any choice. I wish there was another way, but right now it doesn't look like there is one. I need to end this, once and for all."

"I agree. I'd rather people stop taking shots at my family."

Sebastian turned and grinned at me then. "Glad to see that you remember you have family."

"I never lost sight of it."

"Good. Because as family, I'm putting you back in as her guard."

I shook my head. "Are you insane?"

"Maybe. She's not going to be thrilled about it, but it's not as if you are going to let anyone else guard her."

"Yeah, I'll go."

"There's no one else I'd trust my sister with."

"I hear you. I wouldn't let anyone else guard her anyway.

Besides, you're the one who has to tell her the good news. And I can't wait to see the look on her face."

For the first time since he and Penny had gotten together, Sebastian looked legitimately scared. "Are you serious right now? I have no idea if she's going to shoot my nuts off."

I grinned. "Well, there's only one way to find out."

# TEN

*Roone*

THE FLIGHT WAS MOSTLY a silent affair. I and four other guards boarded the plane with the princess. Ariel would join us in two days.

The other guards were at the back of the plane leaving me and Jessa at the front. As soon as we embarked, Jessa made a show of putting her earbuds in and relaxing all the way back. Then she pulled up a blanket and closed her eyes.

So, she was doing the full-on pretending-I-wasn't-there thing. About three hours into the flight, I finally leaned over as she sat up to take a sip of water. "Jessa, we're going to be in tight quarters. You can't pretend you don't know me."

She slid me a glance and fire danced in her eyes. "You'll be amazed at what I can pretend."

My dick stirred because he had no idea what was good for him. "I know you're mad. But we need to work together. And I will point out the hypocrisy because Ariel lied too and you're not mad at her."

"You think this is about the lie? Yeah, that's bad, but you

didn't just lie. You made me believe. I believed you had fallen for me. Ariel lied, sure, but she didn't fuck me, give me orgasms, and pretend to care about me."

**Dick**: I can still give her orgasms. Let me try.

**Me**: Shut it.

I scrubbed my hand over my face because she was right. I'd crossed the line, that was why she was really mad. She didn't know what to believe.

"Jessa—" Before I could finish, she rolled her eyes.

"Oh, it's Jessa now. No more princess?"

"I never meant to hurt you. It wasn't my intention."

"Oh, so I was just an assignment."

"No. You know that's not true."

"I don't know what I know. I do know that I want you to stay away from me. As far away as humanly possible."

I chuckled low. "You recognize how hard that's going to be."

"I know you're my personal guard. I get it. Stay close, that's what Sebastian wants. I will comply, but I don't have to talk to you."

How exactly did she think this was going to go? "Do you realize that we're going to be living together, princess?"

She whipped her head around and glared at me. "Don't call me *princess*." And then it took her another beat to ask, "What the hell do you mean we'll be living together?"

"Yeah, two guards will be placed across the hall in my old flat. Two guards will be placed across the street. And the other guard," I waved, "will be in your apartment."

She shook her head. "There's no way in hell. No way, no how."

"What do you think Sebastian meant when he said that I was going to be your personal guard?"

"I don't know. I thought he meant that you'd follow me around. Wave a gun or what not. I didn't realize that I had to live with you. He can't mean that we have *live* together. If he doesn't know about before, he certainly suspects."

I decided normalcy was what she needed, so I shifted back into annoying-twat mode. "I get it. You care about me. You're pissed off that I didn't tell you the truth, and then I took you into an area that I couldn't explore. And I feel bad about that. I'm sorry. I wish things had turned out differently. I wish I'd been able to help myself, but I wasn't. And now here we are. So the best we can do is try and get along, because right now, you're stuck with me. Flatmates."

She glared at me. "This is not going to last long. I was really clear with Sebastian. No more antics."

"Sweetheart, every time you don't get your way, you think it's some kind of antic, when in reality, you just weren't paying attention. He was very clear. 'Roone is to be your personal guard.' Personal guard means I am with you twenty-four/seven, whether you like it or not. Good luck trying to get rid of me."

"Oh, I'm getting rid of you. I just have to figure out how."

It was nice to see the fire back in her eyes. "You're more than welcome to try."

She shrugged. "I'll do more than try."

**Dick**: I can't wait.

---

*Jessa*

IT WAS WEIRD BEING HOME. It had only been a week, but it felt like a lifetime. Like everything in my life had changed... the things I knew to be true, the things I knew to be *me*. None of it was true. And if none of it was true, then who the hell was I?

I had my keys out, and Roone deftly took them out of my hands. "Sorry, princess, but you don't go in first anymore."

I frowned at him. "I see you're back to calling me princess."

"Well, it *is* your title."

"That's why you called me princess all those times?"

He shrugged. "Well, I called you princess the first time because it was a slip of the tongue. And then it pissed you off, so I kept doing it."

I rolled my eyes. "You're a jackass."

"I think you've called me worse."

He slipped the lock and turned. When he pushed open the door, he immediately ducked, shoved me back, and then tackled whoever it was that swinging something at him.

A round of grappling and "oophs" and "oh shit," and he was back on his feet like a cat. Agile and smooth and gently pulling someone up with him. Someone tiny.

"Chloe!"

Chloe peeked around him. "Oh my God, it's you guys. Do you not realize that, well, after this place was broken into and someone tried to kidnap Jessa, every time I come here, I come with a weapon?" She pointed at the giant umbrella on the floor.

"Yeah, it's a great weapon." Roone nodded solemnly. "You almost had me there."

Chloe just stared up at him. "You're huge. Do you know that? And also surprisingly agile. I didn't feel a thing. You broke my fall, turned around, and were back on your feet in seconds. That's some ninja stuff right there."

Roone just shrugged. "You're not hurt?"

I was pretty sure his muscles had rendered her dumb because Chloe kept staring at him.

"Chloe, what are you doing here?" I asked.

"Watering your plants."

I blinked at her. "What plants?"

She rolled her eyes. "The ficus in the corner. And the orchid I stuck in your bathroom."

"Chloe, you know those aren't real, right?"

"That orchid is real."

I shook my head "No, it's not."

Her brows furrowed. "No, I bought you that orchid."

"Yes, I remember. It was our first year working together. And I made a joke that it was the only plant I could keep. I couldn't have a pet because I couldn't keep anything alive. The only pet I could keep was the plastic kind. For Christmas, you gave me that orchid."

Chloe blinked. "I have risked my life every day to water plastic flowers?"

I grinned at her. "You're a good friend."

"Plastic flowers!"

Roone's lips twitched, and I couldn't help a soft giggle. "Well, they're well hydrated."

She shook her head and bent down to pick up the umbrella. "I have been risking my life for plastic flowers. Well, I hope you two had a great lover's vacation. Now that you've taken several years off of my life, I want to go home."

My eyes went wide. "A lover's vacation? What in the world are you—"

Roone wrapped his arms around me and pulled me close, then placed a kiss to my forehead. "Chloe, you're the best."

I wasn't sure what bothered me more; the kiss or that Chloe thought we were on a lover's vacation.

What the fuck was he on about? He was insane. That was the only explanation. But then he squeezed me even harder and gave my shoulder two squeezes. Ah, he wanted me to go along with this. But why? And then I got it. Chloe couldn't know. No one could know, because if I was actually being bait, everyone would have to think everything was normal, not that I was here on some kind of undercover mission. So I forced a smile on my face, even though I wanted get out of Roone's strong embrace.

*The hell you do.*

My stupid body was loving every second of it. The scent of him was wrapping around me, filling my nostrils, relaxing me, and making me want to ease into those muscles.

To pull this off, it was best to go along. And it seemed he was going to pretend to be my boyfriend, my blooming boyfriend.

Well, for what it's worth, it could have been mostly true. *And you would have loved every second of it.*

Yeah, I *would* have loved it, but it wasn't true now. Now were lying to my friend. *Or, you can look at it as keeping you safe.*

"Yup, vacation. It does your body good." The irony was the Caribbean *had* done me good. I was more relaxed than I'd been in years, but I still didn't know what to make of everyone. I needed time to process.

The girls had been fun, and crazy, and amazing, and I still couldn't believe Ariel was some kind of insane hacker. And she'd made up Meet Cute. Oh God, what did that mean for Chloe's date? Who was he?

Another problem for another day. But first, I needed to figure how I was going to live with Roone.

"Oh my God, you guys are so cute together. Where were you anyway?"

Roone answered before I could. "Hawaii. It was amazing. The water was so clear and blue and warm."

I frowned, why wouldn't he just tell her the Caribbean? *Because, you idiot, first of all, anyone could be listening. Second of all, Chloe might inadvertently say something.*

So, this was to be my new normal, trying to lie and figure out who's lying in return? I wasn't sure how long I'd be able to live like that.

Chloe laughed. "Oh my God, relationship goals. You just whisked her away to Hawaii?"

Roone nodded, still with his arm around me. "Yup. She needed the break."

"I'm going to leave you two lovebirds alone. I'm sure you want to unpack. But it's good to have you back. Evan has been going insane." She slid a glance over to Roone. "I told you he was jealous of Roone. Maybe next time you'll listen to me."

Then she was gone. I shoved Roone away. "You plan to make people think we're together?"

"It will be easier. The whole hate-to-love-you thing, is not going to work for much longer. I need to be with you all the time. When you're at Ben's, I can just protect you with surveillance. And since Ben knows some of the deal, he'll be able to accommodate. But, when we step out these doors, everyone in the world needs to believe that we're together, a happy couple meeting for lunch, a happy couple strolling around town, a happy couple... do you get it?"

But what I focused on was 'Ben.' "When did you tell Mr. Covington?"

Roone winced. "Well, Ben is my cousin."

I blinked. "What? Ben Covington of London Lords is your cousin?" I thought back to that first meeting and wanted to disappear. He was probably laughing his ass off now. "He has more money than God. Covington is your cousin?"

He nodded solemnly. "Yep, lucky me."

"I just can't believe it."

I rolled my eyes. "He knows I'm not in PR, so while you're there I'll have one job."

"What, you're just going to quit Evans?"

I chuckled low. "Well, I'll keep doing what we were doing before. If Evan objects too much to the relationship, I'll talk to Rick about being undercover. We might be able to work it out."

"Wow, you have this all figured out."

He shrugged. "Yeah."

Then suddenly it all crashed into me, the gravity of what was happening, the intricacies, and all the moving parts. This was going to be insane. And then regret weighed in. What had I done? I needed to breathe. I needed some space.

*No, what you need to do is talk to Phillip. He may be able to give you some more answers.*

But I also didn't want to take Roone with me. It would be difficult enough to explain to Phillip what the hell was going on.

Maybe I'd call and make an appointment. In the meantime, I had to figure out how the hell I was going to live with Roone.

# ELEVEN

*Jessa*

MAYBE IT WASN'T the best idea I'd ever had, but I needed to speak to Phillip. I needed help to untangle everything I'd learned, and honestly, I didn't think Roone would allow it.

*There might be a reason for that.*

Phillip wasn't going to hurt me. He was a friend, and he'd cared about my father. It was surprisingly easier to ditch my guard than I thought. I simply told them that I needed to go to Evans PR for something. And once at Evans, I knew the exits better than he and his men did. There was a rarely used service exit in the basement. Just like that, I had a car waiting and I was out the door.

My heart hammered against my ribs. This was really stupid. And honestly, I could have just told him I needed to see Phillip.

*Have you met Roone?*

Okay, fair enough. He'd have insisted on being there, and it just would have been a mess. And frankly, I wanted to tell Phillip about the trip and everything I was feeling. It was strange how comfortable I felt with him. As I sat in the back of the Uber, my phone rang.

*Roone. Shit,* I hadn't cut it off. I turned it off but couldn't figure out how to remove the battery. I had no idea why that was important, but they did it in the movies. But since I didn't know how to remove it from my iPhone, it was just going to have to do.

When the car dropped me off in front of the university, I glanced around. The whole university seemed to be milling about, running to class, or to work, or hanging out with friends.

I wrapped my coat around me to help block out the spike of cold. Even though it was technically spring, there was still a hint of a cold snap every now and again. I took the worn-out stairs, unable to believe that I'd managed to pull one over on Roone. Although there was a part of me that was concerned he'd be worried. Should I have left a note?

This morning, true to his word, he'd mostly kept out of my way. By the time I woke up, he'd apparently worked out and showered already. And he was out of the apartment, waiting outside in the hall. It almost like I didn't have a flatmate.

*And why do you feel so guilty?*

*Stop. It feels weird because of how everything happened.*

We'd figure it out.

When I knocked on Phillip's office door, no one answered. I knocked again, leaning my ear against the door, waiting to hear footsteps. I checked the time, it was 8:30. He should have been here. He had office hours at 8. It was recorded on the website.

I tried the door, and it gave way easily.

If he wasn't here, why wouldn't he lock it? And then I pushed the door open.

There were papers everywhere. His heavy oak desk had been moved off-center. The chairs in the room were upended or strewn about.

Oh God, someone had been here. But who? Every instinct

told me to back away, to run, to turn and bolt and call Roone and beg for protection.

But there was a part of me that refused to believe it, refused to accept it. Something had happened to this man.

Had something happened to him because he'd helped me? Was this related to my brothers? I couldn't just sit here and accept what I was seeing.

I did a double check, and there was no laptop anywhere in sight. Another cursory look told me that there were also no personal items, no coat or briefcase. The room had just been destroyed. Who would do this to him? Who would make this happen?

*It doesn't matter. You need to get out of here.*

But it was too late. I heard the footsteps outside the door. With mere seconds to spare, I had nowhere to hide. My body screamed at me, *Danger is coming.*

Why on earth had I thought it would be a fantastic idea to leave Roone behind? This was dumb. I should have listened to him, but instead, I'd put myself in even more danger.

---

*Roone*

WHEN I CAUGHT up to Jessa, I was going to palm her arse.

She'd slipped the guards on her detail. She had to do one thing, one little thing, which was listen. Follow through. It was all she had to do. But the moment she'd had a free minute, she pretended to go in into Evans PR, slipped out the side, and then dodged our guy on the street. God, she was such a pain in the ass. All of them were. Sebastian used to do it to me. Granted, he'd always text me later and tell me where he was. And

Lucas... Lucas had been the worst. And now her. Was that a Winston Isles bloodline thing?

Either way, I bolted up the stairs toward Phillip Winchester's office, fury coursing through my veins, thinking about all the ways I was going to make her pay for this. But when I found her, she was sitting in the middle of Winchester's upturned office, and she was shaking.

"What the fuck do you think you're doing?"

She looked up at me. "He's... he's not here. I—"

Oh, I wasn't letting her finish. I advanced on her, and that snapped her out of her shock. Fire lit her eyes, and she backed up. "You had one rule. You do not slip your security detail. What the fuck is wrong with you?"

"Stop yelling at me."

"I'll stop yelling when you stop acting like a five-year-old."

"I had to see him. I did not understand some of the things that he told me about. I just wanted to clarify, and I knew if I asked you—"

"Shut up. So you came on your own?"

"You don't tell me to shut up."

"I will tell you to shut up, especially when it involves keeping you safe, protected."

"I feel like I already told you that I don't handle assholes very well, so you're going to have to check your current behavior."

"You, princess, are the one who's going to have to check your behavior. Do you recognize that Sebastian could have ordered you to stay in the Winston Isles?"

"The hell he could have. I'm not one of his subjects."

"If he'd wanted you to stay, you wouldn't have left." I injected just a hint of menace into my voice. In truth, there was no way Sebastian would have stopped her. He could have sequestered her, confined her to quarters, but he would never do that. The thing was *she* didn't know that.

Her mouth fell open. "I wasn't a prisoner. Just who do you think you are?"

"I am your guard, and it's your job to listen to me."

"I am done listening to you. I never should have agreed this. I cannot stand you."

She was backed up against the wall now, and I was still in her space. Amidst the upturned bookshelves and the papers scattered on the floor, our breaths came out in harsh pants and co-mingled. "Let me be really clear with you, princess, you will do as you're told, and you *will* follow directions. You will not ditch your guard ever again. Have I made myself clear? Or should I talk more slowly so you'll understand? You're a smart girl. But you shouldn't think you're smarter than all of us. I just wish you'd use your brain."

That did it. Her hand twitched, and she let lose. She had to guess that I was going to catch and block her slap, but she was probably hoping this was one of those moments that caught me by surprise.

It wasn't. I caught her on the wrist. I nearly growled at her, my fury was so close to the surface. Her other hand flew out. I caught her and bracketed both her arms above her head against the wall and then leaned forward. "I thought we'd already covered this princess. Tsk, tsk. That is not the way to solve your problems."

"I hate you."

"No, you don't."

And then, like the idiot I was, I kissed her. It was less kiss, and more clash of teeth and tongues and lips. I sucked on her bottom lip, gently nipping as I let it go. Her body quivered against mine.

A part of me did a mental calculation. *We don't have time*

*for this*. Like a moron, I hadn't even cleared the room. Anyone could be coming up behind me. As I'd been taking those stairs two at a time, I'd had two guards behind me who had more than likely posted at the door, so we were protected. Which meant I had a minute.

A minute to indulge, a minute to remind her just how good it was with us. A minute to enjoy because I hadn't touched her in over a week. I was desperate. Hungry. And she was fighting me at every turn. I pressed my hips into her, just so she could feel the length of me, feel how much I wanted her.

I was going to let her go. I was. And then she made that sound at the back of her throat, a mewling one. The one she always made when she wanted me to do more of something.

Shit. If we kept this up, I was going to end up fucking her right here.

**Dick:** I am so down for that.

**Brain:** Yeah, so am I.

I switched my hold, so that I held her wrists in one hand. And then I slid my other hand into her hair and angled her head so I could lick into her mouth. I could try and taste my fill, get my fill, because for over a week, I had been willing her to be mine, willing her to forgive me, even if I didn't feel like I was good enough. And she'd been refusing to give in. Which was fine, that was her prerogative. But she couldn't just stand here now and fucking pretend with me.

She slid her tongue over mine, and when mine slid back in, she sucked on it. I groaned low and hitched my hips. She arched her back, angling her hips toward me in slow pumping motion.

*Yeah, that's it. Show me that you want it.* Still restraining her hands, I slid my free hand out of her hair and down her torso. I tucked my hand under her shirt, and her inhale was sharp. Pointed. I immediately stilled, waiting for her response, and she stayed tight and frozen. I'd stop. I'd walk away. It would kill me, but I had to leave her alone.

That was not how I wanted her. I wanted her yielding and so soft she was practically melting. I wanted her on the verge of begging so that I could remind her how good it was with us. So that I could say I was sorry properly. So that I could ask for her complete forgiveness. So that I could hear my name on her tongue again. That's what I wanted. That's what I dreamed of. Those lonely nights in Winston Isles, all I wanted to do was stand on the balcony and point out all the parts of the island that we could see, how each part had become my favorite sites. I wanted to show her how sometimes the Winston Isles felt more like home than London ever did. I wanted to show her all of it. Instead, I'd been by myself on my own balcony wondering what she was doing.

When she whimpered, I knew her answer. I slid my hand up her torso, until it dusted over her nipple.

She shook in my arms. And then I dragged down the cap of her bra, all lace and satin. It tore just a little, but I didn't care. I wanted access and I wanted it now. As long as she wanted it too, I was going to take it.

She tore her lips from mine. "Yes. Oh my God, yes."

I palmed her rougher than I'd planned to. My control was just on the edge. I wasn't going to make it if I kept this up. Holding her firmly, I squeezed. She sucked in a shivering breath and arched into my palm. I rubbed my thumb over her nipple and then gently pinched with my forefinger. And then she was practically begging.

"Please, please just—I just—I want it."

My nose tucked in the hollow of her throat, I whispered against her skin. "You want what?"

"You. I just... I need it."

"If you need something, you're going to have to tell me exactly what you want, princess."

I was torturing us both. I wanted the words she couldn't give me yet. I knew it. But it was fun asking her to say it. She wasn't ready. We needed more time. But if this was what I could have right now, I was going to take it.

"Roone."

"Princess." I pinched her nipple again, and she fought my hold on her wrists, but I gently kept her arms where I wanted them. So she angled her hips up and gently rolled over the length of me.

Holy shit. At this point, I didn't care who fuck came in the room. I was ready to cum. I could cum.

"You're playing with fire, princess."

"Good."

"Oh, is it?"

I released her nipple, and her whimper was audible.

"Oh, I have something else I think you'll like better."

I slid my hand down her petal soft skin to the button of her jeans and snapped quickly, then unzipped. She threw her head back, giving me better access to her neck, and she whispered, "Yes, God. Oh my God."

I tipped the hem of her panties and slid my hand inside. Down the front, over her clit to the wet center—oh fuck. She was soaking. So, so wet. Had she ever been this wet before? Had I ever felt her like this before?

No. This was different. This was raw. I slid a finger inside then retreated slowly, and she dragged her head back and forth. "Yes. Go on."

I sank two fingers deep, but at that angle I couldn't quite work my thumb over her clit. I knew what she wanted. I knew what she needed. She moaned in my arms. And then I kissed her again to muffle her cries. Against her lips I said, "It feels like you've been missing me, princess."

"Shut up. Keep doing that."

"Not unless you ask nicely."

"Oh God, just please, okay? I'm begging. Why isn't it good enough for you?"

"Because I want more than this. It has to be more than this." And even though both my dick and my brain were threatening me, I gently eased out of her and pulled my hand back. Against her lips I whispered, "We could do this. It would be easy. I turn you around, shove your jeans down, slid my dick inside you, and have you scream my name in seconds."

"I vote yes to that plan."

"Yeah, so does my dick. But that's not the plan I want. We're not doing this until you actually want me again."

"You're here. I'm here. Clearly, I want you."

"No, you're just looking for me to get the job done. We're not doing this until you've reconciled what happened before and what you know now. When you do, we can do this. But until then, let's get your clothes back on."

Gently, I released her arms, wary of her hands striking out at me again, but they didn't.

"You're serious?"

"Yeah, dead serious. We've been here before, remember?"

Her gaze narrowed. "Yes, I remember."

"It's not a habit. I'm not trying to make you insane. I just know that if we do this now, you'll still hate me. That's not what I want."

"Why does it have to be so complicated?"

"Because whether you acknowledge it or not, I was trying to do the right thing. You just can't see that."

"Sure, I finally see it."

I chuckled low. "I know, right now, you'll say just about

anything to get off, but it's not happening. And if you do really see it, figure out if you could actually start to care about me again. Otherwise, there is no point. We're just going to set each other on fire and watch the whole house burn."

"What's wrong with that?'

"That's not what I want. Not from you. For the first time in my life, I was personally invested in someone. So, I'm not selling myself short. Come on princess, let's get you out of here and then figure out what the hell happened to Phillip Winchester."

"I don't think I like you."

I shrugged. "That's fine. You'll come around."

She glowered at me, adjusted her clothing and then stomped ahead of me. As I thought, the others were outside the door, silently waiting.

She shifted her glance toward them and then back over her shoulder at me. "You guys knew?"

I laughed. "Princess, you're good. But you're not that good."

# TWELVE

*Ariel*

I wasn't sure I'd ever been more scared in my life.

Where the hell was Dad? I had looked everywhere and so had Matthias, but he was gone. I couldn't sit back and wait with everything that was happening. I'd taken two extra days in the islands to look for him to no avail. Once I was back in London, I knew it was going to be more difficult to trace him from there.

But he wasn't my only problem. Jessa's contact, Winchester, was gone too. Just up and gone missing. No plane ticket, no bus ticket, no train ticket we could find. Nothing on cameras. Nothing on CCTV. Just gone. Given the state of his office, Jessa was worried.

As he was the only one who seemed to have any information on her father or the Heirs of Angelus, we needed to find him. Preferably alive so we could question him.

It was do or die time. And I was going to do... or die. I wiped my hands on my jeans and made the call.

I was one of the few people in the Royal Guard with a direct line to the King of the Winston Isles. As a matter of fact, that circle was small. It was team Winston Isles, basically. Every time he changed his phone number, we all got a new text, saying, 'This is Sebastian.'

Same with Penny. But Penny was my best friend, and if she didn't tell me her new number, I would hunt her down and kill her. Sebastian and Penny changed their numbers about once every six months to a year or so, just in case someone overzealous got a hold of it.

I made the call with my hands shaking. Sebastian answered right away. His voice was wary. "Everything okay?"

"Yes, Your Majesty."

He sighed. "You only ever call me Your Majesty when something is wrong. What's up, Ariel?"

I started pacing around my flat. I opened my fridge, willing myself to find something in there that was edible, but I knew better. That why I spent so much time at Roone's place. "Um, I don't know how to say this, but I have reason to believe that it was my father who accessed to Princess Jessa's files."

There was a beat of silence. "Explain."

Even knowing that I had profusely fucked up, Sebastian's voice was still low, still kind, and there was no anger in it. "Okay, right at the start of this mission with Jessa, I got a call that he needed a place to stay for a couple of days. I know it's against protocol, and I'm sorry. But I didn't think that there would be any harm. I should have said no right away, or I should have called Ethan and cleared it. I didn't think. There was a lot going on."

Sebastian's voice was ever patient. "Okay, calm down. Fine, your father said he wanted to come and stay. Not a big deal. He has a visitor's pass. He'd been cleared for visits in the past."

"I know, which is why I didn't worry. He said something had happened to his flat and he just needed to stay a couple of days. And I gave him the rules. No going to the palace. You know, head right and straight to the parking lot for his transportation to work."

"Okay, what happened after that?"

"Well, what happened after that is, I couldn't reach him. I called and called and checked my security footage, and instead of going right every day that I checked, he went left. I asked Penny to look in on him just to make sure he was behaving. She said that there was evidence that he'd been there, but not that he was really staying there. And by the time she checked, he wasn't there anymore."

"Okay, still really not damning evidence that he has accessed Jessa's files. Besides, from my understanding, we went over all security protocols and risks, and your father is not exactly like you. He doesn't have the skill set to do what you do."

"I know. And the way we set up the firewall, he would need to be some A-grade hacker. And he's not, but I'm still concerned. Once I found out that it looked like *I* was the one who accessed the server, I knew there was trouble because we set it up so that it can't be accessed off site. And I was here, so someone made it look like I did it. I could only imagine that would be him. He wouldn't have access to any of my codes, but if someone spent a little time in my place getting to know me better, they might be able to figure it out."

"Okay, that's a bigger problem, but I'm pretty sure it wasn't him for two reasons. First, how would he get access to our server which is inside the palace? Second, he didn't have the skill set. So, you might be over reacting. We've already had our guards infiltrated once, so it's entirely possible we have another mole."

"Yes, it is entirely possible. But the things that make me nervous are my security protocols being used, and my father pulling a vanishing act." I cleared my throat. "Unfortunately, you know my father. I think I need to step down... at least for the mission, if not from the Royal Guard entirely."

That earned an immediate response. "What the fuck? Think it through. We'll find your father. But you quitting? That's not going to happen. So if you would like to temporarily put Roone in charge while you track your old man down, fair enough. But you're not quitting. You're a member of this team. Until you tell me that you no longer want to be, you're stuck, do you hear me?"

Relief poured through me so instant and swift that I almost choked. Tears stung my eyes, and I blinked them back rapidly. I willed myself not to cry over this. "I – I am so sorry. I know it's impossible to trust anyone right now, and I've broken that trust and I—"

"Shut up. I don't want to hear this nonsense. Find your father."

"I will. And Sebastian, I know what it means if I can't find him. If he's involved..."

"I feel like I told you to shut up already. I have zero interest in hearing this particular line of thought. You're a member of the team."

Why was he being so stubborn? "Listen, I know. But I do have to be candid. I am a member of Intelligence after all. And once I'm done speaking with you, I'm going to call Ethan. But since we're practically family, I wanted you to know first."

He chuckled on a breath. Penny and I had been saying that he was inadvertently in a thrupple, he just didn't know it. And he'd consistently asked what a thrupple was until he finally found out. Then, like an idiot, he wanted to know why he didn't get the full benefits of being in a thrupple and just got the negative elements. But somehow along the way, he'd become family to me, even though he was His Royal Majesty.

"One step at a time, Ariel. If you need to go find your father, temporarily put Roone in charge. You will *stay* on the team, so do what you need to do and come back."

"Sebastian... I mean, Your Majesty—"

"Seriously, if you call me Your Majesty one more time, I swear to God..."

"Sorry... I'm just trying to be as formal as possible since this is bad news. But if I can't find him, you'll be the first to know, and I am sorry."

"Never apologize about choosing to help your family. That's not how this works. So, do what you need to do and keep me posted."

He hung up, and my hand dropped to my side as the adrenaline flooded my body. Jesus Christ, that had been the most stressful phone call I'd probably made in the last six months. He'd stood by my side though, which I hadn't expected.

I knew I *should* have expected it because it was Sebastian, and he always insisted we were family. Outside of Penny and her family, team Winston Isles was my ride or die, the kind of family and friends I'd always wished for. I hadn't known that they could exist when I was younger, and it would hurt to lose them.

But while His Majesty wasn't thinking about the future, I was. Which meant that I had to find my father fast, and I prayed he hadn't done something stupid that would jeopardize all of our lives.

---

*Roone*

BACK AT THE FLAT, things were still tense with Jessa. She was silent on the drive back. Not solemn exactly, just introspective.

It was the weekend, so we hadn't had to go into the office. I'd had Ben cover for me by requesting me for a 'special assignment' while I was gone, so that had explained my absence from Evans PR.

We'd been home for a couple of days, and Jessa still hadn't said a word to me. *Home.* That was a strange word. Especially in relation to Jessa.

Of course, neither one of us had said a thing about that kiss earlier, either. Fuck. What the hell was that?

**Dick**: If you need me to explain... I can't help you. This is probably why I'm not getting any.

Ariel came over to Jessa's flat, and she looked like shit. While Jessa was working in her room, I pulled Ariel aside. "What's going on?"

She glanced toward the bathroom and then lowered her voice. "I messed up. Remember how I told you about my dad?"

"Yeah? What's the problem?"

"Well, the problem is I should have listened to my instincts. Somehow, he has my access code to access our private servers. The one with all the details on the mission, including Jessa's personal information."

My brows snapped down. "The fuck?"

She nodded slowly. "Yes, it was accessed using my code while we were here in London, so clearly, it wasn't me. And before you even ask, no, my father is not some secret super-hacker. He's just a guy. But knowing him, he could have found some kind of unscrupulous help somewhere then accessed her personal information."

Roone blew out a breath. "Shit. Are we sure they have that information already?"

"I don't know. All I know is there was a secure server with all the details about the Jessa mission. How many guards, who they were, personal information, rotating shifts, everything... our whole plan of watching her."

"You have got to be fucking kidding me."

"Well, I made it as secure as possible. It was only accessible on-site, and it was protected by Fort Knox-level firewalls, so none of that information should be accessible by any normal person who doesn't have the right access codes. I have them. Ethan has them. The king and Penny obviously have them. But your average Royal Guard wouldn't have them. I think you're on the list and allowed access, but Lucas is not. He's not Intelligence, so he has no reason to have that information. Bryna certainly doesn't either. Do you see what I mean? Of team Winston Isles, only a select few of us have access to the information on that server, so it took someone with a whole lot of knowledge and a huge set of balls to access it.

"Shit, why didn't you say something?"

I knew we'd talked about her father. I knew he'd pulled a vanishing act, but I didn't know it was this level of fucked up.

"Well, once we got back to the island, I went looking. He's vanished without a trace. Not a hint or a hair. No hits on his passport, nothing."

"You should have said something. I could have helped you look and turned over some hidey holes."

Her gaze shifted toward the bedroom again. "I think you had your hands full."

That was utter bollocks. "You are my partner. If you need me, I'm there. None of this bull shit."

She squared her shoulders and gave me a brisk nod. "Thanks. Which leads me to this... I need to go track him down. Matthias has come through with a lead, so while we're looking, I need you to take point."

I frowned. "This is your mission."

"I know, it's just that right now, I need to find out how we're compromised, or how dangerous this information leak is going to be to us. I have to track him down, and at the end of the day, it's going to require most of my attention. And I can't be in charge of two things."

I nodded slowly. "Look, we'll figure out what's happening, okay? It's fine. The team will sort it out."

She gave a long exhale. "God, this is so embarrassing. How is this my life?"

"I think we all have embarrassing shit in our lives. You're not the only one with skeletons dancing in the closet."

She gave me a soft smile. It was the first time I'd ever seen Ariel truly down. She always had a snappy come back, a quick line, so I knew she wasn't okay.

"I don't know what I'm going to do. If we find him and I find out that he endangered this mission in any way, that he endangered the princess, I'm not going to be able to stay."

What the hell? "Stop talking bullshit right now, and let's just worry about finding him. Then we can ask him all kinds of questions. And even if we find out it's the worst-case scenario, like hell is Sebastian going to let you quit."

She shook her head. "Yeah, he wasn't willing to listen either, but it won't be up to him. The Royal Guard is the Regents Council's problem, and they won't be so forgiving. They will vote me off in a heartbeat, but I can choose to leave before they decide my fate."

"Bollocks. Sebastian has votes. We can force their hand."

"It's never good for a monarch to force their hand unless it's urgent. Me leaving the Royal Guard wouldn't be urgent."

"The hell it wouldn't."

"Roone, you don't understand. The laws are clear. Should any immediate family member commit treason, you're out of the Royal Guard."

"I know the bylaws. I understand them. I just think that

there are exceptions to be made. Besides, there's no way in hell that Penny will let you quit, so this is a moot point."

"Yeah, I know. But still, she might not have a choice."

"I'm not willing to lose another partner. We'll find a solution. We have to."

# THIRTEEN

*Jessa*

I KNEW THIS DREAM.

It was familiar.

I was drowning. It was dark. The water was choppy, crashing all around me. I could see a light in the distance, reaching for me, offering to save me. And I was so relieved. I'd finally be safe. Secure. I will be able to survive.

But it was a lie, because as soon as the boat would come near, my father would be on the other side. He would call me his little princess. And instead of reaching for me, he would place a crown on my head and then tell me I had to swim. Swim to safety. Swim now. And instead of staying on the boat where it was safe and warm, he would jump in with me.

Except my father couldn't swim. So, while I was drowning, I would then expect to see him going down with me as well.

The shrink I had seen in my teenage years had said it was a basic anxiety dream, but there was sort of no point in having a shrink when you couldn't actually tell him the truth. And I had insisted that he couldn't know all the dirty details. He couldn't know what was wrong. But there *was* something wrong with me because I kept having that dream, and my desire to stay perfect, to *be* perfect, was literally killing me.

It didn't matter if it was anxiety or not, I was still drowning. And not only was I drowning, I had to try to save someone else. Someone who, unlike myself, knew all the rules.

It was always the fear that wound its way around me, and every time, I would gasp for air before it would drag me down with a sudden jerky force.

And then my father would hold on to me and tell me, "Swim Jessa, you have to swim princess. Time to move."

I woke in a cold sweat with a scream on my lips, desperately gasping for air and searching for solid ground. I was in the dark, alone, just like in the ocean. Except this time, a big hulking shadow shoved my door open, gun in hand.

I knew exactly who it was before I could even process. I was safe. Safe enough anyway. My body would be safe, but my heart wouldn't be.

"Roone..."

He ran to the bed. "Princess? What's wrong?"

I didn't mean to do it, but I was so desperate for something solid, something well-grounded to cling to. Need fluttered low in my belly.

*How is that sexy? Just look at him. Completely sexy.* I needed him because the world as I'd known it, topsy-turvy and crazy as it was, had come to a crashing halt. And I didn't know which side was up, who my father really was, or how sick he'd been. But he'd been right... there *had* been people hunting me down. Had the threat only exacerbated his illness?

Or, was he never ill at all? Just hypervigilant.

"Hey. Hey, hey. Hey love. Look at me, princess. You're okay. Bad dream?"

I couldn't find the words. All I could do was nod my head desperately as I tried to make sense of it all.

"God, I'm so scared."

"Sshh. Sshh." He ran his hands over my hair and held me tight. Gently he tucked his gun into his back pocket and pulled me close. "You're okay. There's nothing to be afraid of. I'm right here."

I knew I shouldn't have said it. Even as the words tumbled out, I wished I could recall them. Tuck them somewhere I wouldn't have to look at them or face them. "Will you stay with me?"

To his credit, there was zero hesitance. "Yeah, of course. I'll stay until you fall asleep."

I wanted to shake my head and tell him, 'No, I mean stay forever,' but I knew I didn't mean that. I was still angry with him, wasn't I? Shouldn't I be? I didn't trust him, right?

*Yeah, you didn't trust him, but he came running in here and you know you're safe.* I'd deal with that in the morning, but at that moment, I was just relieved he was there and I didn't have to be alone. I'd been holding up the entire ship alone for too long. I scooted over to make room in the queen-size bed. My bed wasn't exactly small, but Lord, the man was big.

He slid right in next to me and pulled me close. Then he stroked my hair. "You're safe now."

"Yeah, but for how long?"

"As long as I am breathing, you will be safe. I will protect you with my life."

"How can you even say something like that to me? How can you be so steady? So perfect?"

"Well, you know. I don't know what to tell you. It's just one of my many skills."

"It's not fair. I'm like a mess all the time, and here you are, knowing exactly what to say and do."

"Hate to break it to you, princess, but I'm faking it."

"Then it'll be our secret."

"Thanks. Now, close your eyes. Try and get some sleep. I'll be right here."

"I don't want to sleep. There're too many scary things when I sleep."

"You've got to sleep, princess. We all need sleep. Tomorrow, you have work. You'll need all the rest you can get."

That little reminder was enough to make me groan. How had I gone from loving my job one week, to hating the thought of going back to it in another? Was it because I had a better view of the truth now? Evan and his machinations? The dull threat he posed? I wasn't sure which was worse; his stalking tendencies or the fact that I actually had *real* homicidal killers who were trying to kill my family.

*My family.*

How long had it been since I could say those words? Even though I didn't know them, even if I was still working on those connections, they were my family.

---

*Roone*

NO WAY in hell was I sleeping. Shit. She was inches away and I couldn't have her. I couldn't touch her.

*Yes, you can. You already have.*

Yes, I could, but not like this. She was clearly scared and terrified and she still wasn't sure if she wanted me.

*Oh, she wants you.*

Maybe. But I didn't want her to be pissed off about it. I wanted her with the core of my being. I wanted everything about her. The fire in her eyes when she got angry, the way her eyes danced when she was happy, and the way she laughed with her full body.

"Roone?"

"Yes, princess?"

"What are you thinking?"

**Dick:** Go on, tell her. I'm real good at bedtime stories.

Fuck no. I wasn't telling her what I was thinking. I went with the tried and true classic. "Nothing."

"Do you think maybe you could tell me something true?"

*Shit.* "What do you want to know?"

"Well, maybe your real background?"

"It might surprise you to know that most of it is actually real. I just left out some important bits."

She rolled onto her side. "Okay. Tell me one thing you left out."

I sighed. "Well, I was British military. Technically, I still am. It was an exchange program. I was meant to be on loan to the Winston Isles. Basically, I was meant to be on loan for Sebastian. Every member of the royal family goes to some kind of military training, even the princesses. Sebastian wanted to see real combat. So he went to some of the most insane places on earth, and it was my job to go with him and back him up, as much as possible."

"Are you serious right now?"

I nodded, even though in the dark she probably couldn't see it. "Yeah. So, I was on loan, and then King Cassius asked me to stay on, and I did. The next thing I knew, it had become a semipermanent position. Although if there were a time that I wanted to return to Her Majesty's army, all I had to do was say the word, and I'd have returned with the post that reflected my military rank, years of service, etc."

"So, you're actually British Military?"

"Yes. But, it's unlikely I'd return to SAS. I've been out for too long. The training is brutal. Really rigorous. And I've gotten used to people not shooting at me. But who knows, one day? I did love SAS. I miss the team, but that's a high-adrenaline environment. Always on the go. It just wears on you."

She whispered, "Wow. I can't say I ever would have guessed that. You seem quite comfortable in a business suit."

I grinned in the dark. "It's because I'm so bloody dashing."

I couldn't see her, but I could almost hear the eye roll. "Can you tell me something else that's real?"

Oh God, what did she want to know? "Well, I'm terrified of heights."

She laughed then. "What? You did trapeze with me."

"Yeah, because Ariel was fucking with me. It was my least favorite training in SAS."

I could feel the shift of her head on her pillow. "And you still did it?"

"Yeah. I knew why Ariel picked it. There was supposed to be trust. Nothing says we can trust each other like me catching you during trapeze."

"You caught me, every single time."

The questions kept coming.

"So, your mother, she really did die?"

I swallowed. "Yeah, she did."

"I'm sorry. I just didn't know if that was all for show or what."

She had a point. "No, it's a fair question."

She was silent for a beat. "Everything you said about her... it seems like you guys were close."

"We were. After my father was gone, we only had each other."

She kept asking about the family angle, which just made me itchy. "And your dad? Is he alive?"

"He died when I was young."

"You said the guy at the gravesite was your brother. Which one of you is older?"

Oh boy, how did I explain this? "My mom was not wealthy. Dad approached her at a museum, if you can imagine it. They were young and stupid. She didn't realize that dad came from money or anything like that. And I guess they were really in love, at least that's the way I heard my mother talk about it. But his family didn't approve. They went ahead and got married and had me anyway. But eventually it got to him, being cut off from the rest of the family. Or maybe he was weak and missed the title and wealth. Either way, he left. He got accustomed to a certain lifestyle as an Earl, I guess, and didn't want to give it up. I was only four when he left. Almost immediately, he married someone his parents approved of. They had a son. A little boy, my brother. He was doted on and spoiled and given all the best things in life. Me and my mom struggled. Although, I guess, we didn't *really* struggle. We were fine, but we weren't rich or anything like that. But I was happy. I had her. I didn't really know quite how much money Dad had until he passed. He was born into the gentry, with a title and all that it came with."

"Jeez."

I shrugged. "Yeah, whatever. I was his first born. So technically, I should have inherited his title, but all that went to my little brother when he died."

"But that's not fair."

I shrugged. "I don't know. Fair or not, it's not like I would have wanted that or known what to do with it. I hadn't attended any of the right schools when I was very young. I did eventually go to Eton though, his alma mater, and then I went to Sandhurst."

"Your mom passed away when you were at Eton?"

I nodded. "Yeah, I was one of the kids that was given a scholarship."

"That's insane. Your father could have easily paid for your tuition."

"I know. But his new wife wasn't into that. So anyway, mom, she'd been sick for a while. But she was a fighter. God, she's exactly what true grit is about. When she died, there was no money to send her off right, you know?"

"I'm so sorry."

"I went to my half brother and stepmother. She had never liked me. I think she envied my mother's place in Dad's heart. Even though my parents had divorced, Dad still came to get me every year for my birthday and a few holidays, you know? He wanted me to get to know my brother, Reese, better. But when my mom died, she refused to give any money to help with the funeral. She told me I was on my own."

"God, that's so cruel."

"Yeah." I swallowed the bitter bile that rose up. I told myself that I'd gotten over it a long time ago, but, oh God, that acid still burned. "Sebastian, he stepped in. He helped me pay for my mom's funeral. I mean, he really didn't need to. My tuition was met and taken care of, so I could have taken her meager savings and buried her, but he insisted, you know. He did the kind of thing that no fifteen-year-old should have to help a friend with. Picking a casket and that sort of thing. He didn't just pay for it, he walked me through it, asked me the questions and took care of it. He made sure I didn't have to do or deal with anything I didn't want to."

"Wow, he truly is your brother."

"Yeah, it sure feels that way. I would protect him with my life."

"I see why now. Was he always like that?"

"That open and giving? Yeah, he is. Kind of a pain in the ass, but he is family."

She was silent for so long I thought maybe she'd fallen

asleep. Then in the quiet of the darkness, she whispered, "Thank you for telling me the truth."

"I won't lie to you. Not anymore. You might not like it, but I'll tell you the truth."

"That's good to know. Roone?"

"Yeah, princess."

"I have a feeling I might regret that."

I chuckled low, and she curled into me. I held her tight, pretending that she was mine. Even if she wasn't entirely mine yet, we were getting there. I just had to take it slow and not rush her. Because once she was really mine, I was going to keep her forever.

# FOURTEEN

*Jessa*

WHEN I WOKE UP, Roone's side of the bed was still warm. It took everything I had in me not to crawl onto his pillow, hold it tight and inhale deeply.

Okay, who am I kidding? That's exactly what I did. Well, first I checked to make sure he wasn't in my shower or bathroom, and then I went ahead on with my inhaling. Sue me, the man smelled like a dream.

It was only after I'd had a shower that I realized he wasn't in the flat at all.

My phone chimed to let me know I'd received messages. And sure enough, there was one from Roone.

**Roone:** *Went across the hall to shower. We'll leave for work at 8:30 as usual.*

He'd saved me from the early-morning awkwards. So what if I'd asked him to stay, to hold me? I'd had a nightmare, but I was fine in the bright light of morning.

*You're an idiot.*

Because there would be no getting over him now. No getting

over the fact that he'd tucked me into his side and held me tight, rocking me and chasing off the scary dreams. I'd slept like the dead after he joined me in bed.

*That should tell you something.*

I hated what it was telling me. That I liked being in his arms. That I wanted to stay there. It would do me good.

But the best part about having Roone stay here was that there was always food. While he was still storing his things in the flat across the hall and he went there to shower and dress, everything else was here. Here, we were pretty much always together, which meant I had my own personal live-in chef and I was taking full advantage of it.

Under a warming plate, he'd left eggs for me. None of that nonsensical runny-egg English stuff either. Real eggs. Scrambled with some cheese and pepper. Instead of toast, there were crumpets with jelly and clotted cream. God, I really could get used to being spoiled.

Another text came in.

**Roone**: *Don't get used to being spoiled.*

My lips twitched. God, it was like the man lived in my head.

*Well, he sort of does.*

There was a knock at my door. Still holding my jelly-covered crumpet and tea-filled sassy mug, I ran to the door. For some reason I assumed it would be Roone, so I stumbled slightly when I saw Evan on the other side. "Oh my God, Evan." I mumbled around a bite of crumpet.

"Jessa. I'd heard you were back."

I frowned, slightly suspicious. "Well yes, I did email the team that I'd be returning to work today. But how did you know I was home?"

"Well, security. You still do live in the company flat."

"Yes. I do." And maybe I would have to change that because what the hell was Evan doing here on my doorstep?

He'd never been here before. "So, is there something I can help you with?"

He looked over my shoulder and glanced around. "Can I come in?"

Ugh, there was no easy way to do this. I prayed to God, whatever mechanism Roone was using to check on me, he was looking now, because there was no way I could refuse Evan. "Ah, sure. Come on in."

"Glad to see you're well, considering the way that you left so abruptly."

"I apologized. And I am still so sorry. It couldn't be helped. I really needed to go. But I'm back now, rejuvenated and ready to get back to work."

He pursed his lips and slid a glance over me. "Jessa, look, if you have a boyfriend, it's fine, we can work something out. You can't just pretend you were off sick."

I'd been sick in a way. "I'm not pretending."

"If you say so."

"Is there a reason you're here?"

As if Evan suddenly realized how close he was to me, he backed away. "Well yes, I came to tell you that I will be joining you on the Meet Cute meeting."

I lifted a brow. "Okay. You could have just texted me."

"Well, I wanted to see for myself that you were back safe and sound. Prodigal daughter returned."

"Is that how you see me? A prodigal daughter?"

"You know what I mean. I'm also relieved to see that you're not with Roone."

My brows went up with that. "What?"

"Come on. It's not a secret, and you two aren't hiding it very well. Your relationship, the secret looks. I know he was supposedly on London Lords business, but it was awfully convenient."

*Shit.* I had no protocol for this, so I held firm with the lie. "I don't know what you're talking about."

"So you're telling me that you're not dating Roone?"

"No. I'm not dating Roone." That, at least, *was* the truth.

I was grateful that I could say it with a level of conviction that he would have no choice but to believe.

He relaxed then. I could almost see the tension roll off his shoulders. "Oh, well then, perhaps I was wrong."

"So you came all this way before I even get back to work to ask me if I'm dating Roone?"

"Well, no. I said I was coming to check if you were okay. And you are."

"Yeah, and I just have thirty minutes before I have to leave for work. So if you don't mind," I marched to the door and opened it for him. There was no way that he could try and force 'the two of us together' scenario. Although, I guess he could try to force the 'let me drive you' option. How had I not seen some of these symptoms earlier?

*You saw what you wanted to see.*

He followed me to the door. "Okay. Well, I'll see you at the office. I look forward to hearing what you have come up with for Meet Cute. I recognize you're a man short, so I'll be helping out."

"Evan, when I want your help, I'll ask for it. I don't need it right now. So, if you want to observe the process, great, but I don't want the impression around the office to be that I can't work without my boss looking over my shoulder."

"Everyone knows how capable you are. I'm just making sure that all T's are crossed and I's are dotted."

Sure he was. "Okay then, see you at the office."

The moment he was out the door, I breathed a sigh of relief and collapsed, sliding to the floor. There was no way I was going to survive this. None. I couldn't believe I hadn't seen it before.

And maybe he wasn't a legitimate stalker, but Evan had veered directly into creepy-man territory.

---

## Jessa

TRUE TO LONDON FORM, the fog permeated the morning air but not enough to actually get us wet on the walk to the office. "I'm not making that up, right? That was weird."

Roone's walk was brisk by my side, his gaze swinging around. I knew the other team members were following us, I just didn't know where they were. It was a bit unnerving to have someone on our tail all the time, but I supposed it was necessary.

"Yeah, that was beyond weird. Which is why we need to be more careful."

"Part of me still thinks it makes more sense for someone else to be posted inside my flat. Ariel?"

"I'd like to accommodate you, but that's not going to happen."

*You've gotten used to him, anyway. And you want him there.*

I clamped my mouth shut before the truth could spill from it. "It's just... that was close today. You could have been in the flat."

His chuckle was low as he directed me to make a left. "Oh, don't worry. I can see through you. I know you like having me around."

*Arrogant ass.*

"Did I say that? I barely tolerate you."

"Oh yeah, that's obvious from way you were wrapped around me like a boa constrictor last night. I tried to get up more than once, but you were clinging on like a baby koala for dear life."

"I was not."

We took another sharp right, and I frowned. "This isn't the way in to work."

"Yeah, I know."

We walked three more blocks, made another left, hooked a right and then doubled back along the main street. It was far more crowded now. Some of the shops had started to open. "Roone, what's going on?"

He tapped his com. "A few blocks back I picked up someone following us. The team spotted him too, but I don't think he knows about the team so we're at an advantage for once. Right now, the word is it doesn't look like Millston."

"It shouldn't be. I sent him packing over thirty minutes ago."

"Yeah, it shouldn't be him following you to work. And not if he actually wants to make it to that Meet Cute meeting that he keeps going on about."

Prickles of anxiety hit me in that same kind of scatter-spray pattern that the stupid misting rain did. Not enough to be real so I could pinpoint it and correct it, but just enough to be annoying. "What are we going to do?"

He took my hand and squeezed it. "We're going to act like a couple in love and jump in here."

Roone tugged me into a nearby coffee shop, pulling me close to him, wrapping my body with his. Surprise! His body was just what I needed to quell my anxiety. I stared up at him. "What is going on?"

He glanced down at me. He smiled broadly, dimples showing, teeth perfect, and a lock of hair fell into his face. That hit me like a gut punch. Jesus Lord, he was incredible to look at. And with his arms wrapped around me like this, I felt tiny. Super petite. Taken care of. *Safe.* "Roone?"

He grinned down at me. "Relax, princess. This is just for show. Anyone looking will report two people madly in love, not two people about to double back. We're going to see if we can catch whoever is following us."

"We're all going to turn around and follow him?"

He nodded slowly. "If you're up to it. We have time before you're due at work."

"Oh wow. I didn't think I'd be—"

"If you're scared, we won't do it. I'll leave the team to try and chase him down. But this way, we get to cast the net."

"Yes, let's do it. If we can catch this asshole, my life goes back to normal, and I'm in for that."

He chuckled. "Of course you're in." With a quick press of his lips to my forehead, he took my hand again and we went back out, headed back the way we'd come.

Our pace was brisker. He kept tapping his coms, quietly talking. We headed back the way we came, but instead of going left the way we'd come from, we went right. Then he pulled me into a little alcove close to a boutique. "I thought we were trying to—"

He pressed his finger on my lips and shook his head. Instantly, he counted, one, two, three, and then pulled me back out. The two people meeting us were the two Royal Guards who had been posted across the hall.

"Oi, what the hell? I thought you had him."

Trevor, the taller of the two, ran a hand through his hair as he muttered expletives. "We fucking did. There was a crowd around the last corner, and we freaking lost him. He must have spotted us."

I glanced up at Roone, and he reassuringly squeezed my hand. "Not today then, but soon. It'll be over soon, I promise."

I just wished I could believe him.

# FIFTEEN

*Jessa*

I WAS SHAKING from the morning's adventure. After Evan's impromptu visit, it was the last thing I needed. And from the looks of it, the day wasn't going to get any better. Evan was in one hell of a mood.

When I walked into the conference room, I expected to see Roone. But he was nowhere to be found.

It seemed Ariel wanted to know what the hell had happened to him too. She glanced around. "What happened to Roone?" Ariel had followed two days behind us to London. Roone hadn't been forthcoming with where she was, but she'd probably been following a lead.

Evan didn't even bat an eyelash. "I've reassigned him. He's only working on London Lords. Since it's a large account, Jessa, you're still primary on that account as well with oversite from me. But I'll be working with you more hands-on, on Meet Cute."

*Hell.* I'd gone straight from the planning meeting with Evan to a debrief with Chloe. Then I'd come to this meeting, so I hadn't had a moment to connect with Roone.

Ariel crossed her arms. "I just feel like since it's my project, that's something you should have discussed with me first."

Evan gave her a smile that was all teeth. "Well, it's my company."

Rick lifted a brow and interjected, "*Our* company? I think that I would have liked some notice too."

Chloe and I both kept our gazes down and let the grownups fight. I felt like a little kid whose parents were about to get a divorce and I was caught in the middle. The Evans were having some side-eye.

Ariel, though she was obviously hip to the scenario, was jumping into the fray.

All I could do was watch. A week ago, I was willing to fight tooth and nail for this job. It was everything. My anchor. But things were different now. How had I gone from loving this job and everything about it to wanting nothing to do with this place, nothing to do with being here?"

*Because you've been home now.*

I shoved that thought aside. The Winston Isles, while beautiful, were not home. London was my home... for now.

*At some point, you have to stop running.*

I inhaled a deep breath and cleared my throat. "Look, Ariel, I'm sorry. I promise you, I'm perfectly capable of handling the account with Chloe. You'll be covered with everything you need."

Ariel lifted a brow, and her lips twitched. Obviously, she knew I was bullshitting and showing off my ability to defuse a situation.

Then I turned to Rick. "I'm sure you and Evan will sort out whatever is happening now, but in the meantime, can we get back to the clients so that Chloe and I can do our jobs?"

Rick visibly *hrmphed* and then settled in. "Fair enough. Let's discuss the marketing plan. Ms. Scott, how are you feeling about the—"

Evan interrupted. "Actually, before we get started, I'm first going to say that from this point forward, everyone needs to stop using the app."

I blinked. "What?"

Rick laughed. "What are you talking about? We should all use the product."

Evan worked his jaw. "Well, I will no longer require my employees to use it for dating."

Chloe asked softly. "Well, if we like using it, can we?"

Evan frowned. "Well, given that it's a premium option, anyone who wants to keep using it will have to pay for it on their own. No more company funds."

Ariel coughed. "I'm sitting right here. If Evans PR no longer believes in my product, then what am I doing here?"

Evan started to walk his decision back a little. "What I'm saying is, the purpose was for everyone to see how the app worked. We've all done that and been on multiple dates. I think it's important that we no longer *require* anyone to use it. Everyone is past their second or third date now. It gets into touchy territory to force them to continue using it."

"Is there something that you're not telling me, Mr. Millston? Mr. Evans? I was so excited when your team had an opening, but now I'm feeling as if you really don't want my business as a client."

Chloe flicked me with her pen as if she was silently begging me to stop mommy and daddy from fighting again.

Evan continued to walk it back then. "No, we value you as a client, Ms. Scott. I'm just saying I'm no longer requiring my employees to use your app."

Ariel gave him a beatific smile. "Fair enough." She turned to

Chloe and to me. "You guys can have access to the app, free of charge, as a show of good will."

Evan glowered at her, and she just smiled back.

I jumped back into the fray. "Okay, like I was saying, I think bolder colors work. More youthful, happy. Think shades in the Easter egg family; the teals, the purples, the bright, happy, sunny yellows."

Ariel smiled. "I like that. That works with my brand coloring which is that lilac-purple, so I like that the marketing matches that. Obviously, I'd love to use women for imagery. But not just sexy young women, women of all ages, beauty at all ages, peppered in with, obviously, some handsome men. But no one too good-looking, because men who are too good-looking scare people off. And no super models. I want real people."

Chloe furiously took notes. I didn't bother, because, well, it wasn't a real app.

Rick asked a few questions which Ariel answered easily. I still couldn't believe this whole app of hers, all the work it had taken to program it, was simply for this job. So that they would have a cover, an in. That was an awful lot of work, and it just demonstrated how brilliant Ariel was.

Evan spoke up then. "I know we have discussed this, but I really do need access to your database."

Ariel smiled at him. "We *have* discussed this, and I've already said no."

Evan didn't let it go, though.

"It helps us do our jobs better if we can at least mine the users, find out who they are. Advertise to them."

"Well, I can't tell you who they are. I have a strict data policy. I don't share with anyone. I find it disappointing that we need to keep having this conversation again. Before I signed the contract, I made it clear you could not have my database. Are we on the same page, or aren't we?"

Rick chimed in then. "Yes, of course. Ms. Scott, your database is yours. I'm sure Evan only wants to make the marketing plan the best that it can be. If you can provide us the general information about your customers, the region they live in, what they do, what they like to do for fun, we can tailor our marketing."

Ariel nodded. "Fine, I can do that."

Evan looked like he'd swallowed a bag of rocks. He was livid, and I didn't know why. I didn't know why he needed specific access to that database, and that scared me. What did he want to do with it?

I glanced around and tried to divert everyone back to the main topic, but I made a mental note to ask Ariel and Roone what in the world Evan could want with that database.

*Jessa*

AFTER THE MEETING WAS OVER, I headed straight for my office. Chloe had another meeting so that left me alone with Ariel, who immediately called Roone.

Roone was on the phone, and Ariel tried to calm me down. "It's okay. Everything is fine."

"Why is Evan acting that way?"

Roone's voice was deep and sharp once he hung up. "What did he do?"

Ariel tried to explain. "He was just very aggressive about Meet Cute. Maybe we're burned, maybe not. At the end of the day, I'm not sure what to do with that angle. Since you're off the account, I'll have to insist on working with Jessa directly."

Roone was silent for a beat. "That could work."

Ariel ran her hands through her hair. "Well, this is the time for a bit of advice. I'm pretty sure I don't have much time before he barges in here, because he's insisting on accompanying Jessa to London Lords."

"You guys. Give me a plan here. If I'm here, trying to be bait, I need to act like everything is normal. Which means I need this job. I'd rather Evan didn't drive me crazy while I do it."

Ariel rolled her eyes. "Evan's just got a hair up his ass. And he's angry. I'm not sure what set him off, maybe it was Jessa leaving for a week, but he's in a mood."

Roone rubbed his jaw. "Okay, I hear you. Jessa, relax. Go to the meeting as usual. I have an ace in the hole I can play, okay?"

"What? I mean, I still have to do my job. What ace could we possibly play? He showed up at my *house* this morning."

Ariel touched my hand. "It's okay. We're going to make some arrangements, for a more secure place."

"But that's my home."

*One that you could leave at a moment's notice.*

I don't know why I was being stubborn. I was the girl who moved at the drop of a hat. My whole life, all it took was a, 'Jessa, get a move on,' and I would strap my backpack on and be out the door, never looking back.

But somehow this felt more intrusive, and I didn't want to do it.

Roone's voice was soft. "Look, him with a burr up his arse is problematic, yes. But let's not do anything drastic. I don't want to disrupt Jessa's life any more than we have to."

I breathed a sigh of relief. "Thank you. What are we going to do?"

"Relax, like I said, we'll go to the meeting as usual, and then we'll keep things from going off the rails."

Ariel pursed her lips. "We won't have enough protection in that room with Evan insisting on going."

Roone lifted his chin. "Don't worry. I have her. She'll have enough protection."

"You guys, he's my boss. Do we have anything to go on? Any evidence we can use against him?"

Ariel shook her head. "No, but, I'm still working an angle. Thanks to Willow, I've located a couple of other past girlfriends. I'm hoping one of them will be willing to give us information on how he acted, what he did. I'm also digging up some old police reports. I don't think he's had any official charges filed against him, but reports were still filed. I'm looking for those, anything to show a pattern of behavior. And then I'm going to stick surveillance on him. Actually, I've already got that going. Any activities that are untoward, we'll know about. If need be, we'll arrest him."

"Jesus Christ, we are talking about having my boss arrested. How is this my life?"

On the phone, Roone's voice was low. "One step at a time. Ariel is going to get surveillance going, and we're going to go to the meeting. I'll be with you every step of the way."

Ariel rolled her eyes. "Oh my God, you guys. Can't you stop with the voice fucking? Roone, your voice is going all low and sexy. Focus people."

There was a sharp rap at the door, and Ariel somehow went from looking relaxed to looking like she was having an intense conversation with me about the product. "I really like this model over here." She pointed at something non-existent on my computer and then glanced up when the door opened and Evan walked in. He frowned when he saw her there. "You're still here?"

Ariel's smile was sweet, but I could hear the undertones. "Yes. Jessa and I took the opportunity to look through some models."

He nodded. "Jessa, the car is here. Let's go to London Lords."

I nodded. "Yup, on my way. Ariel, we'll pick this up later?"

"Of course. Have a good meeting. Evan, pleasure as always. I'll see you later."

He scowled at her. But she walked out with a flounce. When she passed by the massive window in my office that looked out into the cubes, she flipped him off, but he didn't see that. I had to work hard to school my smile and turned my attention to Evan.

Forcing a smile, I said, "Ready when you are."

# SIXTEEN

*Roone*

To SAY it was tense was an understatement. I could tell Jessa's nerves were raw. She was edgy, her shoulders stiff, her lips pressed into a firm line. I'd spoken to Ben before they headed over, and he'd been more than happy to accommodate. He kept asking if helping me out would earn him a double o badge. Sometimes he was a pain in the ass.

*But a pain in the ass that's going to help you.*

We took our seats, and Ben smirked at me. The bloody eejit was enjoying himself. Note to self, don't ask Ben for any more favors.

Ben grinned as he shook hands with Evan then Jessa. "I'm glad you're here."

Evan took the lead and wouldn't even let Jessa speak. "Thank you. I'm actually stepping in as lead again. Evans PR wants to provide you with the best we have to —"

Ben put his hand up and interrupted smoothly. "Actually, I need you to stop there. There will be changes. First, as Miss McLean is so vital to our operation, I'll need her on the account indefinitely. She'll still work for Evans of course, but we are to be her only client. With all the new hotel openings we have scheduled, I'd like to keep everything in one set of hands."

Evan blinked rapidly. "I don't understand."

"Okay, let me be crystal clear. I need Roone and Jessa exclusively. Will that be a problem?"

Evan pushed to his feet. "You will have the team I assign! And you can't have her."

My cousin stepped back and eased into his chair. "Why don't you have a seat Evan? And let me remind you about all the business that the London Lords properties have brought you. I'm sure that you can overlook any personal issues and how I handle my team."

I probably should have avoided smirking, but I didn't give a shit. The only thing I cared about was how stiff Jessa was. I hated that she was caught in the middle. I wanted to fix it for her.

Ben turned his attention to Jessa. "Now, Ms. McLean, why don't you go ahead and run us through the marketing? Actually, you know what? Let's first start with the restaurant. The chef is good, and I want to make sure that he gets the kind of showcase he deserves."

"Of course," Jessa adjusted the folders she was holding and opened one. This was a situation where she was prepared, relaxed. She knew what to do. Anything else was distraction. As she spoke, Evan watched her intently, as if the sun and the moon hung on every word she uttered.

*So basically, how you're looking at her.*

I was not looking at her like that.

**Dick**: *I can look at her if you prefer.*

Okay, fine. But the difference was she actually liked me. I had molded my lips to hers. Evan, not so much.

At one point, Jessa looked up at me. "Roone, you were

suggesting something in terms of the restaurant and the juxtaposition between how we can make it work with the hotels."

"Yes, I was thinking one of those things that we could do to really showcase what London Lords has to offer, especially at the flagship, is to do in-room dining with real finesse, not just with cold efficiency. The number one thing people complain about room service food is that no matter what, it's never as good as if you sit in a restaurant. And the more hotels try to economize, the less gets left in the experience. It might be something you could do for premier clients. A premier in-room dining experience, so that everyone knows what it feels like to be treated like a king or queen while sampling the delights of Ian Talbot. If we paired the restaurant event with stays at the hotel, there might be an opportunity to customize the menus based on a set number of room options. Junior suites get certain meals. Presidential suites get another set of meals, etcetera."

Ben sat forward. "Actually, that's not a bad idea. And we could—"

Evan interrupted. "First of all, the logistics behind that are astronomical. You can't expect my team to do the extra—"

Ben cleared his throat and sat back again, steepling his fingers. "Mr. Millston, correct me if I'm wrong, but London Lords is paying for this, right?"

Evan nodded. "Yes."

"Well, then let us, the client, determine what's within the scope of our budget and what's not. If we want to add to the campaign, and we're willing to pay to do it, what's the problem?"

Asshole shut up then. He really had no leg to stand on. He was just posturing and being a dick. He was good at that.

Jessa took the idea and ran with it. "Yes, and London Lords has each type of room based on a real name, so we could make meals catered to what would have been that royal 'spirit dish,' you know, with a modern touch and flare, mixed with things on the new menu from the restaurant. And then, if it goes well at the opening, we'd incorporate some of those ideas into the new hotels in New York, Los Angeles and Paris."

Ben nodded appreciatively. "Yeah, I think this plan might work."

As we chatted for another few minutes, Evan just glowered at me through the rest of the meeting. Finally, at the close of the meeting, when Evan stood, Ben raised a hand. "There is one more thing. Given that things are about to spike up, and that once the restaurant opening is dealt with Jessa will need to transition on to the hotel openings, I'll need her on-site."

Evan sputtered. "Excuse me?"

Ben nodded slowly. "Yes. I'll provide an office for Evans PR employees, but I am the only client she's working with, right?"

Evan shook his head. "No, she's on Meet Cute."

Jessa saw the question for what it was. "Yes, I'm on Meet Cute, but as it is, I can take my meetings with Ariel here. London Lords, obviously, is a lot bigger than Ariel's account. It only makes sense. And then I won't have to shuffle back and forth."

Evan just glowered at her. "I'm sorry, Mr. Covington, I don't think that we can accommodate that."

Ben wasn't having it though. "Are you sure you don't want to discuss this with Rick Evans first? It only makes sense. Unless there's another reason you won't allow Ms. McLean to work on-site? It's not the first time we've asked for workers to stay on for the duration of a project. We did it for the original London Lords hotel opening."

Evan opened his mouth and then closed it again. He was stuck. He knew it.

Finally, he mumbled. "I'll discuss it with Rick."

Ben smiled and then turned to Jessa. "Ms. McLean, I'm

looking forward to having you on the premises. We'll get so much work done that way." And then as an extra dig, he added, "And you and Roone will be able to work side by side."

I swear, the vein in Evan's forehead looked like it was going to burst, and there was something oddly satisfying about that.

---

*Jessa*

"OH MY GOD, did you do that?"

Roone grinned. "Surprise."

"Oh my God, Evan looked like he was going to explode."

"Good. He's got to stop. Right now, he's unraveling. His behavior is not only uncalled for, but it's concerning. Anyway, this bought you a reprieve."

"Thank you. I don't even know what to say."

Roone shrugged. "Of course. And if we're here and you want to jump my bones, we don't have to pretend."

I sputtered. "What? Roone!"

"What? I'm just saying. Should you decide that you like me again, and you want my mouth on those pretty lips of yours," he inclined his head and his gaze drifted down my body, "those lips, not the ones on your face," he winked, "you just say the word, and we will have a little more privacy here."

"Oh my God, I am not telling you that."

"If you say so."

"You are still an impossible asshole."

"When you say arsehole, I say slightly annoying. But I'm delightful."

"Oh my God, why is it that some things never change?"

He shrugged. "Well, it's not supposed to change. And seriously, at least here you can do your job unencumbered from Evan. And I can do my job. The real one."

It only now occurred to me how difficult it must have been to protect me when I didn't know what was going on. "Wait, so for the last few months or so, you've been working and guarding me?"

He nodded slowly. "Yes."

"But, that must have been impossible."

He shrugged. "Well, there was me and Ariel, and we had a team of four, so we were able to get you covered outside of the building."

"Were there other people I saw every day that were on your team?"

He nodded. "Thomas. The front desk security at Evans."

I frowned as I thought back. I had assumed Thomas was Jamaican, with his dark onyx skin, and his lilting accent. I don't know why it hadn't occurred to me he could have been from anywhere else in the islands, but I suppose it made sense. Everything about him said soldier. His suit had been a little too filled out. He'd been a little too on alert.

"Oh my God, how much did I miss because I just wasn't looking?"

He shrugged as he led me to my new office. Unlike my office back at Evans, this one had a full-length window, one that overlooked the West End. I could see blooming Westminster Abbey from here. "Wow!"

"Yeah, Ben is trying to impress you. Ignore my cousin."

I whooped around. "I like your cousin. Wish I'd known earlier."

He winced. "Yeah, sorry. That wasn't exactly a lie. It was just that I never mentioned it."

"Wait, how did you arrange for Ben to be one of our clients?"

Roone shook his head. "I didn't. That first day when we came into the meeting with him required some fast talking. He didn't answer when I called beforehand, so he was just as surprised as I was."

"No wonder he looked like he'd swallowed worms. How oblivious was I?"

He shook his head. "You weren't. People don't see what they don't need to see. You didn't need to see it. The Ben thing could have been a big problem, admittedly. But you shouldn't have noticed. You shouldn't have noticed your guard. You shouldn't have noticed any of it. Once or twice you did though, which was unnerving to say the least."

I frowned as my brain tried to run through it. "Shit, we're going to have to rehash every single conversation we've ever had."

"I know. We have time."

"Wait, that day I was leaving the tattoo parlor... was that you?"

The lilt of his lips told me that my hunch was right. "You are surprisingly good at picking up a tail."

"Oh my God, I thought I was losing my mind."

Roone laughed. "Actually, I would love to hear how you did that."

"No, no way I'm telling you. I need my secrets. But Jesus Christ, how hard was it to protect me?"

"Not easy."

"I can imagine."

"So, Ariel and Meet Cute... she made a dating app just so she could come in to protect me?"

"Well, Ariel is kind of a tech genius. I'm pretty sure if she wanted to, she could really put Meet Cute on the market."

"Wait, what about Chloe? Her date seems real."

"Yeah, it was real. After studying everyone's profiles, Ariel did an online search on other dating apps to find people who would be good matches for everyone, with the exception of you, of course. And then she did some heavily targeted ads for her brand-new dating app. When they signed up, she put them in the algorithm and paired everyone up. So Chloe is, in fact, dating that guy. So is Evan. So is Rick. I don't know what Evan was doing because that day he caught us at the amusement park, he wasn't there on a Meet Cute date. So, that's a whole other set of issues. But yeah, that little dating app could be a real product."

"Jesus Christ, she's brilliant."

"Yeah, woe be us if she ever decides to use her powers for evil and not for good."

I shivered. "Jesus. When you put it like that..."

"Yup. She could be an evil criminal mastermind. But, that's not Ariel. A pain in my ass, yes. Criminal? No. Besides, she's too loyal. Loyalty is a big thing for her."

I smiled. "Yeah, it seems that way. And you two seem like you genuinely care about each other. How long had she been your partner?"

I wanted to know more about him. Any tidbit I could get, I wanted. But he was in no mood to share any further. "Princess, why don't you go ahead and get to work? I'm going to go and get the security setup going. I'll be right next door. Just remember, you're not alone. Now you can actually do the job you are meant to do without my interference."

"Yeah, at least we'll need to talk about exactly how you have a full business degree. Sandhurst is a military academy."

He laughed as he opened the door and slipped out.

And there was the problem. It didn't matter that I was still angry with him. I liked him a hell of a lot. Hell, I more than liked him. I had started to fall for him before I ever went to the islands, and I was afraid I'd gone and fallen in love.

# SEVENTEEN

*Roone*

I T  WAS  MUCH  EASIER to do my job at London Lords. I still had no idea why it hadn't occurred to me before. I should have just called Ben and asked for a favor.

*Oh, but that would mean you would have to depend on someone.* And asking anyone for help was not in my general vocabulary. *Asking for help would make your job a whole hell of a lot easier.*

Yes, fair enough. I'd learned my lesson. At 6:30, I went and knocked on Jessa's door. "Come in." Chloe had already left, but it seemed the spunky blond was loving the upgraded office as well. She'd brought in photos, a plant, all the things that made it feel like home. I inclined my head toward her desk. "I guess your side kick went home?"

Jessa grinned. "Either that, or she went to hunt down Bridge. She got one glance at him and I think her jaw fell open."

"Ugh, Bridge is a handsome asshole."

"You know him?"

I laughed. "Ben is my cousin, remember? I went to school

with him, and Bridge, and East, the Lords of London. God, if there was ever a broad pack..."

Her eyes softened. "But you weren't part of it?"

"Oh, don't get me wrong. Don't cry for me Argentina. Ben and I got on, but after my dad died, things kind of went to shit with that side of the family. So while Ben and I stayed close, we had different friends at school, and I didn't see him on breaks and such. But we were still mates."

"Oh. It would have made things a whole lot easier if I had known that you knew them."

"Easier? How?"

"I could have dangled that carrot in front of Chloe."

I laughed. "Of course. Do you want to get out of here? I figured I'd take you out and take your mind off of the situation for the day. I know that that's probably difficult to do."

"Difficult but not impossible."

"Come on. You've had a long day. Let's have some fun."

Her eyes lit a little, and I remembered how much fun she'd had at the amusement park. Like she'd been a kid again. It occurred to me that Jessa hadn't had much time for goofing off or being irresponsible, and there was a part of her that needed that.

"I don't know. There's a lot of work to be done. And since I apparently no longer actually have someone helping me besides Chloe, I have to do it myself."

"And imagine how well you can do it when you're fresh and you've had a break."

She chewed on the corner of her lip and I wanted to take over the motion for her. I wanted to kiss her thoroughly and drown out all of her thoughts so she could finally relax.

"Come on. Have some fun."

She sighed, and I knew I'd won. "Okay, but not too late,

yeah? Evan wants a status update by tomorrow morning at 7:30."

I ground my teeth. "He still thinks he is your friend?"

"Can we just not right now? It's been a long day and I really don't want to talk about Evan or his behavior at the moment."

"Fair enough. Come on, let's go." Honestly, I had no plan. I knew Ariel was going to kill me. I had alerted the follow team that had changed shifts at six. I'd told them we were going straight home. Clearly, I'd lied. I shot them a quick text as we left.

I ushered Jessa out of the building once I had a firm plan in my head. When we got in the car, I gave the driver our destination, and we headed into the traffic of London.

"Why do I feel like it's a bad idea to let you be in charge of my social life?"

"Probably because it is. But it'll be fun."

So for fun, I took her to see the latest shark horror movie in the theater in the middle of Leicester Square. When we left the theater, it was loud, rash, and there were street performers everywhere outside. One performer was doing old-school popping and locking, shirtless in his joggers and wearing nothing else but a hat and a smile. He wasn't half bad. He had a crowd.

We meandered in the square with me knowing full well it was a nightmare to defend. But she was having fun. And that tension around her mouth had eased, so I would gladly take the arse chewing from Ariel about my choice.

Several hours later, after I'd fed her, stuffed her full of sweet and salty popcorn, and filled her mind with sharks and blood, we called the car again and headed home.

After we were dropped off, we headed up the front steps into the building then took the elevator up to our floor. We made a left toward our flats and she was still laughing at the absurdity of the movie, and then she stopped short.

My eyes had been on her and her smile. *Rookie move.* I had missed what she was stopping for. When I lifted my gaze, I frowned. Evan Millston was on waiting outside her door.

He glowered at me. "Just where have you been?"

Jessa sighed. "Well, considering I have finished my work for the day, I went out."

Millston turned his attention to me. "You know, every time I turn around, there you are turning up like a bad coin. You're just *always* around. I can't seem to get rid of you."

I grinned and then headed toward my old flat.

Evan frowned. "How are you still staying there?"

I grinned. "Well, the new owner asked me if I'd like to stay on, and I chose to. Did you think I'd get kicked out?"

His narrowed gaze told me that was exactly what he'd expected. He thought that by letting go of the townhouse flats, he would also get rid of me. *But, not so lucky are you, arsehole? I don't just live across the hall. I live with her.* But it was semantics at that point. Helplessly, I watched as Jessa opened the door to her flat. There wasn't much I could do except watch Millston follow her. I hated that.

"'Night, Jessa."

She swallowed hard. The look I gave her was meant to convey that it was going to be okay, that everything was going to be fine. But I couldn't let her walk in without reassuring her, and I knew that hugging her would set off Evan. So quickly, I fired up a text on my phone. She looked down at hers and nodded, acknowledging that she received it.

Then she went inside with Evan Millston. And I prayed to God she was good at following directions. But just in case she wasn't, I prepared to make a call as soon as I was inside the flat.

Two of the other guards, Trevor and Jacob, were already there, and Jacob said, "I've already called Ariel."

I nodded my thanks and headed straight for the monitors. I just hoped Ariel would be in position soon because I didn't like Jessa being alone with that guy where I couldn't keep her safe as I had promised.

---

### Jessa

"FRANKLY, I find your relationship with him inappropriate."

"Oh my God. Evan, what are you doing here?"

"Well, I was going to discuss the situation surrounding the LL project with you. After careful consideration, I think I need to take over."

"Oh really?" I crossed my arms. "Are you sure Ben would agree with that?"

He lifted his brows. "Excuse me?"

"Evan, what is this really about? You gave me the account. You've been riding me the last couple of days. What have I done? Is this all because I asked for some time off?"

"You went on vacation with him." He pointed toward the door.

The vein in his forehead throbbed, and I could see the veins popping on his neck as well. He was angry. This is what they'd been talking about. Roone and Ariel.

"If you'll excuse me, I need to wash my hands." I walked away from him and straight into the bathroom. I ran the water for some noise as I opened the window. I saw a flash of movement outside and a shock of red hair. Ariel. Okay, that's why Roone wanted me to open my window. Fair enough. It was so someone would be here, just in case.

I went back out into the living room and saw that Evan was pacing. "I'm just going to take over your account. I'm the best one to head it up, and I have the most knowledge."

"With all due respect, I've been working on this account for over a year. You've been basically hands-off up to this point, so if you're going to punish me by taking it away, I'd like to know why. Surely it's not just because I went away for a few days."

"With him!"

"Evan, I don't know how to put this, but you have no say over what I do on my personal time."

"Your relationship with him is inappropriate."

"No, it is not. I've already told you we're not dating. And what I choose to do in my free time is my business. I'm off work. I pay rent. And I shouldn't have to feel like I'm always working or that my boss can come by at any time. You've already come here unannounced once today, and now you're here a second time. I'd like to know why."

"You don't understand. Clearly, I need to protect you from him."

Unfortunately, that sounded all too familiar. "I don't need any protection, and when I do, I will ask for it. When I'm in the building at Evans PR, if you want to worry about my protection, great. Matter of fact, I'm all for it. I've had some office scares. But when I'm home, in the safety of my flat, you can't be here. That's what's inappropriate."

He opened his mouth to say something then snapped it shut. After another deep breath, he started again. "I just want what's best for you."

"Well, what's best for me right now is to get some sleep. My *boss* wants a status report tomorrow at 7:30."

"Well, if you'll just give it to me now, we won't have to meet at 7:30."

"I'm not prepped now. I'm tired. It's late."

"We can just talk it through."

What was going on with him? His eyes were all wide, and his pupils were almost pinpoints. I walked to the door and opened it. "I'd really like to be alone now, thank you."

"Jessa, you're making a mistake with him. You need to know that."

"Right now, the only mistake is the one you're making, by being at my flat. This is inappropriate Evan, and frankly, quiet concerning. You're my boss. I'm not working right now."

I wouldn't be able to breathe again until the door was locked behind him. I'd thought this morning was concerning, but this was downright scary. I wasn't going to be able to keep my job.

Not by a long shot. This was insane. I knew that at some point the next day, I was going to have to make a call to Rick. He needed to know about what Evan was doing. I stood at the door and waited. I gave him my best *go on ahead, fuck with me* look. He seemed unperturbed. But finally, he grabbed his jacket and left. Before I could close the door, he turned around. "You know that you're making a mistake with him. He's not what he seems."

I sighed. "People rarely are." Then I closed the door with an audible click and locked it behind him.

When I dropped my head to the door trying to drag in deep steadying breaths, I heard Ariel behind me. "You are never alone, Jessa. You are always safe."

"I know. It's just that I see what you were talking about now, your concern about him. He's unhinged."

"Yes, yes he his."

"I'm not going to be able to stay here, am I?"

Ariel's voice was soft. "No, no you're not."

A second later, there was a knock at the door. A quick glance through the peephole told me it was Roone, and I opened the door for him.

He pulled me in his arms immediately, and I was so worn out from the tension, I just sank into his embrace. *Yeah, sure, worn out, that's what we call it.*

"I might have an idea. It's going to involve Ben again, but it will certainly be safer. Since Evans PR owned this block of homes, Evan may well have a key. And I think we all know that's a dangerous prospect."

Some things never changed. My whole life, I'd been making escapes in the middle of the night, uprooting at a moment's notice, and it looked like I was about to fall into old habits.

# EIGHTEEN

*Ariel*

LATER THAT NIGHT after the adventure with Millston, I'd finally caught a break when I went back to Roone's former flat. It was a lucky break and I knew it, but I was going to take the win. I'd done a search for my father's known associates, and I got a hit in Barcelona on a man renting a flat in Las Ramblas. I pulled video surveillance from a local bank, and sure enough, instead of his friend I found none other than my father, enjoying the good life and hiding in plain sight. I watched him take breakfast at the café and read the paper right out in the open as if he hadn't just committed treason... and betrayed his daughter.

Oh no, he was having a café con leche without a care in the world

Roone came in. "Are you okay?"

I'd been getting a debriefing from Jacob and Trevor when I heard the ping from the alert I'd set up. Jessa was trying to prep for her early meeting before going to bed, so Roone had joined us. "Um, yes. The good news is I found my father. The bad news is I found my father."

"Where is he?" Roone asked.

"Barcelona."

"How did you find him?"

"He's using an alias. Juan Cornelus. He's a known associate of my father's. So, I need to pop over to Barcelona before he runs again."

"All right. I'll handle things here."

I hesitated. "Are you sure this is okay?"

Roone shook his head. "Of course. You're my partner. This is also part of the mission. Go on and do what you have to do. I'll hold down the fort."

I wasn't even sure why I'd ever doubted him in the first place. He may not have liked me being assigned lead on this case, but he was perhaps the best partner I could have asked for. "Thank you. I honestly don't know what I would do without you."

"Well, good thing you don't have to figure it out. Now go. Get a flight to Barcelona. I have things under control here."

"I know that. Try not to get the princess killed or kill her yourself."

He just chuckled as I closed the door behind me. Now all I had to do was find my father.

*Jessa*

AFTER A LONG NIGHT, I'd finally gotten to bed sometime around one in the morning. I wanted to make sure I was ready for anything Evan threw at me. But when I finally had gotten to sleep, the nightmares came at me again.

The doubt, the fear, the worry, the confusion. Again, my father on the choppy water. Jumping in, leaving me to save him but unable to, and then of course, the doubt, the way I'd doubted him, the way I hadn't believed in him. I was ashamed. Horrified. Confused. What if he hadn't been crazy?

But of the recent dangers, all signs pointed toward stalker, not to some grand royal conspiracy. I understood and believed what had happened to Sebastian, Lucas, and Penny. I just wasn't convinced right now that it was the work of the same people. After all, how did they find me? The more Evan acted like a crazy person, the more convinced I was that he was behind all of this and that he was secretly crazy, that he was stalking me. Was he responsible for Toby's death, too?

That was next level. I couldn't even wrap my mind around Toby. I couldn't accept what had happened to him. I couldn't let it go either. I couldn't stand by and just wonder. Was Evan responsible?

All of that running together in my thoughts led to a lovely nightmare cocktail.

Again, Roone came into my room and gently shook me. He didn't say anything, just peeled back the sheets, climbed in next to me, and opened his arms. It was that easy.

I tucked into the crook of his arm. I still couldn't believe that he didn't ask any questions. He just accepted what was happening. He gave me a safe space. I could love that about him

*You already do.*

I could be mad at him. I could still hold on to it. But the truth was I missed him. I missed that easy rhythm we'd found before my whole life went to hell. In the comfort of his arms, I knew that I could easily let it go and give myself permission to be loved, to have someone care about me. Truly care about me. Or I could hold on to my anger and be alone.

*How long does that work out for you?*

My lids were so heavy, it was hard to keep them open with Roone's heat around me, his scent lulling me into a safe comfortable love. My happy place.

I was asleep before I even knew it. To be honest, I hadn't even been aware I was asleep until I woke up sometime later to noises in the living room.

The bed was still slightly warm, so he'd left me not that long ago. I padded out to the living room to find him surrounded by boxes. He was putting my things in boxes. The cold tentacles of panic closed around my heart and squeezed. "What the hell are you doing?"

"Relax, we don't have to leave now. We're not doing this in a hurry. I just want to prepare you. You can't stay here anymore. I hope you're okay with me packing these things for you. But when you mentioned it last night, I knew we had to make a move. Ben, East, and Bridge are giving us a suite at their Soho location, a penthouse. You'll be comfortable. You can still work. But you said you didn't want to stay here anymore. So..." His voice trailed.

"So you're making it all better for me."

"I know it's probably freaking you out seeing the boxes. But I wouldn't just do that to you. I know how important it is to you to have some say in the agenda. I just wanted to get a jumpstart because I want to keep you safe."

I shook my head. "Why are you like this? Why are you so damn—sweet? It makes it really hard to stay angry with you."

"I'm pretty sure I'm the one who gets hard."

I threw my hands up. "Oh my God. I was having a moment."

He chuckled low. "I'm sorry. Go ahead."

I folded my arms and refused to talk.

With a grin, he took my hand. "I'm sorry. Go ahead."

With a sigh, I said, "It makes it hard to hate you."

"You never hated me," he said with finality.

"Yes, I did. When you moved in across the corridor, I hated you."

He grinned. "And then I charmed you with my really big... smile."

I couldn't help a giggle. "Yes, it was your smile that did it entirely."

He nodded solemnly. "Yup, I knew it. I should show everyone my... smile. I'd probably get away with a lot more."

"Eeww. No, I'm pretty sure you'd get arrested."

"Yeah, good point there." His smile faltered a little. "So, are you good with me continuing to pack? Because I'd like us to get you packed up and moved to London Lords as soon as we can."

I nodded. "Here, I'll help." And while I was potentially closing out a chapter of my life, I was okay with that. After Evan had shown up at the flat twice, I knew I couldn't stay there anymore. Even if I had to get my own flat somewhere else in London, it was fine, because staying there was certainly not an option anymore. But somehow, instead of feeling worried, I felt hopeful because Roone was with me.

# NINETEEN

*Jessa*

ROONE STOOD watch like a guard dog. With his unflinching, soldier's stare. There was something really hot and also really foreboding about it. Tight rigid jaw, intensely focused eyes. He was glaring at the Detective Inspector like he wanted rip him a new one.

But DI Spencer didn't seem to notice. "Miss McLean, thanks for meeting with me again. This is my associate, Detective Inspector James. I just wanted to touch base with you on Toby Adamson."

"Yes. Did you find out who hurt him?"

He shook his head. "Right now, the leads have dried up. But, it looks like all evidence points to Toby Adamson having stalked you. We've even got a witness who says they saw Adamson outside your apartment two nights in a row before you were burgled."

My gaze shifted to Roone. Was this true? Wouldn't he and Ariel's team have seen it?

"Is that so?"

"Yes. But the good news is now you'll be safe. No more stalking, no more incidents."

"No more incidents. How about if I don't think it was Toby at all? Why haven't you looked at anyone else? Because it just makes no sense that it was Toby. Maybe the person who killed him was stalking me. Maybe they are responsible for trying to grab me outside the gala."

He flattened his lips, making him look older and more haggard. "And that we *are* looking into. But as far as who broke into your flat, that was Adamson. And as far as who tried to assault you outside the gala, we suspect that was him as well. A trickle of blood found about a hundred meters from the scene matched to him. We almost missed it."

Blood? God, was I wrong? I knew it wasn't Toby who attacked me. At the same time, I couldn't prove it. And it was all about what you could prove. Not a gut feeling.

"I just—I don't believe it."

"Right. These things are usually difficult to comprehend. But if you know of anyone who might have wanted to hurt him, now is the time to speak up. Now is the time to say something."

"I don't know anything." Not anything I could prove anyway. But after what Roone and Ariel had told me about Evan, I wanted to scream from the rooftops that it was him. *He* was the one with the erratic behavior and the stalking tendencies. But I had no proof. "I don't know. But you know, he didn't get along very well with our bosses, so you might ask them if they knew of any reason why someone wouldn't like Toby."

He wrote it down and nodded. "You didn't mention that before."

"Well, you just asked. Last time I was so shocked it didn't even occur to me, so I'm amending my statement." I didn't want to outright accuse Evan, but maybe I could get Detective Inspector Spencer to look at him.

"I recognize that you believe he was a friend of yours. In many of these cases that's how it goes. You want to properly vet *everyone* you bring into your life." He slid a glance at Roone and glowered. "Even if someone seems like they're good for you, they might not be."

I cleared my throat and stood. It was terribly rude. The inspectors hadn't even finished their tea. But I didn't want to hear any more of this. There was no love lost between me and Toby, but no one seemed interested in properly figuring out what had happened to him. Spencer wanted a nice neat clean line, ends he could wrap up. If I pointed at Evan, he wouldn't be able to do that. Not that I didn't think he was good at his job. I didn't know. But so far, they hadn't even looked at Evan. And I had a feeling Evan had planted that evidence against Toby.

*But good luck proving that.*

"Thank you for coming, Inspectors. If you learn anything else, please let me know."

The DI Spencer's gaze narrowed at me as if he couldn't believe that I'd dismissed them. Well, let him put that in his pipe and smoke it. "Of course. Thank you so much."

Roone was all too happy to show them to the door. When he returned, I asked, "Are they ever going to look for the person who killed him?"

He shrugged. "Possibly, but they would need a reason. Millston is smart. Anything he took from here, he planted at Toby's, so it made Toby look like the stalker. The good news is you and I both know what he's doing. You won't be unprotected. He's not going to get his wish."

"So what is his wish? I just wish that I knew what these guys wanted."

"Well, in the case of Evan Millston, he wants *you*. You are the prize. He wants you to look up at him as more than just a mentor. Thus far you haven't. It's extremely frustrating for him.

And as for Adamson, he was just a poor dumb kid that got caught in the crossfire. Millston wants to own your essence, something you're not letting him do. I promise you, I will help you take care of this."

It wasn't much in the way of comfort. But it was all I had. I knew Roone wasn't going to let anything happen to me. He opened his arms, and I stepped in.

Happily taking the comfort I knew would sooth me.

---

*Jessa*

"COME ON, TONIGHT WE DRINK."

Ariel and Chloe had dragged me to the top of the roof bar at the London Lords Soho location. While I was technically on lockdown, it didn't mean we couldn't at least enjoy a girl's night.

Chloe whistled as she took in the ambiance of the rooftop, the plush seats, the gorgeous, spectacular view of London, the strategic placement of heat lamps so that even though it was a brisk spring evening, it felt like a balmy summer day, save the occasional chilly wind that drafted through.

"Honestly, I'm fine. I don't need cheering up."

Chloe rolled her eyes. "Are you kidding me? You've been timid. Jumpy. Questioning yourself. Questioning decisions. Don't let Evan do this to you."

"Please, can we not say his name?"

A pretty brunette with a sweet smile, wearing the bar uniform of all black approached our table. "Hiya, I'm Paulette. I'll be your server tonight. What can I get started for you?"

Ariel gave me a smile and squeezed my hand. "My friend here has a shit boss. The only way to fix it is with shots of Patrone."

Paulette gave me a wink. "I have just what you need, love. I'll be right back."

I rolled my eyes. "The last think I need is shots. "I'm so sorry he's been such a turd. If it makes you feel better, it's not just you. He tried again to force my hand and get my database. I told Rick that if he didn't stop I was pulling my account, which obviously I don't want to do because I think you're the best person for the account." I read between the lines. She couldn't say that she needed to be on my detail in front of Chloe.

"I need to get a new job." Just the thought depressed me.

"Well," Ariel lifted her brows, "I know London Lords would hire you in a second. I also know Ben Covington wants to sleep with you."

Chloe coughed. "Oh my God, you can put me in as tribute. I will ride him until the dawn breaks. Oh my God, and East Hale. I only had a brief glimpse of Bridge, but from the back, I can tell he's delicious."

I snorted a laugh. "Oh my God, Chloe, what happened to Thomas, or Tom, or whatever his name was?"

"He's there. And actually, things are pretty good. He's sweet and he grounds me. But that doesn't mean I can't ogle the merchandise."

"Ugh, you're like that woman that goes after what she wants, but she just wants to fondle every piece of jewelry in the store."

Chloe giggled. "Yes, sign me up for fondling."

Ariel snorted. "Oh my God!"

A round of shots came. We clinked the glasses of tequila per Chloe's request, and I knew it was going to be a long night. Ariel raised hers. "To my new friends, even though I need to leave tomorrow for a little trip, I shall be back, and I just want to say, thank you guys for making me feel like I have a little slice of home away from home."

Chloe grinned. "I'll drink to that."

Considering Chloe didn't know exactly what Ariel meant, her eagerness to drink was comical. But I knew, and I raised my glass in return. "Cheers."

The shot went down smoother than I expected, and I glared down into the glass. "Oh my God, I think these are dangerous."

Ariel just laughed. "Well, we're only going to be having two. Technically, I have to get up for an early flight in the morning, so... not too many drinks for me."

Chloe groaned. "Oh my God, you're such a spoilsport. Where are you going anyway?"

"It's a business thing. An investor in Barcelona I have to go and check on. Make sure the money came from the right place."

I knew something was happening in Barcelona, but it certainly wasn't an investor, so what the hell was going on? Of course, I wanted to ask all the questions, but I couldn't because Chloe wasn't in the know. She wasn't a member of Team Winston Isles.

*But you are.*

I couldn't help the giddy rush at the idea of being part of a team. I'd never really had that before. But now that I did, I enjoyed it. It felt good to not just be on my own. I wasn't a lone wolf. I had backup.

"Well, you are the best girl boss, so I hope Barcelona turns out how you hope."

Ariel clinked glasses with me, and then Chloe called for our next round. "Me too."

Chloe downed hers quickly and set her glass down. "So, are you going to ask the question Ariel, or should I?"

My gaze darted between the two of them. "What question?"

Ariel giggled. "Well, what the hell is happening with Roone?"

"Oh that."

The truth was I had no idea how to answer that. Me having a nightmare had become a habit, as had his sleeping with me. All we did was hold each other and sleep, but it had gotten to the point that he'd just started going to bed with me. That had happened two nights ago.

I'd brushed my teeth and climbed into bed. Roone had come in, brushed his teeth, taken off his shirt, changed into his pajama bottoms, and climbed into bed with me. I'd had the benefit of the bare-chested Roone in my bed, easily wrapped around me like he owned the joint.

And he clearly did. The suite we'd been given at the hotel had two bedrooms, a massive chef's kitchen, a living space that looked over Soho and Piccadilly, but we usually ended up in the king-size bed together, half-naked, and unfortunately, doing nothing but sleeping.

*It's not like the guy knows you've forgiven him.*

It wasn't even so much about forgiveness as it was about me processing all that he was and all that I was. And truth be told, I had no idea how to bridge the topic with him. He seemed in no rush, which I was grateful for, but I was also beyond frustrated.

Every night when we went to bed, my pulse raced, and I throbbed between my thighs. I ached and willed him to touch me. I'd lay awake for a while in his arms. His breathing and his scent made me want to be touched, but I was too afraid to ask for it.

*If you want it, ask for it.*

But what if he said no again? What if he knew as well as I did that it was a bad idea, and that I was going to get hurt. What if he said that? What if he refused?

All the 'what ifs' in the world still didn't change the fact that I wanted him or the fact that he knew it. I was only mildly comforted that as I slept wrapped in his arms, his body also responded to mine. Every morning, I woke up to the thick ridge of his erection pressed up against my ass. Every morning, he'd kiss my temple, roll away from me, and head straight for the shower, as if I hadn't noticed the giant baseball bat in his pants. Oh yeah, I just ignored the anaconda wanting to come out and play because that was an easy thing to do.

"Honestly, I don't know. I'm starting to process how I'm feeling about him."

Chloe shook her head. She didn't know the whole story, so what I told her was that he'd wanted to move things a lot faster than I had, instead of opening up because I couldn't deal with her knowing the truth.

"I just don't get it. He's so good for you. He takes care of you. He won't let Evan creep on you. What has Rick said about the whole Evan situation?"

"I mean, he gave me a pat answer and apologized if I felt uncomfortable. He said he would reassign me to other projects. I spoke to him because we have a relationship, but I should have just gone to HR, I think."

"What happens if you no longer work for them?"

I met Ariel's gaze levelly. "Nothing, I guess. I just feel like I'm quitting."

"You're not quitting love. They let you down. They're supposed to take care of you, protect you, and they haven't done their job, especially when the predator is the one in charge. The problem is he hasn't done anything overt. Just enough to be creepy, but nothing obvious to anyone but you."

"Well, there's not a lot Rick can do, and all HR can do is have me reassigned, but London Lords is a big account that I don't want to lose."

"Oh honey, why do you want to stay again?" Ariel asked.

"Because when I joined the company, I really needed it. It felt like family. And obviously, Chloe works there."

Chloe laughed. "Honey, I would quit in a heartbeat if you

didn't work there. I still need money from my father to pay my rent on my flat. Those guys pay me so little. Always have. My father was disappointed that I didn't join the family business, so he tries to lure me with expensive vacations and paying my housing. Honestly, I'd rather just get a job that I really liked that pays decently. And at Evans, while the work is great, I really just stay because I never wanted to leave you in the lurch," Chloe added.

"I guess you wanted that sense of family too."

Ariel winked at me. "I think you've both already got that. You don't need you jobs at Evans for it."

Despite my mood, I smiled. "I think you have a point there."

# TWENTY

*Roone*

How MANY YEARS had it been since I went to the Biltmore Club?

It was so long I had forgotten what it was like, the level of service, the way you're treated if you're accepted.

*You're a member of the club.*

Tonight, I was Ben's guest. So that meant from the moment I checked in at the door, I was Mr. Ainsley. Several of the staff members did a double take when they saw my name. It was to be expected, because like it or not, Reese and I looked a lot alike. And obviously, the name. The staff was far too well trained to ever notice, to ever comment.

When I was led to Ben's private booth in the back corner, my cousin stood and grinned. "Cousin."

"Hey, mate."

"Sit, sit. What do you want to drink?"

I nodded at his glass. "What are you drinking?"

"I like to keep it simple. Old school and old fashioned."

"I'll have one too."

The server who appeared out of nowhere nodded politely and scuttled away.

"I forgot what this place was like."

Ben laughed. "You know, I don't actually even like it here that much, but I had an earlier meeting with Bridge and East. East fucking loves this place. I still don't know why. I 'd rather be at a pub, mate."

I laughed. East was the one who tried the hardest to fit in, to comport to societal expectations. Bridge and Ben though, well... my cousin leaned toward not ever giving a fuck. And Bridge, it was always hard to read him. But he had a different code.

"That's fine. I'm guessing the steak here is going to be incredible, and the drinks will be too."

"That's what I like to hear. I figured it might have been a while since you've let yourself relax, and all I need as repayment is double o status."

I chuckled low. "You know I can't do that."

"Oh, come on mate. You're a double o spy, why can't I be one too?" He made a petulant face, causing me to laugh out loud.

He grinned as I covered my laugh with a cough. "Ah, there it is. It's good to see you laughing, mate."

"Yeah, you're outrageous as usual."

He shrugged. "Well, gotta play to our strengths. And how is the lovely Jessa McLean?"

I wrinkled my nose and considered that. "Fine, I guess."

Ben laughed. "Shite. You have it bad."

"Is it that obvious?"

"Yes, it's that bloody obvious. I watch her because, well, I'm a dirty bloke. Can't help it. She has really nice tits."

I glowered at him, and he held his hands up. "I'm just saying it objectively, but *you* watch her, and I can see it in your eyes. You mean that shit."

"Yeah, well, she's still mad at me because I lied about the whole double o thing, so she's coming to terms with it all."

"Nah, mate, I see it. She's in love too."

I coughed. "No one said anything about love."

Ben tossed his head and laughed. "Mate, how do you not see it? You are so bug sappy stupid in love with that girl."

"I—" *Shit*. My heart raced, but then a weird calm fell over me, like that was exactly the revelation I was supposed to have. From the corner of my eye, I saw someone I wasn't expecting, and then I glowered at Ben. "Is that your doing?"

Ben looked up from his drink. His immediate frown told me that it wasn't, in fact, his doing. "No. I didn't even know he was going to be here."

"Fantastic."

Reese spotted me right away and came over. "Cousin," he said to Ben.

Ben inclined his head but said nothing. And then Reese focused on me. "Roone, all right, mate?"

"I'm not your mate."

My brother sighed. "Ben, a minute, would you?"

Ben slid me a glance and then shrugged, sliding out of the booth. "I'll be back. I'll order you the veal."

I nodded my thanks, and my brother sat. "I've been trying to reach you."

"Well, I've been busy."

He sighed. "Look, I know you don't want to see me or talk to me, but this is important."

"So you ambushed me?"

"Not intentionally. I was already here. I had a meeting, but then one of the butlers approached me and mentioned that you were here. I couldn't pass up the opportunity."

"What is it you want?"

"I wrote you a letter, mate. Did you not get it?"

"I've been here. I haven't gotten any mail. Then I went back to the island for a while, and now I'm back. Maybe it was forwarded. I don't know where anything is."

He nodded slowly. "So, you don't know."

"Know what, Reese? What are you doing here? Why were you at my mother's grave?"

"I told you, she was kind to me when she didn't have to be. I appreciated it and..." He cleared his throat. "I'm appalled by what my mother did to you."

I scowled. "I don't know what you're talking about."

His mother had been cruel. When my father was alive, she tolerated me. But as soon as his back was turned, she was absolutely terrible to me. And then when he passed away, during the time that he'd dictated that I spend with Reese, she was always there, interfering, never allowing us to bond. Then, when my mother was ill, she'd been very clear that no money that father left was ever going to come to me. And when mom died, she said that to bury my mother, I just had to do it the old-fashioned way, with a shovel. The word was, Reese's mother was mentally unstable, in and out of hospitals. But none of that excused what she did to me then. The pain still sliced.

"Look, Roone, my mother—"

"There's no amount of apologizing you can do on her behalf that will change anything."

"I don't imagine there would be. She was alone, but it doesn't matter. You weren't the one who was in love with someone else. None of it was personal, and she shouldn't have taken her anger out on you."

"I was a child."

His voice went quiet. "I know."

"If we're done with this walk down memory lane, I'd like to get my drink now."

"No, not quite."

"What the fuck do you need, Reese?"

"In that letter, I was trying to tell you about the changes to his estate. With Mum's last stint at the facility, there were so many things to go through before I saw the paperwork she'd filed."

"What paperwork?"

"The one that allowed you to have access to your inheritance."

I frowned. "What inheritance?"

He sighed. "Dad... I think he always regretted letting you and your mum go. He always regretted being forced into the life he had with my mother."

"That's bullshit. He loved you."

"Yes, me he loved. Mom, not so much. And she certainly never loved him. I was overindulged, I know. I'm kind of a twat. A wanker, in its finest form. When Dad died, he left you money. Well, you and your mother. He left you money and the title. Lord Roone Ainsley, the Earldom, he left it to you."

I blinked at him. "Shut it. You're taking a piss now."

"I wish I was. My mother got wind of it from the lawyer. Since she was the executor of his estate, she and the lawyer were in on it. But they couldn't completely keep the money away from you. They just didn't have to give it to you until your twenty-fifth birthday."

"So she—she kept me from being able to properly bury my mother out of spite?"

He sighed. "Yeah, she did. I was horrified when I found out. That's when I started—" he cleared his throat, "—that's when I started going to her grave. Putting flowers there, making sure it was clean. She had it fixed so you never would have found out either until she died or you reached the age of inheritance. Although, I guess you're twenty-six now. I've been trying to reach you basically ever since I discovered what was going on."

A year. He'd been trying to reach me for a year. That would account for the letters that I'd burned.

"Fuck."

"I know there's no amount of apologies I can make that will ever make up for it. But I just thought you should know. Now that I have informed you, I can get you the paperwork to sign at any time. The title, the money, it's yours."

"But you... What about you?"

Reese laughed. "Oh, he left me more money than I know what to do with. I don't even want the lands, or the title, or any of that bullshit. I'm better with my nose in a book anyway. I don't want all the trappings."

"Fuck."

Reese nodded slowly. "Look, I know I'm just your half brother and you don't much like me, which is fine, and I probably deserve that."

I swallowed hard. "I guess I don't really know you."

He shook his head. "No. And I don't really know you. But once I graduated from Uni, I took some time and traveled. I went to a whole bunch of places in the world where there were people less fortunate than me. I got rid of most of my stupid. It still flares on occasion, but yeah, building wells for people who need clean water to drink daily gives you some perspective."

I stared at him. How was this my brother? He'd always been the favored son, the one who got everything. Toys. Love. Attention. Nothing that I'd had.

*Yes, you did have it from your mother.*

That was true. And in that moment, I started to look at him differently. "You really have changed, haven't you?"

He shrugged. "I certainly hope so. I'm nothing like her. I wouldn't have kept this from you. I'm so sorry."

The refusal to forgive anyone surrounding my mother's death, the cloud of it, just dissipated in that moment. I couldn't hold on to it any longer, all because my brother had actually tried to do the right thing. "I don't even know where to go from here."

Reese nodded slowly. "Well, I for one would like to get to know my big brother better. You know, it doesn't have to be a big thing, but maybe I can come see you on the island sometime."

"Yeah. Maybe that wouldn't be the worst thing in the world. And maybe you can help me figure out how to run an earldom?"

He laughed. "I figured you might have some questions. Somehow sorry doesn't seem like enough."

I shook my head. "But you know what? Sometimes it's a start."

"Well, I don't know if it's ever been done before, but I think you'll probably be the first Winston Isles Royal Guard with his own title."

It was only then that it occurred to me. I was gentry now. Not a single person on the Regents Council could object to me being with Jessa. And somehow that scared me even more than the prospect of *not* being with her.

---

*Jessa*

MY HEAD WAS BUZZING. Those two tequila shots were making me warm and fuzzy. Roone walked in the door, and I sidled up to him. "Well, there you are, handsome."

I could tell something was wrong. For once, his gaze was distant. He didn't have that signature smirk on his lips, the one I'd like to kiss off all the time. "What's wrong?"

He shook his head. "I just, um, I got some unexpected news tonight."

"I thought you were with Ben? What happened?"

"I saw my brother."

"Shit. What was he doing with Ben?"

"He wasn't. I just—" He shook his head. "I'm sorry. I'm here. Go ahead and get ready for bed. I'm just going to chill tonight. Reese said something about my dad, and I just need to process it for a bit."

I'd never seen him like this. He looked lost, like he needed something. "Okay. Well, why don't you have a seat? Would you like me to bring you something to drink?"

He nodded slowly. "Yeah, I think I need a scotch."

I ran to get it. "What did Ben say?"

"He was as surprised as I was. I could barely eat I was so out of it."

"Are you hungry?"

He shook his head. "No, I just—sorry. Why don't we get ready for bed?"

"You enjoy your drink, okay? Just take a little bit to clear your head."

He nodded. "Yeah, I'm just going to take a few minutes. Decompress."

Not exactly what I'd planned for the night, but this was about him. I hopped in the shower. I wanted to see if I could get him to bed. Give him kisses to make me feel good. But wait... that wasn't what this was about. *He* needed to feel good. This wasn't about me. And it was time I took a definitive step.

I knew just how to do it.

I took the shower cap off and opened a decadent lotion that was provided in the suite. And to my joy, I found out it smelled just like roses. Sort of like my perfume. And delightfully, there were some sparkles in it, so I would shimmer like a Grecian statue.

I wrapped myself in one of the big plush robes, then I padded back out to the living room. Roone was exactly where

I'd left him, drink in hand, except the drink was mostly gone now. He raised his head, and his brows lifted. "Princess?"

"I feel like you've been taking care of me, and now maybe it's time I take care of you."

He shook his head. "I—what is happening?"

"All you have to do is relax and sit back." The nerves fluttered in my belly. I'd started down this road, and I was saying something very definitive. I was taking that step into the terrifying unknown abyss of staking my claim, of saying I wanted to be with someone.

I'd never done that in real life. I was so scared. But I was going to do this, and there would be no looking back, because for once, I was taking charge of my own life. My fingers went to the knot in my robe. Roone's gaze went heavy lidded, and he sucked in his bottom lip, grazing it with his teeth.

"What are you doing, princess?"

I undid the robe and parted the thick cloth. "I'm finally taking what I want."

---

Roone

MY HANDS SHOOK, I wanted her so bad.

"I—I'm in a weird headspace, princess. I'm not sure how gentle I can be."

"Roone, I want this. I want you. You don't have to be gentle. Maybe I won't be gentle on you."

Despite the cocktail of confusion, despair, and raging desire in my blood, she managed to make me smile. How did she always do that? "I look forward to you having your way with me."

Sure, it sounded like I was going to let her lead. But she was so close. I could smell her faint perfume. I knew how I'd feel with her wrapped around me. Whole.

I slid my hands into the hair at her nape and fisted, angling her head and kissing her deep. I kissed her with all the love I didn't know how to express. My tongue sliding over hers, demanding she respond to me. And respond she did. She made my favorite little mewling sound, and I was lost.

She moaned, rocking her hips over me. Why was this always so good? Was it supposed to be this good? It was like the two of us just fit together in a way that made me feel as though my skin was on fire, like my hair was in flames.

I kissed her deeper while my cock twitched inside my boxers. She could feel how much I wanted her. There was no hiding that.

"Roone," her whispered moan was harsh and throaty.

Our movements were frenzied and quick as we devoured each other. With a frustrated groan, I tore my lips from hers and made quick work of my shirt. I needed skin to skin contact, and I was tired of the tease.

I ducked and suckled her breasts as I whispered homage to them. Her fucking tits could occupy me for days. I licked. I teased. With my tongue and teeth, I tormented and pinched her nipples gently. Her sharp pants told me I was hitting the mark.

Jessa dug her nails into my back as she rotated her hips. My cock was searching for entry even through my pants. Like the fucker knew she was naked.

**Dick**: I'm not dumb. I know where I belong.

She met each shallow thrust with a roll of her hips, making my balls ache. "Roone..."

I grinned as I nuzzled her neck. "Can I make you come from just this, I wonder?"

I gripped her hips, my fingers digging in as we ground against each other. *Shit*. I wasn't going to be able to hold this. I moaned low, throwing my head back. Fuck, this sensation was everything.

Sliding my hand between us, I found that spot she needed me to touch. That secret place that was the key to everything. Gently, I stroked my thumb over her clit.

Bloody fucking jackpot. With a low moan, Jessa threw her head back, convulsing in my arms. I lifted my head to watch her in awe. Just the look on her face was enough to send me to my knees.

I stared up at the woman on top of me with breasts worth paying homage to, her skin practically glowing in the dim light of the room. With every glance from under her lashes, and every tentative touch of her fingertips, my whole body felt like it was on fire, being stoked to full blaze.

Her mocha-tipped breasts swayed as she shifted her straddle further down my legs. Her hands came into contact with the elastic of my boxers, and the buckle of my pants and my cock throbbed and strained. Involuntarily, my hips rose, and I tried to school my breathing.

With some wiggling, we worked together to shed my trousers, then I lay back watching her.

She supported her weight with her hands on either side of me.

"Has anyone ever told you you're very big?"

I grinned. "Nope. You're the first."

She cocked an eyebrow, then resumed her inspection of my body. When she leaned directly over my straining cock, her long hair brushed against my skin, and her breath floated over my dick. It only took two puffs of breath from her, and my control snapped.

My hands banded around her biceps, and I hauled her up against me and flipped us over so I could kiss her.

She trembled underneath me. Against my thigh, I could feel

the moisture of her slick core. I tried not to think about how soft she would be. I needed to go slow. My cock, on the other hand, had a mind of its own and pulsed against her thigh.

I gave her another peck on the lips before tracing feather-light kisses along her jaw. When I nuzzled her neck, she giggled. When I went from muzzling to nibbling, she moaned. My hands enjoyed free rein of her breasts, testing the weight of the full globes, teasing the tight buds to a pucker. Her hips rose to meet me every time I tugged on one of the tips.

I placed open-mouthed kisses on her clavicle and her chest, eventually making my way to her breasts. But no matter how much she shifted, I didn't kiss her nipples again. Not even when her hands tried to pull my head to her breasts. Though I wanted to taste them again, there was somewhere else I needed to be.

My lips continued a path down her ribs to her belly button. When the tip of my tongue dipped into the tiny crevice, she parted her thighs on an exhale.

"Princess, I want you so much."

Her eyes fluttered closed, and she moaned. "I'm yours."

My cock strained against the material imprisoning it, and I growled. Since we'd moved to London Lords, the cameras were only outside of the suite to see who came and went, so I didn't have to worry about not having privacy.

I wanted her so bad, but I wanted to take my time in bed with her. Pushing off of Jessa, I stood and tugged her with me. I made quick work of the rest of my clothes, then I pulled her to her feet and shed her robe. The moonlight streamed into the suite, making her look incandescent.

Picking her up easily, I carried her into our room and gently placed her on the bed. Her delicate fingers reached for me, and she found her target easily. She pumped my cock with her palm once, then twice. The trembling in my body started in my legs first.

"Love, I—"

She pumped me again, but this time she brought my cock to her dewy center. I hissed a breath and squeezed my eyes shut, praying I didn't come before I was inside her. Blinking rapidly, I gazed into her eyes. She owned a part of me. Completely. And she knew it. And I owned her too.

With a growl, I shoved a hand under her back, grabbing onto her waist, then I flipped her over onto her stomach, and she squealed.

"This okay princess?" I glided a hand down her smooth back to her perfect, round ass. I drew her limp body up onto her knees. Leaning into her, I whispered, "Hold on to the headboard."

She flicked me a cocked eyebrow over her shoulder, but she complied.

"That's a good girl. Now spread your knees for me." When she parted her legs, I bit back a groan. She had a truly spectacular arse. Shifting behind her, I covered her body with mine again. I inserted one finger in her still slick pussy, and she moaned.

I kissed a freckle between her shoulder blades. "You are so perfect."

"Roone, please..." She muttered as she moved her hips in time with my questing finger. When I added another finger, she sucked in a quick breath of air but then moaned as my fingers retreated.

"Please. I just need—"

"Oh, I have an idea of what you need, princess." I lined my dick up with her sweet opening and whispered as I slid my cock into her pussy. "I know because I need you too."

There was no way I could last. This felt too good. As I held her hips tight and rode her, she called my name. Leaning over her as our hips locked, I played with her breasts, relishing their sweet response to my touch. Just by hovering over the sensitive skin of her nipples, they puckered in anticipation, inviting me to touch, to tease, to pinch.

She let her head land between her braced shoulders as she pushed her hips back to meet my every stroke. "God, that feels, so—"

I knew the instant she started to come. Her pussy began to milk my cock, and her whole body shook. I could only hold on for the ride, digging both hands into the curves of her arse.

As she shattered around me, my vision started to gray at the edges. The tingle that had started in my spine felt more like someone had hooked me up to thousand-volt electrodes as I pumped inside of her. So close to heaven.

As blinding light exploded my vision, my whole body erupted in electric bliss.

# TWENTY-ONE

*Jessa*

Somehow, being with Roone was even hotter now. I couldn't explain it; it just was. And being here at London Lords... Well, while I was still professional, it was hard not to take full advantage of unfettered access to him.

Over the last few days since I'd made my feelings clear, Roone had been... attentive.

Letting myself fall was the push I really needed. Letting myself feel, letting myself trust. It felt good, actually. Every morning I woke expecting sheer panic, the need to flee, to course correct, but it didn't come. I just woke up in his arms with him kissing my neck, my collarbone and then travelling his way down and back up and making love to me. It was delicious.

Then we'd have breakfast together. One of us was on food duty and the other was on coffee or tea duty. We'd switch. He'd make me breakfast one day, I'd make it the next. Okay fine, I would put on either crumpets or toast when it was my turn, but the point was we were happy.

Then we would walk down to the car hand in hand, letting our fingers interlock while driving to London Lords. It was idyllic. Completely insane. And Rick had become my main point of contact at Evans PR. Evan was not speaking to me. Which was —well, it was what it was. Maybe there would be a time when I could speak to my mentor again, but I didn't know what was going on with him and didn't want to ask.

Roone nuzzled my neck. "Okay, have a good day."

"I will."

Chloe snorted as she brushed past us. "Ugh, Christ, would you two go get a room?"

Roone just grinned against my lips. "That's my cue. You go do your thing. Be great."

"And you watch my back."

"Well, technically, I already do that every day."

I frowned. "Are you seriously watching my ass all day?"

There was that smirk of his again. Except this time, I didn't want to smack it off. I wanted to lick it off and then do inappropriate things to his body. But I was working, so I was going to focus on work things. I gave him one final kiss and then went to my office.

The tasting event was scheduled for that day, and we had a lot to do. The caterer had so much work, but we got an agreement to do the in-room service menu as well as the themed lunch. We all had to deliver like clockwork and in rotating shifts. It was going to be insane, and Chloe and I were running the logistics.

I was finding it hard to focus on the job I loved because I was freaking *in* love.

*Love?*

*Don't be silly, you know it.*

I did. I was completely in love with him. I had been since before I found out who he was. I'd been falling for him then, and now it was cemented. That first night he'd held me in his arms, keeping the nightmares away, I was a goner. I was completely in la-la land, but Chloe was stepping up.

"Okay. Do you have everything you need? Because I need to get to the restaurant and meet with the chef. He's got the sous chef ready to go, and meals are already being prepared. Can you follow behind me with catering needs?"

I couldn't help but grin at her. "Well, look who's all grown up."

"Well, I was taught by the best."

"Fabulous. Okay, you go to the restaurant. I'll follow with Katy. Most of our staff are already at the hotel, and the auxiliary staff we hired is ready and willing and just waiting for us. Everything has been prepped and polished, and everyone looks the part. Then tonight will be the special tasting, and the faces of our party, the London Lords themselves, will be present to give their big speeches and announce that the restaurant will be part of the new hotel and the partnership. We got this?"

Chloe grinned. She really did look like she was in her element. "We got this. And the moment you fell in love, everything else sort of fell into place, so I am digging this new you. You were good before, but man, you're firing on all cylinders now."

"Who knew orgasms were good for productivity?"

As soon as Chloe was out the door, Roone was knocking. "Hey, I realized something I forgot before we were separated so rudely by your assistant."

I lifted my head. I had my clipboard, my folders, everything I needed. I grinned. "Yeah, that was rude of her, wasn't it?"

He laughed. "How much time do we have before we need to leave?"

I checked the clock. "It takes three minutes to get downstairs. The car will be ready at a moment's notice. It takes fifteen minutes to get there. And since Chloe is already handling Ian, I have ten minutes before we absolutely have to leave."

He nodded, stepped into my office, and closed the door, locking it behind him. I leaned around him and glanced at the door. "Uh, why is the door locked?"

"Because I realized I forgot to tell my beautiful princess that I am in awe of her. From all the changes in your life and everything you have found out to how well you do your job, you amaze me on a daily basis, and I think tonight is going to be your crowning achievement. I am in awe of you."

"I don't know why." The flush crept up my neck, and I didn't know where to look until he placed a finger underneath my chin and tipped it up so that I was forced to look him in the eye.

"Look at me."

"I don't know how to accept a compliment."

"Just take it and know that I love you."

"What?"

Fucking Christ on a Jaffa Cake. He'd just said I love you. I knew there were several ways to respond to this, and I needed to think through a rational response, the right protocol. But my brain had other ideas. My brain basically said fuck it and tumbled out the words, "I love you too."

He grinned. "Uh, God, that's a relief. But I knew that already."

I frowned. "What?"

"Yeah, you are completely in love with me. That first time you saw me at the party and refused to buy me a drink. Then again when you saw me across the hall."

"Oh my God, I was in love with your abs. You had a very nice—"

He quieted me with a kiss and then whispered against my lips, "We have ten minutes. We both just said I love you. Since I can't keep my hands off you, and I can't seem to think, let's use the rest of that time wisely. And then you'll be nice and relaxed for the event."

"Oh my God, we cannot do this in my office."

"The doors are already locked, princess. It's still your choice. My mouth, my fingers, my dick—"

Oh, fuck it. "Dick. I vote dick."

He chuckled low. "I thought you didn't have time for this."

"Nope. I have time."

"Well, it seems I will have to accommodate the lady then."

"Screw the lady. The lady wants to be screwed."

He grinned. "Then by all means, I have just the thing for that."

---

## Jessa

HE HAD HIS PLANS, but I made it clear that I had some of own. My hands shaking, I pushed him back until his gorgeous ass hit my desk.

He cleared his throat and gave me his cockiest smirk. "Okay, princess, you have me at your mercy. Do your worst."

And I had every intention of it. "Stay there. Do not move. Do you understand?"

His eyes flashed with mischief and need, but he nodded. "Yes, ma'am."

Hastily I tugged my blouse out of my skirt, unbuttoned the tiny row of buttons, then shrugged it off my shoulders. His gaze homed in, and he turned that laser focus to my breasts. With every movement, jostle, and wiggle, he licked his lips.

"I know what you're looking at. You're only torturing yourself."

"Woman, you're the one who said she has a party to go to. My patience can only take so much before I jump you."

"Well in that case, I better get down to business." I slipped out of my skirt, leaving only my thong, stockings and shoes on. When I stepped over to him, he groaned low.

I began working on his shirt, my bare hands tracing the planes of his chest, and he hissed. "Princess, you're killing me."

I slid his shirt off his shoulders and pressed a kiss to his nipple.

"Jessa..."

"Hush. I'm busy."

He cleared his throat and then dropped his head back. "Yeah, I can see that."

When his shirt dropped to the floor with barely sound, I kissed across his pecs, and then shifted down to kiss each of his ribs and over his abs, sinking lower onto my knees.

"Oh God. Princess—"

"Sssh. Woman at work here. Try to focus."

"Fuck, I am focused. You're all I'm focused on. I just—"

I was in no mood to listen to him. I just unbuckled his pants. Once free, his cock bobbed in front of my face, fully erect, completely at attention, and begging for mercy. "My, my, someone has been missing me."

"It's been too long," he muttered through clenched teeth.

I chuckled. "We shagged this morning."

Roone groaned when I teased my nails over the skin of his balls. "So long ago. I–fuck." He panted as I stroked him up and down gently, teasing the head then stroking down and cupping his balls.

"What were you saying?"

"Fuck. Jessa I need—" But he was done talking when I leaned forward and wrapped my lips around his dick. He stopped talking altogether. All that came from him were a series of moans and groans, as I worked him over with my tongue and my lips, and occasionally very gently with my teeth.

He dug his hands into my hair, and I relished every moment of it. The possession of it, the visceral nature of it. He tried to pull me back, but I wasn't having it and instead took him deeper, forcing the back of my throat relax and take more of him.

"Oh my God, I," he growled. "I'm going to come."

Instead of drawing back like he wanted, I planted my hands on his hips and dug my nails into the top muscle of his ass and took him deeper.

His muscles tensed and bunched as he held me in place, and finally, he let go. When I eased back, Roone's harsh pants tore out of his chest as he stared down at me. "Jesus, Mary and Joseph, woman."

"See, you like it when I'm in charge." But before I knew what was happening, Roone had me on my desk, thighs splayed.

He didn't bother removing my thong, but instead shoved the flimsy fabric aside and sank into me deep as he kissed me.

I gasped. "Roone."

"You didn't think we were done, did you? I still have a few minutes and I plan to spend them inside you."

The thing was... I was so down for that.

It didn't take long. Two deep strokes, a quick flick of his thumb over my clit, his tongue sliding over mine, and I was flying.

I jumped with him into the abyss of bliss, finally letting go of the fear and the worry and the panic from today. He was home, he was safe, he was mine. And I was never letting go.

# TWENTY-TWO

*Jessa*

WE ARRIVED AT THE VENUE, with time to spare. Roone squeezed my hand.

"See, I told you we'd have plenty of time."

I swatted at him. "Somebody was trying to make me late for my own event."

He grinned. "Well, you were taking your time. You knew that was supposed to be a quickie."

I rolled my eyes. "You are impossible." I pushed open the door.

He shook his head. "You forget, that's not how this works."

"Oh yeah." I would have grumbled, except he was right. That wasn't how it worked anymore.

*It's only temporary.*

He opened his door and got out first. He something into his com and then came around to my side of the car. He opened my door again, and I climbed out. His grin flashed. "See, was that so hard?"

I giggled. "You said hard."

He gave me a long blink, and then he barked with laughter exploding from his throat. "See, I'm having a positive effect on you."

"You sure about that?"

"Yep. Absolutely."

Our lead team went first, followed by me, followed by Roone. When we reached the kitchen, Chef Ian Talbot ran up to me. "Where is she?"

"What are you talking about?"

"I've been waiting for her for half an hour."

My gaze snapped to Roone. "Who are you talking about, Chloe? She came ahead. She should've already been here."

Ian shook his head. "No. I don't have a final guest list to complete the meal personalization. We've been holding, waiting for her, but we're going have to get started."

"Shit, shit, shit."

Roone squeezed my arm. "I'll find her. You do this."

I had no choice but to watch him go as I pulled my laptop out of my purse to work with Ian. "Okay, we can do this. Let me get you going." Unfortunately, my brain was only half there because I was worried about Chloe. But thanks to planning, there wasn't much I had to do, just confirm final names and all the dinners. Which was basically just a quick scan back and forth.

We could do this. I just hoped Chloe was okay.

---

*Roone*

WITH AN EYE ON JESSA, I barked orders at the others. "Find Chloe. She got in an Uber nearly a half hour ago. Someone find that car."

Trevor inclined his head toward the exit of the kitchen. I left Jessa where she was and followed. "Boss. We checked with Uber. According to them, Chloe was a no show for the car that was supposed to pick her up, but we all saw her get into a black Mercedes. Same make and model as the Uber car."

Fuck. "Did we get plates?"

"Not from our cameras, but we have someone pulling CCTV."

JACOB WAS SPEAKING into the mobile at his ear. His gaze flickered to mine, and I read trouble. The tightness around his mouth and the hushed tones he was using as he spoke were a dead giveaway. When he strode over, the pit fell out of my stomach.

"We have a problem."

"Where is she?"

"In the hospital."

I kept my voice measured. The one time Ariel had left me in charge, I'd fucked up. Too wrapped up in Jessa. Now a member of the team was in danger. "What the hell happened?"

"Car accident."

"In the car that *wasn't* her Uber?"

"Yeah. An ambulance took her to the hospital. Looks like they were broadsided. Basically T-boned. It's not good."

I forced the sawdust in my mouth to go down my esophagus. "Is she alive?"

Jacob nodded. "Yes, but she needs surgery. The driver is less injured, but he's got broken bones. He's talking now. Someone paid him a hundred quid to take the Uber job."

"Shit. Okay, let's get one of you guys to the hospital. Jacob, did the driver say what happened? Who hit them?"

"It was a hit-and-run." His brow furrowed. "But the driver

did say that after the accident, someone came out of the other car over to Chloe's side and looked directly into the window and said something along the lines of, 'Tell the princess this is just the start. She should give herself up or other people get hurt.'"

And string of expletives flowed off my tongue. It was my own special blend. Gaelic curses intermixed with English ones. My maternal grandmother was Irish, and she'd taught me all the best ones before she died. "What the fuck?"

Jacob's jaw went tight. "I'll go check on her."

"I need to tell the princess." I would rather do anything than that, but she needed to know. A part of me would rather wait until after the event to tell her, but I'd promised I wouldn't hide things from her anymore. Even the bad things.

Jacob nodded. "Yes, boss." He said that as he and Trevor ever-so-wisely backed away.

When I approached Jessa, she gave a smile. "Got tossed right in. It's madness. Any news on Chloe? Where she went? What did the driver say?"

I took her hand and pulled her to the side. There wasn't much room for privacy in the kitchen, but at least we were out of the chaos. "Listen, there was an accident."

I expected her to cry, or at least to break down, but instead, she said, "Damage?"

"What?"

With a heavy sigh, she clarified. "How bad is she hurt?"

I blinked. Wow. She was straight to the point, straight to the facts.

"All I know is she's in surgery. But there's something else."

"She's alive though?"

"Yeah. She's alive. But there is something you need to know."

"Oh, God."

I placed both hands on her shoulders. "Listen."

She blinked up at me, finally still. "What?"

"Someone came over to the car and said something to her before driving away."

She blinked rapidly. "You mean it was a hit-and-run?"

"Yeah. But it was no accident, Jessa. Someone came right over to her and said something along the lines of 'Tell the princess more people will get hurt if she doesn't give herself up.'"

Jessa staggered backward. "Wait, this was because of me?"

"It certainly looks that way. We'll find them. I swear to God."

"We'd better. Because when we find them, I'm going to personally make them pay."

---

*Jessa*

I STILL WASN'T sure how I made it through the rest of the event. There was no choice really. People were counting on me. So, like it or not, I had to keep it together, but all I wanted to do was collapse in a corner and give in to the tears.

East and Bridge both made it point to come over and congratulate us. Ben looked thrilled. I couldn't enjoy any of it though. My best friend, the first friend I'd made here in London, was hurt because of me. There was no denying it. This wasn't an Evan thing. This was a royal thing.

It all came crashing down on me, that comfy denial I'd been living in. It all sank in. There would be no going back to my normal life. This was my new reality.

Chloe was my best friend. Someone thought they could manipulate me, force my hand. Someone thought they could make me bend to their will. And what? Give myself up?

I would. I could. That wasn't the problem. That was no hardship. I was more than ready to do that for my friend.

Granted, there was a part of me that wanted to rail against the idea that I needed to give in to these assholes who'd hurt her.

I hated them. And I wanted them to burn. So sure, I could give myself up. I would absolutely do that if it meant no one else I loved would get hurt. At least she was already somewhere safe where we could keep an eye on her. Jacob sent me a picture of Chloe from the hospital giving me a weak smile and a thumbs-up after her surgery. Jacob was going to watch over her personally.

Chloe sent me a text from his phone.

**Chloe:** *Thanks for sending me a hot guy to help me recover.*

**Jessa:** *Anytime.*

**Chloe:** *Honestly, it was only my spleen. What does one need with a spleen anyway?*

I knew she was going to be okay, and I was very relieved. But still, I couldn't chase the worry away.

By the time we arrived back at the hotel, my nerves were frayed. We were going to have to figure something out because I couldn't live like this.

Once Roone did all his checks, we Facetimed my brothers. "Are you okay?"

I don't know why it was such an odd question to me, but it was, because nothing felt okay. Nothing felt like it would ever be all right again. All I could do though, was nod my head. The words refused to come out, still caught in my throat and far too raw.

Lucas shoved Sebastian out of the way, and his hands and face popped in front of the video. "I need to see for myself. Well, you look okay. So, let's find out who hurt your friend and kill them, okay?"

Somewhere in the background, Ethan's voice, calm and steady as before, said, "No, we can't kill them."

Lucas scowled.

Penny ignored them all as she came onscreen. "Listen, if you want, we can bring your friend to the Winston Isles and keep her safe here."

"That's really sweet. But Chloe's life is here. Her parents moved to Mallorca a few years ago, but this is Chloe's home. She's grown up here, all her friends are here. I don't really think she'd be down for displacement in a foreign island."

"Well, it would only be temporary, but I understand. Lord knows I wouldn't exactly be thrilled about it."

Finally, someone moved the camera so that we could see all of them at once. I couldn't help but smile. They were in Sebastian's office. The room wasn't tiny, but with men as large as my brothers, plus Ethan, Penny, and the Queen Mother in there, it looked like a sardine can had been stuffed full of people.

Sebastian's frown now was familiar. It was weird. These people I'd met a couple of weeks ago had started to feel like... family. Like people I cared about. Like people whose opinions mattered to me. Like people I would miss. It didn't matter that I barely knew them. Each and every one of them was willing to jump into the fray. For me.

*Yeah, no shit. It's called family.*

It was weird having that feeling. From age ten, I'd only had my father. I knew he loved me, just maybe a little too much. I wondered just how sick he actually was, though it didn't really matter. He'd kept me alive to this point. And I would always be grateful.

"Listen, in light of what's happened to your friend, Lucas and I were talking. There's no reason that only you should be bait. If someone wants the royal family, they'll have to come and get us."

I furrowed my brows. "Say what now?"

"What I'm saying is we're coming to London. *All* of us."

I shook my head. "No. That's insane. That's dangerous, and you'd be putting Penny and Bryna at risk."

Penny chimed in. "Hey, I can take care of myself."

I looked at Roone for help, and he just shrugged.

*Asshole.*

"No, Penny, I think we all know you can take care of yourself, but that's not the point. The point is you shouldn't have to. And Bryna isn't trained like you are. She's going to need a full-time guard. Someone just threatened our family. Do you think it's wise to walk right into their hands?"

Sebastian shook his head. "Look, I know. But we're at DefCon 1 here. We need to prime the pump and keep things moving. If someone wants to come after us, let's force them to come at us head on. That way we'll all be together. Because we're far stronger together than apart."

I shifted my gaze to Roone again, but he seemed unperturbed by the crazy. "I've learned when Sebastian says something outrageous, it's better to just go along because he's going to do it anyway. At least this way we have a chance to mitigate some risks."

"Oh my god, I'm going to regret this aren't I?"

Sebastian chuckled. "No, you won't. Because your family is on their way. Hang tight, and we'll help you make sure Chloe is okay."

"It's not your fight. No one asked for you; they asked for me."

"If someone comes for my sister, they're coming for me. And they're about to discover a whole hell of a lot about how much I dislike that."

# TWENTY-THREE

*Ariel*

I HATED the fact that I had to go get my father myself. He'd managed to evade the team I'd taken with me when he was in Barcelona, and we'd had to chase him to Dublin. From the airport, I went straight to the meeting with the staging team I'd reached out to. Thanks to Matthias, I had some extra assistance from local police and Interpol.

A Sergeant Bustalo met me at my hotel and gave me a nod. "I understand you need some help."

"Yes, well, I always need a little help. I guess he was behind a robbery in Barcelona, which means Interpol is now involved. Which means you."

He nodded. "Yes, well obviously I'd heard about his petty crimes in the Winston Isles, but he hasn't been on our radar ever."

"No, up until recently he's been strictly a petty criminal, so there was no need for Interpol."

"Well, it's too bad for him that he took the ID of someone

we've been pursuing for a long time. So, either way, we're making an arrest."

"Well yes, but Winston Isles has jurisdiction. I understand that was the arrangement made."

He nodded. "Yes. Of course. As long as we get to question him, that's all I care about."

My shoulders relaxed. "Okay. Let's get going."

We climbed into his Fiat, and I might have given him a slightly judgmental look. How was that thing supposed to go fast enough if we had a car chase? But that didn't matter. It was enough that my father wasn't hiding. He was sitting in plain sight in a café enjoying his coffee, even knowing what he'd done.

At the café, I was out of the car before Bustalo could even stop me. "Wait."

I didn't listen. I just marched right up to my old man.

He stood as I was approaching. "Sweetheart. It's good to see you."

"Dad. Want to tell me what the hell you're doing in Dublin?"

"Well, you know I've always wanted to see Dublin."

"You're full of shit. We're not Irish."

"How do you know? You've got all that red hair."

"That's from mom. Come on we're going."

He shook his head. "No, I don't think so. It's a very sunny day. I'm going to enjoy it, drink my coffee, you can't touch me here."

"Are you insane? This isn't a non-extradition country. You're actually in the United Kingdom. And the Winston Isles has an agreement with them, so we're going."

"Well here, *I* haven't committed any crimes. And you're going have to get extradition papers. Which you don't have."

I raised a brow. "Are you sure I don't have those?"

He grinned. "Sweetheart, if there were extradition papers they wouldn't have sent you to serve them. They would have sent very official-looking people. Not someone who actually cares about me."

"And what if I suggested that I *wanted* to be the one to bring you in?"

He shook his head. "You wouldn't. You can't. I'm your father and you love me."

"And you took advantage of that."

"I didn't take advantage. You're my daughter. You knew I needed you. And when it's all said and done, you'll understand why I did it. You and I, we don't belong with *them,* with their royal intrigues and succession lines. You and I, we're normal, average. The sooner you realize that the better. And they will cast you out of their gilded tower in no time. I did you a favor."

"You *used* me."

"I'm trying to save you." He leaned forward. "You've gotten so embroiled with them you can't see the infighting and everything that's going on. All of a sudden you think you're better than us. You're not." He sat back again. Sipping quietly.

I just stared at him. Maybe he was right. Maybe I couldn't do this. "Stand up."

He laughed. "What, as if you're actually going to take me in?"

"Yeah. I am."

He grinned. "This I would love to see. You can try to take me in. But you and I both know that you don't have the stones for it."

It was my turn to grin back. "I might not have the stones for it, but you know, *he* certainly does." I inclined my head at Bustalo, who was about fifteen yards back. My father's brows furrowed and then lifted. "You brought thugs?"

"No, Dad, I brought Interpol."

Next thing I knew, the post box on the corner about twenty

yards away popped, made a loud booming sound, and caved in on itself.

Smoke blew out, and immediately everyone in the vicinity took cover. The second that explosion went off, my father jumped back in his seat. The chair clattered to the ground, and he was off.

"Shit. Bustalo, he's running."

Bustalo was right on my tail. We were running through the crowd. Everyone was screaming, running, and ducking for cover. Dad made a turn behind a pub, into a narrow alleyway. Bustalo huffed behind me. "I'll go around."

I didn't even hear him. I could barely process what he was saying. All I knew was that my father was within arm's reach, and he was getting away. I could do this. I could take him. I could bring him back and make sure he stood trial for treason.

*Yes, and loose everything you've worked so hard for?* It didn't matter. Because it was the right thing to do. I didn't care that he was my father. All these years I'd spent begging him to do better, to be better. He just wasn't capable.

*You know what it would mean. It would mean that you couldn't be Royal Guard anymore.*

But none of that mattered. Because that man, *my father*, had threatened my family. My *real* family, the ones who cared about me and loved me, the ones who would do everything in their power to help me. That man wasn't it. That man was selfish. We might be bound by blood, but that didn't define family. He'd used me.

I squeezed through the opening, still running. I thought I had him cornered at the bank of River Liffey, but he glanced back at me, still running full out. Bustalo met me at a dead sprint, and I watched in horror as my father climbed over the embankment onto the bridge and jumped.

"No!" I ran to the edge. Bustalo was already on the phone. "I need a search team. Get the divers, the local police, get everyone. He's probably still alive and we need to get him."

I stared at the water, but he wasn't in it. Just below us, there was a boat, and I ran to the other side of the bridge. It was a barge, and on a pile of boxes or something covered with dark material, somebody was moving. He'd landed safely on his feet, just like he always did.

"He's gotten away."

---

*Ariel*

I COULD BARELY MOVE my feet. I dragged ass all the way back to my flat in London, my overnight bag hitched over my shoulder. When I trudged up the stairs to my flat, I found an unexpected face waiting for me, even though Roone had warned me they were all coming. "So, were you going to call?"

*Penny.*

"Pen, not now. I'm tired. I just got back from Dublin."

Penny's dark gaze met mine, and she searched it. "You didn't get him?"

I shook my head.

She stepped aside and let me open the door.

When I stepped through, I dropped my bag right at the door and just went straight in to the couch. I didn't bother to offer her anything. If she wanted anything, she knew full well that she should have gone to someone else's place. My flat barely had basics; vodka in the freezer, sweaters in my oven. I didn't cook.

"Tell me what happened."

"He jumped off a fucking bridge, Pen. A bridge. To get away from me."

Her eyes bulged. "Are you serious right now?"

"Yeah. Dead serious. I had Interpol with me, and he was just as calm as you please and did a runner off a bridge. I didn't know it, Penny, but he really hates the royals."

She frowned. "If that's true, he never would have let you join the Royal Guard."

"His mind has been tainted or something. I don't know what it is, but that man, he's not my father. Or maybe that's who he's always been, and I have just never really known him. But he jumped off of a goddamn bridge."

"He literally ran from you. That's intense."

"Tell me about it."

"Is he okay? Are they drudging the waters?"

"No need. He jumped onto a barge. Now, whether or not he knew that barge was there, is beyond me. He must have. I don't know. But why run unless he knew what the hell was going on? He obviously did it on purpose, Penny. He used me, and I let myself be used like a moron."

"Babe, he's your father."

I hated how much my eyes stung. I hated the heat behind the tears. I hated the hot, wet splashes on my cheeks. I hated it all. I loathed it. But it was what it was. I was crying. "How did I make such a bad calculation?"

"You didn't make a bad calculation. Your father called and needed a place to stay. Even if I had your father, I'd have done the same thing."

I considered her. "I know."

"Cool, then cut yourself some slack. We'll figure this out. Did you call Matthias?"

I nodded. Weller had been taciturn, but he was helping. "He's already tracking him as best as he can, keeping an eye out for any known aliases, but none of this makes sense. Just why?"

"What do you mean?"

"I mean he was already in Barcelona, already further away

from the UK and the Winston Isles where he'd be more likely to get caught. The whole scenario is just insane."

Penny frowned. "Unless, now that we've cracked the whole conspiracy, maybe that was what they wanted all along?"

I shook my head. "No. Because you had to all be together. They didn't know you were all together in the islands already."

Penny laughed. "And the islands are basically a fortress. That's our turf. You know how difficult it would be to grab one of us there?"

I rubbed my eyes. "Penny, I just I think I don't know who that man is at all. All these years, I knew he was shady. I mean, he's my father. I know him. But that kind of hate? He was never capable of that before, ever. What am I going to do, Penny?"

"Well, let's not panic, okay?"

"This is the time for panic, Penny."

"Oh, my God. Why have we swapped roles right now? Look, you and I, we know how to do this. Just take a break. We can figure this out, you and me."

"Except it's not going to be you and me much longer. My father committed treason. My days are numbered."

"First of all, there's no way I'm letting the Regents Council boot you. I will kill anyone who tries to separate us. Do you understand me?"

I couldn't help but chuckle, even though my heart was being sliced into a million little pieces. "Yeah, but you need me to move the bodies."

"Honey, I can move my own bodies."

I grinned. "Yeah, but you have a tendency to leave parts behind."

She shrugged. "Look, as long as I move most of the body..."

"No, you need to move the whole thing, do a thorough job. That's why you have me for these things."

She looked at me and smiled. "Besties till the end. Don't

worry about what's going to happen in the future. You and I, we will figure this out. But you need to rest first. After you rest we can talk about it. We'll find your father, and when we do, Sebastian will figure it out. And don't you worry. He's not letting you go. Even if you weren't a valuable member of Team WI, you're my best friend, and he would do anything to see me happy. And the one thing that's going to make me happy is having you by my side, so stop worrying about it. You and me till the end... that's how this goes."

"I can't just let it go. I can't pretend it's not a problem."

"Is it a problem right now? Or is your best friend just a girl, standing in front of her bestie, with a bottle of vodka chilled in the freezer, asking her to love her?"

"I'm pretty sure that's not the way the actual movie quote goes."

"Well, it doesn't matter if that's how the movie quote goes or not. That's what I'm saying. You and me. I'm not letting you make yourself insane. We're going to be okay. Okay?"

"I certainly hope you're right. Because, right now I'm done. I got nothing. I have no hopeful, snarky remarks. I'm worried, because at some point, someone's going to get hurt. I just have to catch him before he does anything else to completely damage all of us, before he burns every bridge."

"You're Ariel. You will. I promise."

"I hope you're right about this, because right now, I have very little confidence."

"Good thing I have enough confidence for the both of us."

# TWENTY-FOUR

*Ariel*

I THOUGHT the worst part of this thing would be having to explain to everyone that my father was guilty of treason.

I was wrong. Now, I thought the worst was seeing Roone's face. He watched me closely. After talking to Penny last night, I was trying to focus on the facts. Just the facts, no letting emotion get in the way. Those leaky hot tears from yesterday were more than enough for me. But the team needed to know everything so they could be better armed to protect themselves.

Ethan gave me a sympathetic smile. "Why don't you get started, Ariel."

I shifted on my feet, casting my gaze around. These people were my friends. My family. I fought alongside them and helped protect them. But my actions had put them in danger, and I vowed I would never do that again. "Okay guys, the news isn't good. Dublin did not pan out quite how we thought."

Jessa was the only one who looked confused. "Dublin?"

I tried to quickly catch her up. "My dad went missing when we started this mission. Wanted a place to stay. He abused that, used my security codes to get someone access to the server. They, in turn, gave everyone our entire Jessa plan. Protocols, everything we use, they have it all. So it's pretty bad."

Jessa's mouth hung open. "Holy shit."

"Yeah, but not to worry, Ethan's too smart for that, so we've taken all plans and protocols offline, and we're keeping it very need-to-know. Which is what I want to talk to you all about." I took a deep breath. Jessa still looked floored. I wish there was a way to reassure her, but there wasn't. It was all bad. Really, really bad.

"Jessa, I know you're getting up to speed, but we did locate my father, just not the man he's been working with. Dad's been using several aliases across Europe, and we know he's in Dublin, or at least he was as of yesterday. As far as we know, he has at least one partner, probably more. And from my brief conversation with him, he's all-in with team conspiracy. He is so *not* team Scooby Gang, and in my opinion, he won't be reasoned with."

Ethan, forever a real father figure to me, said in his calm voice, "Let's cross that bridge when we come to it. Right now, the important thing is finding him. How did he escape?"

"We had a pretty good net with Interpol. But you guys, he wasn't even hiding. We found him in a café. Like he'd been expecting us, expecting *me* to show up. So someone was giving him that intel, but I don't know who or how anyone could have known I was going anywhere, since that information wasn't on the server at all. The only people who knew I was going are in this room, and none of you would sell-out yourselves, so we need to figure it out. But—"

I turned my head toward Sebastian. His gaze was direct, and I could practically see him willing me not to say the words. I continued anyway. "I think I need to recuse myself."

Penny stood up. "What? No. We just had this conversation."

"I'm sorry." I glanced around to the people I considered my family. "I am compromised. This isn't going to work."

Penny immediately tried to rally Sebastian, but I was ready for her.

"Your Majesty, you know this doesn't make sense. As soon as I'm off the team, I stop comprising the operation. My very own father has committed treason. You know that's career suicide as far as the Regents Council is concerned."

"Why don't you let me worry about the Regents Council."

"Oh my god, why can none of you see that this is a problem? Ethan, talk some sense into them."

But Ethan, my boss, formidable and austere, but above all a patriot and a loyal subject, frowned at me. "Penny's right. You can't make rash decisions."

"Why are all of you working against me? I'm trying to do the right thing here. My father is working with the conspirators. He's conspiring to take down the monarchy."

Ethan shrugged. "You are not your father, and as far as I am concerned, you're still part of this team."

"Look, I can be part of this team on the outside, but you need me off this team officially because they're using me. My father expected me. Only when Interpol got involved did he run. And even at that, he jumped off a bloody bridge to get away from me."

Jessa's eyes went wide. "What? Oh my god, I'm so sorry!"

I shook my head. "No, he's too ornery to die. He had some kind of barge waiting down below. He's perfectly fine."

Her brow lifted. "Oh, wow, okay. So he saw you coming?"

Lucas sat up. "What did you say?"

"What, about my father doing a runner off of a bridge onto a barge?"

He groaned. "And he was at a café?"

"Yeah. Why?"

He covered his face and scrubbed his hands up and down. "You guys, I think we've been so busy worrying about Jessa and someone coming for her that we weren't paying attention to what *other* files were accessed. The people coming after us, they don't just know things about Jessa. They know me. They know all of us."

Sebastian frowned. "Lucas, explain?"

"The bridge-barge thing, I've done it."

The room went silent as we all stared at the prince. I was the first one to find my voice. "Say what?"

"Yeah, a few years ago when I was still running games for Tony, the getaway was a barge jump off a bridge. I made the jump, but I shattered my ankle. I needed to have surgery to fix it."

Sebastian stared. "You've done it?"

"Yeah, I have."

"Who would know that?"

Lucas shrugged. "Well, I don't know. I'm sure Matthias does, but then he eerily knows everything, so that's no surprise. But I doubt our own external security firm is trying to help anyone overthrow the monarchy. And basically, anyone who knows any of the angles Tony used to run probably knows about the barge jump."

I rubbed my temple. "So basically, anyone with half a brain who knew enough to research your past would know?"

He nodded. "Yep. It's kind of a disaster."

So they weren't just looking for Jessa, they were looking for dirt on all of us, our weaknesses, anything sketchy we'd done before. Ethan sighed. In some cases, they were using our past exploits to work for them. And we'd been a step behind the whole time.

"See, even more reason why I need to recuse myself."

It was Jessa who said what we were all thinking, though. "So basically, I'm not safe and neither is anyone else. They're coming for us with everything. Your father's moving closer to the UK. This might have been their whole plan all along, to get all three of us out of the Winston Isles because back on the island, it's a fortress. Just like you guys were saying. Completely protected."

I tended to agree. "Here though, there's less body coverage, easier access. Here there's room for mistakes."

Sebastian wasn't having it though. "Here, we're ready for them. We've been playing defense for too long. It's time we went on the offensive."

---

*Jessa*

"JESSA, THIS ISN'T A GOOD IDEA."

Roone was trying to change my mind about visiting Chloe, but I didn't care. "Look, I know the risks, but I need to see her. Someone tried to hurt her because of me. I have to see her."

Roone threw up his hands and turned to Sebastian. "You're her big brother. Tell her. Tell her she can't go."

Sebastian shifted on his feet. It was the first time I had seen him when he wasn't completely sure of himself. Everyone had crowded into our flat. Breakfast was brought in, and the living room in our suite had been turned into a war room. We were working with Interpol on how to capture Ariel's father, and we were also trying to figure out where we were at with the tattoos and what role, if any, Evan played in all of this.

Ariel's thought was that Evan was a run-of-the-mill stalker. Point blank, he was just cuckoo for Cocoa Puffs, and we had to treat him accordingly. He still posed a threat, obviously, but it was a threat that was somewhat manageable because at least he was the devil we knew. My main concern was Chloe. She'd been hurt because of me, and everyone seemed to be focused on the wrong things. Team WI was far too focused on *our* future plan and not thinking about who might get hurt in the crossfire.

"Look, I get that you're worried. I understand it. Hell, I'm worried too. But Chloe is my best friend, and she's in the hospital because of us. I need to see her. We need to get somebody to protect her."

Sebastian nodded. "Listen, that one's already handled. We have men on her."

"Oh, well, I didn't exactly know that. Fair enough, but like it or not I'm going to see her."

Roone looked at Sebastian like he was supposed to know what to do with me. My oldest brother looked to Penny. And Penny, well, she just sighed. "Look, Jessa, is there any chance you're not going to do something crazy if we say no?"

"No. No chance in hell."

"Okay, in that case then, why don't we do this... Lucas, remember that job you were telling me about, the Bundaberg plan? Was that the one?"

Lucas sat up straighter. "The one where Tony had us use a double?"

Penny nodded. "Yeah, that's the one. Think it could work?"

He frowned. "Work with what? I mean, it's not like we have a double for Jessa."

Penny grinned. "Well, Jessa's a little fairer than I am, but we're about the same height, though her hair is longer and less curly. But with a little work with a flat iron on my hair, I think we can make it work."

Sebastian stood up then. "Oh, absolutely not. You are not going to do this."

All I could do was glance between the three of them. Then I leaned over to Ariel. "What's happening?"

Ariel shook her head. "Right now, Penny's trying to give you what you want. She's volunteering to go as a decoy so that whoever is following you, whether it's your psycho boss and/or these treasonous assholes, will follow her instead so that you can still see your friend Chloe."

I wanted to see Chloe, of course, but there was no way in hell I was putting my new sister-in-law in danger. "Oh no. You're not pulling me into these shenanigans."

Penny rolled her eyes. "What do you mean? You want to see your friend. Sebastian is as worried about you, just as Roone is. And they should be. And while I think you can give Roone a run for his money, I'm better trained at countersurveillance. And I know how to fight. I have experience with these assholes, and I have a score to settle. That makes me the ideal candidate."

Lucas blanked. "That's why you were asking me?"

Penny sighed. "I swear to God, Lucas, for someone so smart, sometimes you are not all there. It must be hard being so pretty."

Lucas winked at her. "You know you love me for it."

Sebastian looked like he wanted to hit Lucas, and Lucas looked like he didn't give two shits.

Roone was still pissed off at everyone in the room. "You guys. Bloody focus, will you? My girlfriend is taking the piss and thinks she can stroll into hospital and see Chloe. One of you needs to tell her that needs not to happen. Sebastian, you need to do it more forcefully. Lucas, chime in, would you, mate? And Penny, stop encouraging her."

Penny shrugged. "Sorry, Roone. She's going to do whatever she wants anyway. I'm just trying to mitigate the danger."

"Yeah, and my mate here," Roone glanced at Sebastian, "will fucking kill everyone in his path if something happens to you."

Ariel shrugged. "Personally, I say bring Chloe to us. We should all just pack it up and go back to the island because at least then we can protect the fort."

I shook my head at that suggestion. "No. She certainly didn't ask for this. We can't just uproot everybody. And just what are we going to do, kidnap her from the hospital?"

Ariel shrugged. "Well, that's one idea."

Penny leveled a look at Sebastian. "You know I'm right. She's going to go, regardless. This way I can protect her."

"Love, who's going to protect you?"

Penny just grinned. "I don't need protection. I'm pretty badass all on my own."

Sebastian looked like he wanted to throw up. "What is wrong with you?"

"Nothing."

I sensed there was something else going on there, but I didn't dare butt in.

Penny just ignored him. "Look, at the end of the day, you want to see Chloe. I can help you see Chloe. If it means keeping you safe and out of trouble, then I'm all for it. It also means that no matter who is after you, whether it's your idiot boss or these other assholes, you'll be safe. That makes both your brothers happy, and it makes me happy."

I sensed that there was danger in this plan. I didn't know how it would all play out, but I didn't think things were going to end exactly how we all thought. "Penny, maybe we should ask Ethan."

She sighed. "Oh my God, my father's not here, so I'm who you've got."

She was right. Her plan was all I had, and she had me by the balls. It wasn't exactly what I wanted, but honestly, I didn't really have much choice. "I'm all for Penny's plan."

Sebastian sighed. "Of course you are."

Lucas however surprised me. Lucas was usually the joke-ster. Between him and Roone, the snarkiest things came out of their mouths. But there was something serious and sincere about the way Lucas looked at me. "I trust her. She wants to see her friend. It's important."

Sebastian groaned. "I'm not saying it's not important. I'm just saying it's asinine. And she's right, Ethan should be here to weigh in on this."

Penny ignored him. "My father wouldn't stop me either. Sometimes he'll surprise you."

Ariel pushed herself to standing from the couch. "So, when and how are we doing this?"

Penny grinned. "God, it's been so long since I've been in disguise."

Sebastian just mumbled under his breath. "Something tells me you're enjoying this."

So that was it, I was finally going to see Chloe. While I wasn't exactly worried about it, I had a feeling it could turn out to be a bad idea.

The plan was easy. Penny and I dressed in identical clothing. She left first, out the front door with Roone. They were holding hands, and she was sort of tucked into Roone's arm so that nobody could see her closely. I left under the cover of night crouched down in the back of Ariel's car. Not the most comfortable drive I've ever made, but still not bad. Everyone was on coms. Sebastian and Lucas stayed back at the hotel. It was supposed to be in and out. Everything was fine, quiet for the twenty-minute ride. But when I stepped into the hospital and gave my name, pandemonium started. I could hear the shouting on the coms. "What do we got?"

Roone was shouting. Penny was cursing someone out. All I heard was, "Take that. I told you not to touch me."

I could hear the scuffling and the grunting and the hitting and the punching. Ariel pulled me off to the side. And then she pulled out her tablet from her jacket pocket. She'd had a follow team tail Roone and Penny, and those guys were armed with body cams. She pulled up the screen, and as she spoke, she was calm. No yelling no shouting. She just tucked me in a seat, and in the middle of the hallway, she started running logistics from there. So, this was her *real* job. It was kind of terrifying how good she was at it as she instructed, "Okay, Trevor, take Roone's flank. James, go around from the south. See if you can get behind them."

I watched in horror as Roone grabbed some guy by the collar and slammed him up against a brick wall. Where the hell were they? It was a little dark and hard to see, and all I could make out were Roone's profile and his hands.

It was what was happening on the other side of him that I *could* see. One of the guys tried to grab Penny in a headlock from the left. She shifted her right foot to step into the headlock, which made no sense to me, but then she also wound her left arm until it was on her forehead facing out. And then she did something to him. I didn't know what it was exactly, I couldn't see all the movements. But his head snapped back, and then her knee was in the guy's lower back. Oh, that look like it... *ouch*. As he started to go down, she delivered a hammer fist.

I needed her to show me that release. The guy had no choice. He went down like a ragdoll. It was what Penny did after that amazed me. He might have gone down, but she started delivering blows to him. Basic round-and-pound, but it was spectacular. Penny was a queen I could get behind.

One of the other guards, Trevor I think it was, screamed at her. "Protect the queen." Penny legitimately evaded their grasps and went after the asshole who was trying to grab Roone. She ran up to him from behind with her own guard chasing her, and then she delivered a swift kick to his nuts... really wound it up and delivered. It was as if the whole world stood still for a minute. I didn't know if the guy was going to go down or if he was going to attack Roone, but as he stood there, Roone delivered a backward elbow that caught him right at the temple. And then it was as if the guy passed out standing up. His whole body just slumped and withered down.

Roone slammed the other guy up against the wall one more time and hit him with his fist. Then that guy slumped too. Roone turned around and grinned at Penny. "Ah, it's nice being in the field with you. You're badass."

Penny shook out her hand. "Yeah, I know."

Roone just laughed then tapped his coms. "Ariel, bring her back. I don't think we can do this today. They might have other teams."

I knew what was coming before before Ariel even said anything. I stood. "Yeah let's go back. I'm just going to run in really quick."

Ariel reached for me. "Jessa."

"I'm sorry." And then I ran into Chloe's room. When I saw her, there were machines and wires and, oh God, was that a cast on her arm?

She blinked slowly. "Hey, there you are."

"Shit, Chloe. I'm so sorry. I am so, so sorry."

She shrugged. "Um, if you wanted me to take a vacation, you could have just said so. This is the most relaxed I've been in years."

"Yeah, except for all these machines."

She shrugged. "Yeah well not for much longer. I go home tomorrow."

"Are you sure? They operated on you. They had to remove your spleen or whatever the hell that thing is."

She laughed. "It's fine. How are you? Those assholes. What's happening?"

"I wish I could tell you. But I can't stay here too long. I just wanted to make sure I saw you."

"You've got to tell me what's going on Jessa. Right now everything feels crazy."

"Right now, everything *is* crazy. But I promise we'll talk about this. You just get well, okay?"

Because we were on a time clock with nowhere to turn, I had to leave my best friend behind. Praying she understood.

## TWENTY-FIVE

*Roone*

BACK AT THE HOTEL, I had to be patched up. Which was humiliating. I'd had my ass saved by Penny. I'd been so busy kicking the ass of the guy who tried to grab us, or rather tried to grab who he thought was Jessa, I had let my emotions get in the way, and I'd missed the guy coming up behind me. My queen had literally saved my ass, which was just humiliating. God, I should have known better than to let my emotions take over, but because they'd threatened the woman I loved, I hadn't been able to see through my fucking anger. Which was just stupid and dangerous. I was an idiot, and the queen had almost been hurt because of it.

I needed to be more careful, more aware. It was hard to remember, fucking impossible to remember, but I needed to. Thank God, Penny had been there. Which was just confusing. Seriously, who needed their queen to save them?

She came up to me and said, "That looks like it hurts."

I tried to hold back the wince but that didn't help. "Well,

maybe if you hadn't been so busy kicking ass you would have noticed that arse-wipe coming for us."

"I did notice. I just was busy doing other things."

"Yeah. About to get your ass kicked."

She laughed. "You missed a perfect shot to the groin. You should have seen it."

I sent my gaze over to Sebastian for help. He just shrugged. "Watch your six man. And also, don't take my wife out."

I shrugged. "She volunteered."

When Jessa and Ariel walked in, I darted around Trevor, who was still trying to add the bandage to my stupid cut. He'd already sutured it, but I was in no mood to wait for the bandage. I needed to hold Jessa.

"God this is my fault. I should have listened." She glanced around at everyone. "Is everyone okay?"

She didn't even hug me.

I scowled.

When she finally walked over to me, her gaze searched my face. "I'm going to hug you. I just need a second I just need to thank Penny and the team."

That I'd allow. "Okay."

When she did wrap her arms around me, she held on tight. "My God, I'm being stubborn, aren't I? I can't stay here."

Everyone else in the room was silent. They understood what was happening. They knew what the truth of it was. Until we handled the threat, she couldn't stay here. I'd been tiptoeing around the fact. Trying to not tell her what she could and couldn't do and let her come to her own conclusions.

"I have to leave."

I looked back at her and nodded slowly. "Well, for the time being."

"So my life, all this that I've built, I have to leave it behind."

What was I supposed to say? 'I'm sorry baby, it sucks, but you don't ever get to come back?' No man wanted to say that to the woman he loved. But I needed to say it because it was the truth. "We can protect you in the islands. All of us. And maybe Penny won't take such stupid risks."

Penny decided not to comment from the peanut gallery, even though I knew it was killing her. Jessa blinked up at me. "I'm ready. Let's go. But, since they've already tried to hurt Chloe, should we bring her with us?"

I glanced over Jessa's head at Sebastian, who shrugged. He'd be willing to protect her in the Winton Isles, but she might not want that. "Listen, we can, but you have to remember she has her life here. She might not want to leave."

"Well, we have to try. We can't just stand here and pretend like she's going to be okay. Those people tried to grab Penny off the street."

She wasn't wrong. "I know. Just understand that we are going to do our best to convince her, but she's not obligated. She doesn't have to come with us."

"We just need to be very persuasive, because after seeing what just happened, there's no way I can just walk away from her. Those people were savages."

"Okay, we'll do our best. I promise."

And then she did the one thing I needed her to do. She wrapped her arms around me and settled in. Just knowing she was safe made my whole body relax. I planned to never let her out of my sight again. I didn't care what had to happen. The idea of losing her nearly killed me. That's what it meant to be in love.

Well then, so be it, because she was mine, and I would do anything it took to protect her.

## *Jessa*

"I STILL CAN'T BELIEVE any of this."

Chloe sat in her flat staring at me as I laid out the rest of the story. "I know. It's crazy."

"So all this time, you've been a princess?"

I shrug. "I don't know what I am. Technically, I guess maybe I'm a princess. Officially, not even. No matter what, I'm still just Jessa."

"But some crazy people are after you."

I nodded slowly. "Well, when you say it like that yeah, crazy people are after me."

"Jesus Christ, Jessa."

"But listen, all I want is to keep you safe. I'd like you to come with me."

Chloe raised her brows. "With you. To the Winston Isles? To the Caribbean? For a holiday?"

"I guess, but maybe we'll stay longer than for just a holiday. You're always looking for new adventure, and I don't feel good about leaving you here. Sebastian said that he'll give you a guard, but it'll be easier if you're just with me and I know you're safe."

Chloe chewed her bottom lip. "Listen, babe. I know you don't like change."

I laughed at the understatement. "Uh, yeah. Who does?"

"But I can't just drop everything. You're about to embark on a whole new adventure. A whole new life. You have to embrace it and do this. I am so proud of you to no end. You have taught me everything I know, but I can't just drop everything and move to the Caribbean."

I knew she'd say that. I knew it. But I still had to try. "Chloe, at least maybe come for a few days. A week. Until we can figure out who these assholes are that are trying to kill me."

"Honey, I'm just going to get in the way. You've got a whole new life with a whole new hot-ass man. You can't have me tagging along."

"You sure about that? Because I feel like I can. Chloe, this is a dangerous situation. There are people who have vanished the moment they've given me information, there was a fire at Hope House, and now someone t-boned you with a car. I just—I'm terrified. I'm scared for the people I love. Please just come with me. Even if it's just for a little bit, I just want to be able to protect you."

"Okay, I get it. You're scared. Hell, now that you've told me, I'm scared for you. But I can't uproot my life. How's this idea... I'll take off for a week. I'll go see my cousin in France. Your gorgeous brother can feel free to send someone with me to, you know, protect my body."

I had to chuckle. " Why are you so brave? Braver than me?"

"Well, I'm not brave. Matter of fact, I'm insane. But this is your life, and you need to live it. And you can't be worried about me. I know that if I let you, you will obsess about my safety. So, we're not going to do that. You're going to go live your life, be a princess. I'm going to come and visit you occasionally, and it's going to be awesome. It'll be great, and we're going to enjoy each other for a while, and then I'm going to come home. I think you and I both know that your whole life has been about other people. If I come with you, you have to take care of me. And while I would love for you to take care of me, I have to live my own life too. You know?"

I hated that she was making sense. "But Chloe, someone tried to hurt you because of me. I'm responsible."

"Oh Jessa. You are responsible for no one else but you, and that's about all you can manage. I watched you be responsible for your father, responsible for everyone. Evan acted like a twat for years, and somehow you put that on yourself. It's not your responsibility. He's a grown-ass man. He stalked you, acted way creepy, and still you thought somehow that was your fault? That's insane."

"I didn't think it was my fault, I just—"

She put up her hand. "No. Not listening. You get to be a princess. I could not be happier for you. I'm so proud of you. So you go do that and don't worry about me. For once, live life how you want to live it."

"I want to live it with my bestie."

"You get mad respect for that, love. But I can't come with you on this journey. It's not my place."

"I hate this. I hate that I have to walk away."

"I know. It's not really what you do, but you've got to do it this time. Otherwise, you're never going to know what kind of life you would have led. Okay?"

"You're my best friend."

"I know, so let me be a best friend. Let me be the one to tell you that you've taken care of too many people. Maybe it's time someone took care of you. Maybe it's time someone paid attention. Maybe it's time someone did what *you* needed. Let that gorgeous man of yours be in charge. I know, it's not real feminist. But you deserve someone taking care of you. For once."

"I don't even know what to say."

"Well, how about for starters you say I love you. I'll miss you."

I was going to cry. I sniffled and swiped at my nose. "How about I say come visit real soon."

Chloe grinned. "You know, that, I think I can manage."

I stood and squeezed her hand. My guard was waiting outside the door for me. They were also ready and waiting to protect Chloe for me. "I'll see you soon."

As I walked away from the only real family tether I had to London, I pulled out my phone to sever the last thread. The resignation letter had been sitting in my drafts for days.

But now I finally had the courage to hit send.

# TWENTY-SIX

*Jessa*

Leaving was harder than I thought. I don't know why I thought it would be easy, I just did. You know, move to a Caribbean island, become a princess. Clearly, I did not think these things through. It was all a lot. That room I'd been given when I'd first turned up in the islands hardly compared to the room I was given now. It was a suite, right next to Roone's. And it was three times the size of my flat in London. I had my own balcony, that coincidentally connected to Roone's. Lucky that. Funny thing, I could still work for London Lords from there with the agreement that I would fly back to London whenever we needed face-to-face meetings. But I could handle most of it from the islands. Sebastian and Lucas and Roone thought of everything. There was something so crazy about my life being managed for me that I didn't even know how to deal with it.

Penny was great. She was actually fantastic, and I adored her. Every time I had one of those moments where I thought I was going to panic from all the changes and all the differences, Penny was right there. Turning up to find out how I was or wanting to take a walk. It had been three days. Three days of my whole life being turned upside down.

*Just like when you were 10. Or 12, or 12 again, 14, 15, 15, 15, 16. 17.* It was like all those times my father had moved us in the middle of the night or when I'd gone to bed thinking everything was fine and the next morning I'd wake up to find our meager bags packed. Everything was just like that. Roone had wanted me to be able to bring everything from my flat. But honestly, all I needed were my photos, the one of me and my mother, and a few changes of clothes. Nothing much. I also brought along some sketches my father had done. But that was it.

When I'd turned up for the flight with so little in hand, Sebastian eyed me wearily. "This it?"

I nodded and told him that 'If I couldn't carry it, it wasn't worth bringing.'

The furrow in Sebastian's brow had been somehow sad to watch. Because he had no idea what I meant and no idea why I even felt that way. I wasn't sure what was sadder though, because Lucas seemed to know *exactly* what I meant. He simply nodded, grabbed my bag, and handed it to one of the luggage handlers. That was that.

Luckily, even though Chloe refused to join me, Ariel was there, Bryna and Jinx too, so there were at least a few familiar faces. Along with Penny, they were at the ready to fill my social calendar.

But I barely saw Ariel if I was being honest. I knew she had a job to do, including finding her father, so that was that. I knew eventually I'd work it out and figure out what in the world to do. I just needed to get used to being here, and I needed to prepare to meet with the Regents Counsel pretty immediately. It seemed they were deadly serious about the whole princess thing.

I knew my brothers were kind of a big deal. They were a prince and a king, but I didn't think the monarchy was that serious. It wasn't like any of those crazy fairytales where I could just walk through a looking glass and be like, 'I'm a princess.' Despite the support of my new family, it was weird.

As I was working on some of the upcoming events for London Lords, there was a knock on my door, and I frowned. I didn't expect to see Roone. He, unfortunately, was back at work, and he was not on my personal detail. Now that we were back in the islands, I had a whole team. Seven men to be exact. Scratch that. Six men and one woman, but she wasn't nearly as fun as Ariel. I put my laptop down and darted to the door. Even though it was a palace, old habits died hard. I searched the peephole and found someone unexpected on the other side. Lucas.

I opened the door with a smile. "Hey, am I late for some appointment?"

He shifted on his feet. "No. Sorry, I should have called or texted. I don't know, whatever the kids are doing these days. But I just wanted to spend some time with you."

I didn't know why, but a slow grin spread over my lips. "Really?"

He nodded. "I know in these things Sebastian is usually primary. He's the one in charge and tells us what to do, where to go, how to be. But I actually know the position you're in. That awkward what-do-I-do-now feeling. And I know you're probably freaking out about the Regents Council meeting."

"Oh my God, all the studying, the protocols, the who's-who, the faces. I keep thinking about the pictures and how people on Instagram never look the way they do in real life. You know they put their best face forward with their pictures and things, and then you're left trying to be like 'is that you?'"

Lucas chuckled a little. "Exactly. But why don't you take a break from all that. Let's go play on the beach."

"What?"

He nodded. "There's a path straight down to the beach, completely protected. And the armed guard outside can follow us."

"How come you don't have an armed guard?"

"That took some time. Plus, I ran away from my guards once or twice or... you know what, that doesn't matter."

I chuckled. "Oh, so you're an escape artist?"

"Well this one time, I found out some stuff, and I had a hard time dealing with it."

I stared at him. "You know I feel like I'm going to need to hear this story in its entirety."

"I'll tell you the whole sordid story."

For the first time since arriving in the islands, I felt a little more normal. Like this life could be my life. Like I could make this work.

For the first hour or so, Lucas regaled me with stories of the shenanigans he'd pulled, running away from his guard, repelling down the side of a building to make an escape and protect Bryna. That was complete insanity. But then he posed a question that, so far, no one else had really asked. Even Roone. "So, how are you feeling?"

I had no idea how to answer that. "Um, worried, scared, anxious. Trepidatious. All the stresses."

He laughed. "That's normal. I just wanted to tell you that I think it's amazing that we all have each other. And I know it's weird because you have this family that doesn't really feel like family yet. But we will. And if you need anything, I'm here. And you know, cut Sebastian some slack. He's actually a pretty great brother. He just feels like he has to have the weight of the whole world on his shoulders and protect everyone, so sometimes he doesn't listen the best. But he's trying to do the best he can. Which is why Penny's important. Penny keeps everything on the rails."

"Yeah, that makes sense. She's great, and I actually really like her a lot. I just hope I can live up to all this."

"That's just it, Jessa. All you have to do is be yourself. In this place, there are going to be people who try to make you feel like you're not enough. You know, because dear old Dad was sticking his wick in other wells and all that. In the end, he *did* want us. He did *want* to be part of our lives, but he wasn't allowed to be. So now, we get to be part of this family. And don't let them make you feel like any less."

And there, with the sand underneath my feet and the ocean lapping up over my toes, I felt at home for the first time. I was exactly where I belonged.

# TWENTY-SEVEN

*Roone*

I WASN'T sure why I was nervous. After all, this was just Sebastian.

Yeah, just Sebastian, the current king, not to mention the big brother of the woman you're sleeping with.

Sebastian leaned against the billiards table and gave me a shrewd, narrow-eyed gaze. "What's wrong? You look like you swallowed something bad and/or experimentally jammed a stick up your ass. In which case, no judgment."

"Shut up, you twat."

My best mate grinned at me, looking younger than he had in over a year. "Well, you're the one making the face. I just call it how I see it. What's the matter? You did what you were supposed to do. You brought my sister home. You should look thrilled."

"I am thrilled. We can keep her safer here."

Sebastian nodded. "But there's still a threat?"

I nodded. "Yeah, that's unsettling. There's something else too."

*I love her.* "I talked to my brother while I was in London."

Sebastian's brows drew up. "What? Way to keep that secret."

"Well, we had our hands full with more pertinent things at the time."

"Yeah, mate, like trying not to get killed. Trying not to get my wife kidnapped." He shrugged. "You know, typical week for us."

I couldn't help but chuckle. "How is Penny?"

He rolled his eyes. "You know Penny. She's Penny. I tried to talk to her about volunteering for dangerous missions, and she ignored me."

"I don't think you'll ever change that. What happened to the sweet, bubbly artist?"

"Oh, you think she's gone? No, Penny barely sleeps. She wakes up for the best light, or with an idea, and she has to get painting right away. She comes to bed with paint still on her fingers and gets it all over the sheets. The other day I woke up with blue on my nose. She laughed and laughed, and I had no idea why for a good 30 minutes until I went to brush my teeth. So she's still Penny, but she took her oath to protect this land to heart, and I'm not sure I *should* change that. Because she's her. But keeping her safe is a challenge."

"Tell me about it. You okay with all that though?"

Sebastian nodded. "She is who she is, and I'm not going to change her. I'm just glad she's rarely in the field any more. Sometimes you have to take your wins where you can get them."

"Yeah, I get that."

"Now, back to your brother. What the hell?"

"Yeah, I don't know, it was weird. He cornered me when I was at dinner with Ben."

Sebastian looked kinda sad. "Covington? How is he?"

"You know, he's good. He and East and Bridge are still thick as thieves. London Lords is doing well. Obviously, Jessa is on the team to help with their publicity and marketing."

"Yeah, yeah. I just didn't realize you and Ben had gotten to chatting."

"Yeah. But Reese was there one night, and he cornered me."

"And?"

"Apparently when Dad died, he left me some things."

Sebastian frowned. "What did he leave you? Like an heirloom or something?"

"Sort of."

"Okay..."

"He left me an earldom."

Sebastian lifted a brow. "What?"

"Yeah."

"But no one told you?"

"Nope. Imagine my surprise. It seems that when Reese turned twenty-one and took over management of my father's assets, he noticed there was a trust that was unidentifiable. The old man had left me his title, which was supposed to be mine from the start. And he left me some land out near Somerset, which honestly, what am I going to do with that? But I guess it's part of the inheritance, so I have to manage the land and the people and whatnot. And he left me a boatload of money."

Sebastian blew a whistle low under his breath. "Jesus Christ. That could have fucking come in handy when your mother passed."

"Yeah, tell me about it."

"But why didn't you know? The lawyer should have—"

I shook my head to interrupt him. "My stepmom. She didn't want me to have any of the money. She worked it out with her lawyer to extend the terms of the trust. Told him I was unfit to manage it. She would only have been able to keep it hidden until I was twenty-five, which she managed to do."

"You're twenty-six now."

"Yes, well, Reese found out about it a year ago and has been trying to track me down, but I haven't exactly been available. And I don't exactly take my brother's calls. And you yourself don't want him to have access, don't want anyone from his side of the family to have access to me, so... There you go."

Sebastian cursed under his breath. "Fuck, mate." He ran his hands over his face and stared at me. "You could have had your money and title last year?"

"None of that matters, honestly. It's money. I make a damn good salary, and it's not like I pay rent. I'm a member of the Royal Guard, so I follow you around, and I basically get to fly anywhere I want to go. I have money. Money's not a problem."

"Then what's the reason for the face?"

I swallowed hard. It was do or die time. "Well, being an earl looks real good on paper. It makes me an eligible match."

His brows furrowed. "For what?"

I swallowed hard. "An eligible match to marry Jessa."

He blinked at me once. And then again. And then guffawed hard. "Mate? What are you on about? Any idiot can see you love her."

It was my turn to blink. "You know?"

"Oh what, you two thought you were being slick? With the way you were eye fucking each other? And the way you fight? Like the stakes are high. And you hold her like you would rather die than let her go. Yeah, I know."

"And you're okay with it?"

"Yeah, dumbass. I think it's fantastic. You love her. Clearly, she loves you. So why are we even talking about it?"

"Well, okay, if it doesn't matter to you, it will certainly matter to the Council."

Sebastian rolled his eyes. "You guys don't listen. I control the Council."

"Yes, you do. But we don't ever want to do anything where you play your hand when it's not absolutely necessary. You and Lucas got to do what you wanted, be with who you wanted, but you're the king and the prince and kind of uncontrollable. I don't know how it works with princesses. You could have attempted to force her to marry someone to forge allegiance, for all I know."

Sebastian shook his head at me. "No. Women's lib has made its way down to the islands even. There's no way Penny would let a law like that sit. We, between my father and myself, we were able to pass a law to make illegitimate children heirs here. The princess can marry whoever the fuck she wants. And I happen to approve of her choice if she says yes."

My body relaxed. Everything I'd been concerned about dissipated. "You'd back me with the Council?"

"There's no need to back you. I'll just walk in and say, 'This is the lost princess. We found her. Fantastic. Oh, by the way, she's getting married. This is her husband-to-be.'"

"You know as well as I do they need to sign off and make her official. Maybe you don't mention the part about where she's getting married just yet? At least not until I ask her anyway."

He chuckled. "We can make a big old announcement or no announcement at all. It doesn't matter. My point is, you don't need a title. You never did. You were already my brother."

All of a sudden, the spot between my nose and my eyes hurt. It stung a little. My eyes were filling with... oh mother-fucker, I was not crying.

I sniffed deep. "Yeah mate, cheers."

Sebastian angled his head to look at me more directly. "Mate, you're not crying, are you?"

"No. You're crying."

Sebastian guffawed. "Bring it in. If you're going to cry like you're on some bloody American talk show, we might as well hug. I want a hug. Come in."

I backed away. "No, we are not hugging."

"Don't make me chase you down."

I squared my shoulders. "I swear to God, if you try to hug me it's going to get ugly."

He grinned at me then. And I knew just like when we were children, that it was on. And as we wrestled like schoolboys in the billiards room, I could feel the warmth spread through my chest. An empty hole that I had been carrying around for years, was suddenly overflowing. Far too full. I'd always had family. I just didn't know it.

---

### Jessa

I SHOULD HAVE KNOWN it was Roone at my door. The incessant banging, and then barging in as if he owned the place.

I lifted up my laptop. "Hey, you can't just walk in here."

He lifted a brow. "I'm sorry. This is my girlfriend's place. I was here last night. I gave her several orgasms. I figured that gave me permission to walk in whenever I damn well please."

"They're still my quarters."

He grinned at me. "Right next to mine. You're lucky I just didn't come through the bathroom, but I figured that would scare the shit out of you."

"Yes. Yes, it would."

"Get your things. We're going on a tour."

"What? I have work to do. You know I still have a job."

"Yeah, but it can wait. I happen to know your boss, and I approved some time off for you."

"You're insane. Approving time off is not in your job description. Also, I generally need to be told about time off." He was being impossible. "What do you want?"

"Well, I'd very much like to give you another big O, but I want to show you your home."

"Well, Lucas took to me to the beach the other day already. Maybe we can do this tomorrow?"

He shook his head. "Nope. Come with me. We are going to have fun today. I'm taking you to all the isles."

The islands? "What like in the whole Caribbean?"

He laughed. "What? No. The Winston Isles."

Why had I never considered that there were more islands? I knew that there were two, but more than that was never even a thought in my head. "Wait, there's more than two islands?"

He nodded. "Yes. Some of them are so small, they really just qualify as barely inhabited landmasses, but there are eight islands in all, and we're going to see them all today."

"Well that's insane. I don't have time."

"Well, you have time now. Come on."

"But can't I just—" I really wanted to lounge in bed, get some work done, and nap. I was exhausted. I'd had protocol meetings for the Regents Council, and our Queen Mother awoke me early for breakfast. She was lovely. A part of me wanted to resent her, but I couldn't. She was beyond nice to me. Chloe was sending me work for London Lords and filling me in on all things Evan. Apparently, he had taken an unexpected vacation as well, which was good for him, because maybe that would loosen him up a little a bit and stop his insane stalker tendencies.

And then, Penny, Bryna, Jinx, and Ariel had taken me out for tea in the rose garden, which had been fantastic, but it had also taken up a lot of my work time. I was so tired from all of the activities, and the protocols, and the rules, and all the things that I needed to do and see.

"I want to hold my girlfriend's hand as we walk. Put your laptop down and come on."

I really didn't want to protest, but this was my new life. I lived in a beautiful place, and I was spending so much of my time working. "Fine. Let's go."

He took my hand, and then he gave me the sweetest kiss, brushing his lips against mine. I sank into it, letting my body and my brain relax. The way it did every time I was with Roone. With him I felt amazing. With him I could do anything. With him I was just me, he was just him, and none of this other craziness existed. He groaned and pulled back, "I know what you're doing. You're tempting me with your feminine wiles. Trying to keep us in this room. But we're going out."

I laughed. "Oh, you caught me."

As it turns out, I was happy I'd gotten the opportunity. First thing's first, of course, we left with a massive guard. And by massive, I meant two follow cars, and the lead car.

"Way to announce who's in the car."

He laughed. "Oh, this is just for show as we leave the palace. Watch what happens."

Fifteen minutes away from the palace, our car veered harshly to the right as an identical car took our place. And what a ruckus they made. As they headed toward the city center, I looked through the windows. I noticed a pretty black girl in the back seat. Hair straight, just like mine. She looked... like me.

"What is happening?"

Roone laughed. "Decoy. I've already told the guards where we're going, so the pomp and circumstance decoy is to throw anyone off. Now we get to enjoy our day as if there's no one following us. We won't see them, but they'll be there."

I grinned at him. "You did this ahead of time for me?"

"Yeah, of course. Besides, they're your guards now. You could tell them, 'Hey, I want to go naked on the beach,' and they would be obligated to clear one for you and make sure not a single passerby saw your gorgeous tits."

"Are you serious right now?"

"As a heart attack. This is your life now."

He was right. I didn't notice a single guard. It felt like we were by ourselves.

On the ferry across to one of the smaller islands. I wrapped my arms around him and hugged him tight. "I just can't believe any of this."

He squeezed me back. "Believe it, princess."

I chuckled into his hard-as-hell pecs. "I still can't believe you were actually calling me by my title the whole time."

"Well, the first time it was a slip. Every time after that was because you liked/hated it, so I kept doing it. Now it's just a term of endearment."

I sank into his embrace, letting the heat of his body wrap around me along with the smell of his sandalwood cologne. The scent of hibiscus on the air and the sound of the ocean waves lapping against the ferry relaxed me. I was so content. I could do this forever. Lazily, I let my gaze wander as the ferry pulled away, and I saw something on the shore. I picked my head up and searched the shoreline again, a bit more alert and half-convinced I had seen something that wasn't supposed to be there.

"What's the matter, princess?"

"Roone, I swear to God I just saw Evan."

His body went stiff. He tapped his ear immediately.

"Sighting of Millston. Repeat, potential sighting of Millston on the shore of the big island."

"Wait, you have a mic in?"

He nodded. "Yeah. The security firm we work with when we travel to New York, they're sort of friends of the palace. They help us out with stuff, including some pretty crazy tech."

"Oh. Maybe I was overreacting. It's just that guy on the shore, he just looked like—" *No, you're crazy. There's no way Evan is here. All of that is behind you.*

"No, you have to have follow your instincts. If you think you saw him, chances are you did. So let's focus on confirming that instead of confirming that your crazy, okay?"

"Okay." As much as I didn't want it to, a feeling of uneasiness fell over me. I kept wondering what the hell he was doing there and why he'd followed me.

*Or maybe I didn't see him at all. Maybe I'm just confused.*

No. I no longer thought I was actually going crazy. Knowing now that my father was actually my stepfather helped a lot with those *I've lost my mind* feelings. But in so many ways, this was almost worse because I knew it was real. I knew I wasn't losing my mind and I wasn't going crazy. There was actually a boogeyman, and he had my number. I still tried to force myself to relax, to take a breath.

Next to me, Roone had relaxed some. He still held my hand, held me close, but I could tell there was a tension in him that hadn't been there when we left the palace. He was busy trying to follow my crazy hunch, and I felt bad for ruining the day.

But he didn't relent. He insisted we were still going to have a good time. And we did. By the time we hit the second small island with only a couple handfuls of residences on it and the best gelato in the islands, he was relaxed again. There had been no confirmed sighting of Evan on the island, and nothing else out of line had happened. Roone did do a time jump though, and said, "We have just enough time to do another brief walk through, a quick boat ride, and then I have to get you back. We'll do that other island another day. Does that work?"

"Yeah. I'm just happy to spend some time with you. It's been a little crazy. Since we got back, you've actually been working. I'm not used to that."

He chuckled. "Yeah, well, I have to earn my keep. I can't bring nothing to the table when I'm dealing with a princess."

"You bring everything to the table." I looped my arms around his neck and planted a kiss on him. As I pulled back, he stiffened. And then his gaze bore into mine. "Jessa, come on."

There was a small part of me that wanted to argue, that wanted to fight him, that wanted to ask questions, but that instinctive part of me that knew to trust him didn't have to think twice. His fingers gently pushed me in the direction I needed to go, and I took off. It had been a minute or three since I'd hit the gym, but it didn't matter. The instinct to just survive kicked in, and I bolted as he told me to run. I had no idea where I was going, no idea what I was running from. All I knew was that Roone said run, so I ran.

I ignored the burning of my lungs and the pain of my burning thighs. I ignored my elevated heart rate and the dizziness. I ignored the graying on the edges of my vision. I just ran. I forgot to breath, I forgot to fight, but I ran.

It wasn't until I rounded a corner where I made the fatal mistake of turning back to see if Roone was behind me, and I hit a roadblock. I ran straight into someone, my whole body seizing, going tight, every part of my muscles engaging, and it hurt. I stumbled back, nearly falling until someone caught me by the arms and pulled me to them. But the grip wasn't familiar. It wasn't a grip I knew. Finally, I blinked up, confused, expecting to find Roone. Instead I found another familiar face. "Phillip?"

A man who'd been so kind to me once, so sweet, now gave me a smile that was all teeth. "Hello, princess."

# TWENTY-EIGHT

*Jessa*

My body knew I was in danger before my mind knew. My mind kept trying to make excuses or mental rationalizations for what was happening.

Things like 'Oh, this makes perfect sense.' I kept trying to think of scenarios that made sense for why Phillip was in the islands. But I couldn't think of one.

"But your office. It was a mess. I thought someone had taken you."

His grip on my arms only intensified. You were supposed to think that. But that's you, Jessa. Always convinced you know better. You're a fanciful one, aren't you?"

"I—"

"After everything that's happened, you still can't see. I must admit, it was hard at times to get your father to believe too. But with a push in the right direction, I always seemed to do the trick."

"What are you talking about?"

"Like father like daughter, right?"

"What do you know about my father? You said he was your friend."

His grip only intensified.

"You have been a pain in the ass. You vanished for a week on us, running off with your boyfriend."

"Why does everyone think I ran off with Roone? I didn't."

"Doesn't matter."

"You set off this whole chain of events, didn't you?"

"If you had only stayed in England, if you'd only listened to me when I told you about your father, about who *they* were, about how they got power and how they held on to their power."

I shook my head. "This is about power?"

"It's always about power. That usurper doesn't belong on the throne."

"I don't understand. Sebastian's not a usurper. He's a legitimate son of the king."

"The usurper's son was never a king. He took the throne when it was supposed to go to the regent. We believe in the true heir to the throne."

I couldn't believe this insanity, How had I missed all of this? How had I not seen it?

"*We?* You're with them?"

"It's not about being *with* them. It's about what's right. God, your father was so furious when he found out who you really were. I'd never planned to tell him. But wow, did he love you, because he tried to do everything to protect you. We thought we'd lost when he ran away with you. But it turns out all he needed was a little push to make him think he was crazy."

I struggled in his arms. "What?"

"Yeah, the first time you went to a psychologist when he thought he was losing his mind, thinking that he was being followed, he *was* being followed. And when he called me for help, I made a point to suggest someone in Canada who was sympathetic to our cause."

"Oh my God." My stomach roiled, and the bile threatened to erupt. "You did this. You helped make him sick?"

"It wasn't hard. He was already in hyper-protection mode about you. He didn't run because the royal family was terrible, those ideas and thoughts were planted. All he knew was that men were coming for his daughter, and he needed to save you. I gave him the push he needed when he took you to Canada."

"So you were the one responsible for my childhood? You made him sick."

"You're being melodramatic."

I couldn't believe it. All these years, all this time, my father hadn't *been* sick, he'd been *made* sick, but I'd committed him.

I fought against his hold, but his grip only tightened.

"Ow you're hurting me."

"Sorry, princess, but the time to be gentle is over. You didn't stay in England. Oh, you brought your brothers to you, but you didn't stay. If you'd only listened, we could have talked you through it. We would have let you have a position in the new monarchy. Made you a duchess or something. But you had to side with them, so your culpability is the same as theirs."

"You're insane."

"No, I'm not insane. I'm a true believer."

He hauled me up. My feet practically dangled to the ground.

"Let me go."

"You're not going anywhere. Do you understand? We had a whole plan. Take out your brothers in the UK, have you on our side, but then you all had to come here, making things all the more difficult."

"I said, let me go."

"No, princess. You're going to act as bait. Then your

brothers will come, and then all of you are going to die and the true heirs will take their rightful seats."

"And who do you think is the true heir?"

"Me. I'm a direct descendant to Angelus. Duchess Maria is my cousin. I am the one who belongs on the throne."

"You? You're a professor. Not a prince. You're nuts. What is wrong with you?"

"Unlike daddy dearest, I am quite sane. You just picked the wrong side. Don't be mad. You and your brothers are going to die."

The harder he gripped me, the more it hurt. Finally, I remembered what my father had taught me, and I kicked him swiftly in the balls. When he didn't let go, I headbutted him.

He let go of me then.

Heat pounding, head spinning, I took off running, but his hand reached out and he snatched my wrist again. "Where do you think you're going, *princess?*"

Then I heard a familiar and welcome voice, a low rumble that was more warning growl than anything. "Where she's going is back to safety. I can't say the same about you."

*Roone.* He'd come for me.

---

### Roone

PURE UNADULTERATED RAGE was all I could feel. That fucker had his hands on her. And they were pulling her and grabbing her, and she was fighting to free herself. He was touching my woman, and he expected to live through the night? He was going to die.

Jessa saw me. She stepped forward, delivering elbow number three right up under Phillip's chin. His head snapped back, and he let her go. She staggered back, posturing herself against the wall in the alley.

What happened next was nothing short of amazing. With her back to me, she literally watched my six.

I grabbed Winchester and slammed him against the wall. I delivered a fist. I heard her grappling with someone else. Shit, how many men had he had with him?

She delivered a couple of knees and elbows of her own.

All I heard was grunting and oofing as I dealt with Winchester. He wasn't some soft professor. He was a trained fighter. He blocked one of my blows and landed one of his own. A straight jab to the nose. He rung my bell, but I kept fighting.

*Fighting for her.*

Fighting for *us*.

When I was done playing around, I opened my arms wide even as he delivered a couple of punches to my gut, and then I rung his bell properly with a sharp slam of my palms over his ears.

Immediately, his hands flew to his ears as he tried to calm the ringing. But when he did that, I pulled him down by his ears, elbowed the back of his neck, and delivered a Muay Thai kick to his face, and he went down.

No moving, no groaning. I suspected I'd killed him, but I really didn't care. Jessa was fighting someone I didn't know. Lanky. Average height. Knew how to fight though.

I narrowed my gaze at him. He was familiar. And was he wearing a wig. Whiskey, Tango, Foxtrot. My mind tried to place him as maybe one of the Royal Guard. He fought well, but not that disciplined.

He was still fighting and grabbing for Jessa.

There was something about his voice too. It was thin and reedy. "I'm trying to save you. Why don't you understand that?" he whispered to her.

Jessa's response was classic Jessa. "When I need saving, I'll fucking tell you."

She punched him hard, and he sank down to his knees. But he still tried to wrap his arm around her leg. I helped her out of his grip and extricated her. Well, more like performed a surgical extraction on him. I looped an arm around his neck and simply pulled. When he didn't let go immediately, I applied pressure. And more pressure. Finally, he clawed at my arm and then went limp.

Jessa wasted no time stepping back away from him and definitely further away from Winchester. She plastered her back against the wall, looking around, presumably for a weapon.

I dragged the bodies out of sight in the alley and placed them against the wall so that they were in the shadows behind the dumpster.

I took her hand and tapped my coms, but when I plugged into the channel, all I heard was chaos. Shouting, running. People out of breath.

"Call sign Viper. What the fuck is going on?"

Ariel muttered. "Call sign Red. We're coming for you. We had a little trouble. Get to a car. Get back to the palace. We have two guards down."

I cursed under my breath. I glanced at Jessa, whose eyes were wide with panic. But she was holding it together, being so brave. My princess was beautiful and brave and brilliant, and I was going to fucking marry her if it was the last thing I did.

"Come on, Jessa. We gotta go."

She didn't even question a thing. She just placed her hand in mine and looked up at me. "Let's go."

I dragged her toward the opening of the alley. But when a shadow stepped forward, I frowned. I noted one of the bodies I'd dragged into the shadows was starting to stir. That meant not dead. *Bummer.*

I didn't recognize the newcomer, but there was something eerily familiar about him.

"Oh, princess, you're on the wrong side of things. It would have been a lot easier if you'd chosen our side."

Jessa, true to form and unable to keep her mouth shut, rolled her eyes and said, "If you assholes thought I was ever going to choose you, you're insane."

I grinned at her. "Ah, princess? It might not be a good idea to antagonize the crazy."

"I'm not scared of shit, dude."

A smile tipped to my lips, and I wanted to laugh. "Right, of course. Do you want to handle him, or should I?"

Nonchalantly, she said, "I can do it. Why don't you get us a car?"

I shrugged, letting go of her hand. Maybe that was crazy, but I wanted her to feel strong. And I was pretty sure she could take him.

But then I heard movement behind us. I turned, and someone blindsided me. I hadn't even heard his footsteps until he was entirely too close. I'd been so focused on getting Jessa out of there that I hadn't been watching our backs. It wasn't Winchester and his scrawny buddy this time. There was someone else with a big meaty fist, enormous. And he was taller than me, six foot six at least.

My head nearly snapped off my spine, and I tried to recover it. Jessa didn't wait for me. She knew how to handle herself. She had a pipe in her hand and went for the man in the alley.

"You're just like my daughter. You think you can be strong, but you can't. Well, just like her, your mistakes will cost you."

As my vision started to dim, I realized who the man was. It was Ariel's father.

He'd come back to the island. And just like Ariel had said, he wasn't just dirty, he'd committed an act of treason, sided with these nut jobs against us. Obviously, he thought he was on the side of right.

I didn't have time to worry about Jessa. I kept part of my brain on her fight, but I knew she could handle herself. I actually had to fight for my life with this guy.

At one point he grabbed both of my wrists and was yanking me toward him. It was hard to remember my training, but I went with the flow and followed him. I swung my arms out and snapped them together quickly, which forced the release of one hand. I placed my free hand on top of both of ours that were still connected and gave him a twist. He howled, and his knees buckled, but not enough. His leg swung out, and I went toppling with him.

On the ground, we rolled. All I could think was, *shit, do not let him roll on top of you.*

I could hear Jessa grappling. Ariel's father was cursing, and she was muttering things to herself like 'elbow to the nose. Knee to the groin. Stop.'

It was hilarious, but I couldn't be bothered to laugh. I had to think through other things.

Like the motherfucker dragging me down. I did a release move as best I could and worked on wedging a knee between our bodies, then I pushed with all my might. That fucker was heavy though. And he was coming back for me, trying to get those meaty paws around my neck again. I was coughing and wheezing. And the next thing I knew, he was falling. Falling on top of me. *Oh shit.* I tried to roll, but it was no use. He tried to reach for something to stop his fall, but it was out of his grasp and he didn't get ahold of it. Then he sagged fully. Out like a light.

When I shoved him, I saw Jessa standing over both of us, the pipe raised over her head again.

It was covered in blood. Then I touched my face and realized so was I.

*Fantastic.*

But Jessa wasn't watching her back, and Ariel's father grabbed her by the ankle, and she fell, kicking and screaming. I tried to roll, but the big motherfucker was on my feet. I reached for her, trying to grab her hand.

Then Ariel's father was kneeling over her. He rolled her face down and put his hands around her neck, squeezing.

Oh fuck, I needed to get to her. She was clawing at his hands, but it wasn't working.

I could barely talk myself. "Baby, release hold. Release hold." I coughed.

I don't know what did it, but she finally understood and did a pluck on his hand the right way. She brought her knees to her elbows, and Ariel's father went flying. Not as far forward as he needed to go though, because he turned right back around and tried to grab for her again. But then there was a gunshot, one single crack of fire, and he fell on top of her, blood pouring from his temple.

I finally got the big brute off of me and then dragged the body of Ariel's limp father off of the princess.

I saw someone running down the alley with a gun poised to fire, and I covered the princess.

I tried to move her, roll her, do something to protect her, but the only protection left was left was my body.

And then I heard a voice, one that was all too familiar, one that worried me.

"'Target dropped."

I turned my head, and there was Ariel, standing over the body of her dead father. She'd shot him. She shot him to protect the princess.

# TWENTY-NINE

*Jessa*

MY PALMS WERE SWEATING. "What if I make a mistake?"

Roone smiled softly. "You're not going to make a mistake. This is your birth right. This is your family."

"I know. You say that, and I know it's true. But I just—this whole thing—I just didn't expect it. What if I let everyone down?"

"There's no chance of that. You didn't know King Cassius, but when he decided on something, he decided on it for good. For years he listened to the old guard who said any sort of scandal would ruin the family. They were determined to keep things the way they were. But eventually, he was determined to do things differently, to stand for the right things. And Sebastian started his quest as a way to get back at the old man for not believing in him or something. And when he found out that he wasn't alone, he was even more determined. And sure, he was charmed because he thought one of you could be king or queen instead, but once he found Lucas, he sort of found his purpose. So, no matter what, you are wanted. This whole journey of yours has led you right here, so own it. You are no longer the lost princess; you are the found princess. You are home."

Tears pricked my eyes, and I blinked them rapidly away. The makeup artist, Helga, she would only berate me if I ruined her perfect makeup job. Thanks to Penny, she'd actually had the right shades for me. There was nothing worse than getting your makeup done when the color wasn't right. You ended up looking ashy.

"I don't know how to be a princess."

Roone grinned again. "Well the good news is, you still just get to be you. You still get to work and just do what you would normally do. The only difference is that you have a direct connection to the throne. That's all. And you get to wear a tiara."

"But I don't want to be a princess. What if I'm expected to act princess-like? You already know that's a recipe for disaster."

Roone grinned at me. "Yes. It is. But the good news is you get to be exactly who you are. Sebastian and Lucas don't expect anything more. Be a modern princess. Stand for something, just like Penny does."

"I like that idea. That I can stand for something instead of seeing this girl in a tiara. People could see a woman who fought her family. Fought for what she believed in. I think I can do that. I worked hard."

"Of course you can. Now, if you don't mind, everyone's waiting. A lost princess has come home, and her adoring public wants to see her."

"I hardly doubt the public is adoring."

"You underestimate them. There are people who have been waiting a lifetime to see you. There are people who may have heard rumors of you, people from the old days, but to actually see you in person, to know that anything is possible no matter their station, that gives people hope."

"I never thought of myself as giving anyone hope."

"Well, you gave me hope."

"Yeah, because you knew I was the princess."

"No." He shook his head and took my hands. "No matter what, you have been feisty, determined, and you never let me win. You never give up. You are incredible, and stubborn, and irritating, Jesus Lord. But you are also one of the strongest women I've ever met in my life. After everything you endured, to be able to still look forward, that's incredible. I, for one, am excited about it."

He opened the French doors of the waiting room into the expansive hall of the dining tower. Just across the way was the ballroom. When given the signal, the sergeant at arms would open the doors, and I would step through those doors by myself. Roone would still be there, but he wouldn't be holding my hand.

I was going to have to do this on my own. And I was terrified.

But something he said reminded me that I *could* do this.

I wasn't lost anymore. After all this time, I finally had a home. I finally had family. I had roots that would be sticking with me. I had a place to call my own where I had purpose. For once in my life, I would have more than two pictures to my name and more than one friend. I would have everything I'd ever asked for. All I had to do was standup and grasp it. I glanced over at the man I'd come to love. The man I was once sure I'd kill eventually. Granted, there was still time. I lifted the skirt of my ballgown then stood on my tiptoes and gave him the biggest of kisses. I let myself linger for just a moment until he groaned low. "Princess, if you keep kissing me like that, when they open those ballroom doors all of your subjects are going to see you doing very inappropriate princess things."

"Promise?" I asked with a saucy smile.

"Do you want to dare me?"

I giggled and eased back onto my feet. "I do dare you. But I just wanted to say thank you. Thank you for fighting for me even when I didn't want you too. Thank you for never giving up on me."

"I didn't really have a choice. I loved you from the moment I saw you. You were the most infuriating, annoying woman I had ever laid eyes on, and I wanted you to be mine."

"You are a crazy man, you know that?"

He laughed. "You know it's strange, but I've been told that."

"Well, looks like I had better get going."

He grinned at me. "Yeah. You better."

I rushed back to the entrance and nodded at the sergeant at arms. It was time for me to take my place. I was a princess, and I was going to own it. Tiara and all.

---

## Jessa

I WASN'T GOING to lie, I intended to wear this tiara everywhere. Even to check the mail. Wherever the hell one checked one mail around here. Actually, that was a really good question. Where was I going to get my mail?

Not like I couldn't ask my brothers, but still. Inquiring minds.

I was still in my coronation outfit, ballgown, tiara and all. I really did look like a princess. Me, the girl with no family and no home. Someone had stuck a crown on my head. And these crazy people were calling me *Your Highness.* No way any of this was real.

"Oh, it's real princess."

I whirled around. "Roone. I didn't think anyone was in here."

He chuckled low. "I came to check on you since you

vanished from the ballroom. I was looking for my dance partner."

"It was all so overwhelming. You know, everybody was staring at me and watching me as the prodigal daughter returned. Except I never even knew that this was a thing or a place I could be. It was just a bit, I don't know... much. So I came to hide." I shrugged. "Also, I really had to see myself in this tiara."

He laughed again and stepped forward. "You look like you were born to wear it. And you were. Own it."

I grinned up at him. I stood on tiptoes and kissed him gently. "What have I done to deserve you?"

"Oh, you know, just being gorgeous, and beautiful, and smart, and pretty badass, if I must say. My girl can throw a punch."

"Yeah, and don't you forget it."

He shifted on his feet, rocking back and forth slightly. "Jessa, there was actually something I wanted to ask you. I tried to do it the day of the attack, but you know, someone tried to kill us so that thwarted my plans."

"What's wrong? You've suddenly gone very serious."

His smile lightly played over his lips. "Well when you want to tell the most beautiful girl on the planet how much you love her, you should be serious."

I grinned up at him. "I love you too."

Roone cleared his throat, and started to bend...on one knee and I reached for him. "What the hell do you think you're doing?"

"I'm telling the woman who fills my soul with light that I would die with out her."

*Oh shit. Oh shit. This was happening.*

"Princess. I know I don't always say the right thing. I know, we don't always agree. But I hope you know that I would happily hand you the sword to slay your own dragon, every day for the rest of my life. I will lay my life down to protect you, not because you are the princess, but because you are my queen. I will be your partner. I will be your friend. I will be the one you want to occasionally punch. I would be honored if you would call my your husband. Will you marry me."

In that moment, I want completely ineloquent. My mouth open and closed like a guppy and I couldn't find the words. It took several moments for me to manage the nod, then the string of nonsense after. "Oh—Roone—What? How? I—Yes. Oh, my God, yes!"

His hands shook as he pulled the marquis cut diamond ring out of its velvet bed and took my hand. The ring slid on easily and I stared at my left hand. The rose gold band hugging my finger, bringing out the russet tones in my skin. When he stood, he pulled me to him and whirled me around.

Holy shit, I'd just agreed to marry Roone.

He drew me to him, sliding his hands down over my ass, and I could still feel the heat radiating from him even through all the layers of tulle. I was so used to the heat of him. So much so that I needed it to breath.

"I love you, Princess."

"I love you, Roone. Also, you need to stop calling me princess."

"You're right. I'm going to graduate to calling you my queen."

I did like the sound of that one. "You're impossible."

"It's strange. My wife to be has told me that before."

"Wife to be does have a certain ring to it."

Roone kissed my deep. With his lips on mine, I completely lost track of where I was or what I was meant to be doing. It was just be and Roone. Everything else in my life might be crazy, but he would forever by my rock.

We heard the chiming of the church bells and he pulled back with a groan. "You have to get back."

"Nope. I refuse. I'm staying here with my fiancé."

"I love how that sounds. But you really do have to go. It's time for you and your brothers to do the royal family portrait. It's tradition."

Tradition be damned. I was getting bloody married. But then there was a buzzing between us.

"Um, I'm pretty sure your dick is not supposed to do that."

He tapped me on the bottom with both of his hands. "Scamp. You need to get back and I'll need to take this. I'm right behind you."

"Fine. I'm going to head back. I'll see you back in the ball-room." I stopped. "This is all real right?"

"You better believe it."

I was Princess Jessa of the Winston Isles. And the love of my life had just put a ring on it. I had once been very, very lost, but Roone had found me. Seen me. Loved me.

I took a deep breath. Then I stepped out into the larger room. But I wasn't alone.

"Well, isn't this a sight? I always knew you were a princess. But for you to be a real one, that's even better. We will make such beautiful children."

I froze, heels planted into the carpet. "Evan. What are you doing here?"

"What? You thought you could escape to a tropical island, and I wouldn't follow you?" He slammed his hand on the desk in the outer office. "There is nowhere you go that I don't follow."

"Okay, alright." *Think, think, think.* "Evan, I'm just surprised you didn't tell me you were coming. We could have had them prepare a room."

His brows narrowed. "Prepare a room?"

"Of course. I mean obviously, I know that we should be

together, so of course I would want you with me. I was very upset about how we left things."

He shook his head. "No. You chose that bumbling asshole Ainsley. I know you've been fucking him."

*Shit. Good God Roone, hurry up get off the phone. Hurry up get off the goddamn phone. Think Jessa."* I lowered my voice, using the same tone I would use to speak to my father when he was ranting. "Look, we all make mistakes. I thought I wanted him, but after being with him, I realized that you were the one I wanted. You are the only one who truly understands me. You're the one who gets me. He doesn't understand. He's a boy. You, you are a man."

*Flatter. Don't lay it on too thick. Be self-deprecating.*

He frowned. "You chose him."

His hand was in his pocket. What was he holding? Or worse, a gun?

"I made a mistake. I know that now. Do you see him with me? No."

"I saw him here, in that ballroom along with the others, wearing crowns and things. They can't have you. You are *mine.*"

"I know. I *am* yours. I know this. I wouldn't have it any other way. The men with the crowns, those are my brothers. And if you'll let me introduce you, they'd be more than happy to welcome you. But, you didn't tell me. I didn't know you were coming. So now I have to scramble. I'll get a room made up. And then you and I can spend some time together down on the beach by the ocean."

"You want to spend time with me?"

"Of course."

He stepped forward.

It was a knife in his pocket. He pulled it out slowly. The sunlight that poured in through the windows gleamed on the metallic blade.

"Easy does it. You don't need that."

"I'm not going to hurt you. I'm just going to take this off."

He was pointing the knife at my dress.

Instinctively, I wrapped my arm around my belly. "But it's such a beautiful dress, though."

And then I saw he held something else. A white sweater dress? I had one like it.

"What's that?"

"It's your dress. You were wearing it the first time I saw you. I'm sorry, I stole it from your apartment, but I'd like you to wear it now. Take that off."

The last thing I wanted to do was be naked in front of this man. "I just—I'm feeling shy."

The frown was back. Deeper than before. "There's no need to be shy. I'm yours, and you are mine, so we are going to be together now. You have to learn to get used to it."

"Evan, you're not going to force me, are you? I know that's not who you are. You love me."

The hand holding the knife wavered, but he still held out the dress. "Start unbuttoning. You're going to wear this."

I tried desperately to think of all the ways I could stall this, when unexpectedly, I saw movement behind Evan. Was the bookcase moving? A center panel that looked like a shelf started to recede. Holy shit. Were there secret passages in this place?

"Okay, Evan. There's no need for the knife. I'll unbutton. It will just take a second."

"I am tired of being patient. You put this on, we'll get on a plane, and we'll go back to London. Enough of this princess nonsense. We're going to live together."

The shadow moved slowly, efficiently. And then he stepped into the light, and I saw who it was. *Roone.* How the hell had he gotten from the ballroom to here without Evan seeing him? Was the whole palace connected with a series of tunnels?

He put his finger to his lips and indicated I should keep Evan talking.

"Okay. See, I'm unbuttoning."

I reached for my side and pulled down the zipper. Wincing as the fabric started to part. Then I started on the tiny pearl buttons on the ice blue gossamer fabric. It was so delicate, I didn't want it to rip it. I knew that Sebastian would have me a million dresses made, but I wanted this one. The moment I had put it on, I'd known that I belonged. I belonged to a family. I had people who cared about me, cared about my well-being, *loved* me. Just because. And to ruin the first real symbol of that would break my heart.

I moved as slowly as I could. Gently, I undid the buttons, but Evan's impatience grew as he shifted on his feet. "Goddammit, I told you to hurry." He stepped forward, reaching for me with the knife, and I squeaked and jumped back. And as he lunged for me, the knife inches from my belly, he suddenly jerked back.

Roone had an arm around his neck, his other arm behind Evan's head, and he was pulling him backwards. His gaze met mine in a flat, blank stare. Oh, this was soldier Roone, and he was not fucking around. Not when it came to my safety. He would, in fact, do anything to protect me.

Evan flopped, slashing the knife in the air. He tried to bring his arm back, aiming for Roone, but no way would I let that happen. I yanked up the skirt of my dress and kicked out my foot, connecting with Evan's wrist and sending the knife flying.

Roone blinked then, his gaze meeting mine properly, suddenly going hot. Full of emotion. He jerked tighter.

I saw it in his eyes. He was going to kill him.

"Roone. No. You're not killing him. Not for me. Incapacitate only."

He narrowed his gaze at me. I thought he might resist, but

then he didn't. I watched him inhale deeply and then release Evan's body. Evan fell to the floor, passed out cold.

Roone tapped his ear mic. "I need a clean-up in Queen Mother Alexa's office. We had an uninvited guest."

He checked Evan's pulse, and then he stood, slowly moving toward me, hands up as if to show that he was no threat. "Jessa, it's okay. I'm here. I have you. You're safe."

As if the gravity of what had just happened finally sunk in, my hands started to shake. Uncontrollable tremors shook my whole body, and I just stood there.

Roone wrapped his arms around me. Pulling me tight. "I have you. You're gonna be okay. I have you. You're going to be fine."

"He, he got into the palace."

"I know. We had lots of guests. He could have come in as anyone's driver. It's okay. You're safe. He's smarter than most, but now he's on our turf. He's never going to hurt you again. Me, Sebastian and Lucas, we will all see to it."

"God, part of me wishes that you'd killed him."

I couldn't see him because my face was pressed into his chest, but I could feel the movement of his head on top of mine. "No. You were right. I wouldn't want you ever not being able to look at me. I'm not sure I would have known to stop if you hadn't said something."

"Now I wish I hadn't told you to stop."

His chuckle was low. "You're just mad. And you have a right to be. This man has terrorized you. But it's over now. I have you. In my arms, you are always safe."

And I knew it to be absolutely true.

# THIRTY

*Ariel*

I wasn't even nervous when I knocked on Sebastian's door. I knew what had to happen. I knew the Council had met yesterday. It didn't change the fact that I didn't *want* to go in, but I knew what I had to do. If I let Sebastian walk in and save me, the council would never respect him. Ever. And I knew that what he was trying to do was far more important than me and my career. I wished to God I could just let him see my fear. I wished to God, I could let myself walk in and have him save me. But I knew better.

That wasn't what was right for my home. And it wasn't what was right for my friends, either of them, Penny or Sebastian. I couldn't be that selfish. I couldn't make that request. I knew that he would see it as something that he was doing completely voluntarily, but still, I couldn't let him do it. That just wasn't who I was. He would save me without my asking. He would make that choice, that sacrifice, for me and for Penny too. That's the kind of man and the kind of king he was.

But no. I was a big girl. I'd made my bed, and I was going to lie in it and take the punishment as it was to be doled out.

"Come in."

I pushed the door open and gave him a smile. "Your Majesty."

He sighed. "Ariel, I swear to God, if you're walking in here to quit on me, I just won't accept."

I loved him a little bit when he said that, but I still had to do the right thing. "I'm sorry, Sebastian, you know I need to."

"For fuck's sake, Ariel." He slammed his hands on his desk, and I jumped a little. "Do not fucking do this. I will talk to the members of the council. They know what you've done. You were on the team that brought me back."

"I know. And I know what you're willing to do for me, and I'm grateful, I am. But I need to do this for you. After everything that's happened in the past two years, your father's death, the assignation attempts, finding your siblings and having them legitimized, you need peace. And defending me to the council will be the thing that sets everyone off. This is a choice you don't have to make. I know you would do it, you'd take that hit for me. And God help me if I don't love you a little for it myself, but I can't let you do that."

I pulled out the letter from my jacket. "I'm just going to leave this right here. Please don't do me the disservice of refusing to accept it, because I've already dropped one off with Ethan. I did that first, so he would have to at least start the process and you couldn't refuse me."

"You're tying my fucking hands. And what about Penny? She'll never understand your insistence that this is the best for everyone either. I know it's hard. I feel terrible. I don't want do this."

"I knew you'd feel that way, but it's the best choice for this family."

"There has to be something else we can do. I refuse to just accept this."

"Look, I can get another job. Private security or something. But let's face it, even if you don't look at me any differently, there will always be those who will question my loyalty because of my father. And that's not what we're about. We are a team. We do what needs to be done. We make it work. I'm willing to do my part, and you need to let me. Be my king. Be the one to stand forward and lead."

Sebastian ran his hands through his hair. "Okay look, what if you consult? What if I change your status so you're no longer a full-time employee, but you're a special attaché? I thought of it all."

I shook my head. God, I could see why Penny loved him. Hell, I loved him a little bit now. "Your Majesty, thank you, but no."

I turned in my resignation along with my ID. My hands shook a little as I did it.

"Your Majesty, thank you for allowing me to serve you." I turned to leave.

"Ariel."

I glanced over my shoulder at him. God, why couldn't he see that I was about to fucking cry? My eyes were stinging, and the tears were brimming. I wanted to run out of there before I completely humiliated myself. Why was he insisting? "Yes, Your Majesty?"

" We have one other option. At least hear me out. Maybe this doesn't have to be how your service ends."

"Your Majesty, I've made my decision. You're just making it harder." As I turned to face him, there was something in his eyes that told me that this might be worth listening to. "Fine, I'll listen, but I can't be an employee of the palace. You know it, and I know it."

He shook his head. "No, this is something different, a new possibility. Are you willing to hear me out?"

"I am, absolutely." It was weak, but at least there was a chance I wouldn't have to leave my family. I sat down in the chair across from him and prayed for a miracle.

# THIRTY-ONE

*Jessa*

So, this is what family was. Roone, Lucas, and Jinx were in an epic, trash-talking battle about who was going to win at Rummy 500. They were all clutching their cards, getting in each other's faces, and talking serious smack.

At one point I actually thought that Roone and Lucas were going to get into a fist fight. Lord knew that Penny and Sebastian had almost gone at it, and not in the fun kind of way, when they had a disagreement on how many points the ace was going to count for.

Ariel was uncharacteristically quiet. I knew what was happening, and I couldn't believe it. Sebastian said everything was going to stay the same. I couldn't see how, though. She was leaving the guard. She was leaving this place.

She was one of the one's who knew me best. She and Roone. And she wasn't going to be in the palace every day. Everyone else was awesome and great, and Penny and I were getting close, but no Ariel? I couldn't believe it. All because of things her father had done? That hardly seemed fair.

The Queen Mother just watched the shenanigans from her seat by the window. When it was her turn at cards though, she stepped forward to the coffee table, picked up her cards, and then proceeded to kill everyone.

No lie. She completely slayed, making pairings and trios and quattro's left and right. Dropping cards for Rummy against everyone seated. Every single one of us.

My mouth hung open. "How in the world?"

She shrugged. "I can almost guarantee the boys will fight with each other. One of the girls will start trash talking, and I can quietly sit here and pick up cards that I need."

I had only made three trios. We'd played with a double deck since there were so many of us, but it wasn't looking good for me. I still had eight cards in my hand. This was not going to end well.

She dropped her final card, and the game was over like that.

Ethan chuckled as he strolled in with a snack cart. "Ah, I missed Alexa handing all of your asses to you. Damn."

The Queen Mother grinned at him. "Oh, it was epic."

I'd asked Penny why her mother wasn't here, but she was on assignment, as was her brother. I still marveled at how it was a whole family business for them. Penny came from a long line of badasses, and she was one herself. I still couldn't believe that at one point she hadn't been a complete and total badass, but Ariel and Sebastian assured me they could tell the tales.

Roone wrapped an arm around me. "Ah, I'm sorry you lost baby."

"I prefer to see it as quietly learning the game."

He laughed. "Yup that sounds like you. Putting the positive spin on it." He laughed again and kissed my nose. "Now what are you really thinking?"

I lifted my brow. "Clearly you cheated. You're such a pompous ass. You can't stand to have a girl beat you."

He laughed. "Yeah, there's the girl I love."

I tried to squirm out of his hold, but he held on tight and then planted slobbery wet kisses on my cheeks. And I loved every moment of it. I was home. And for the first time in my life I had family. For now, the threats against us had been neutralized. We didn't have to run, we didn't have to hide. I spent my whole life running and hiding. It was nice to finally sit down and enjoy the family around me. I wish my father had lived to see this day. He would have been so proud.

Sebastian checked his phone. Lucas noticed right away and was on lookout for it. "What's wrong."

Sebastian shook his head. "Nothing. Winchester just asked his lawyer to put a deal together."

I frowned. "Are you going to give him one?"

Sebastian shrugged. "I'm going to do whatever it takes to put this to bed. But at the end of the day it won't be entirely up to me. It will also be up to the Council. But for now, we know one of the main conspirators is in jail. And he's willing to deal and give everyone up. We're finally safe. That's all I've ever wanted."

Lucas seemed unconvinced. "I'll believe it when I see it."

My oldest brother put his arms around us. "For now, let's enjoy it. Our father wanted us together and we are. And we are all safe and sound in our home, surrounded by friends. For a while, we can stop fighting."

I smiled up at him. "Even though the way we came together was crazy. I wouldn't change it. I love you both. It feels incredible to have a family."

Out of the corner of my eye, as everyone got up for snacks and stretched their legs, Ariel pranced around smiling at everyone as she quietly backed out.

She was leaving. And she didn't want to say goodbye.

*She was just going to go?*

Maybe it's better for her that way.

I considered this. I knew that I wouldn't want to have to endure goodbyes. Hell, I endured goodbyes my whole life. I got it; I got her. Her gaze met mine, and I gave her a soft smile. She nodded at me and blinked rapidly, and then she was out the door.

I excused myself from Sebastian and Lucas to pull Roone aside. "Ariel is trying to run, so if you have something to say to her, now would be the time."

He glanced toward the door and then around the room. Before muttering a curse under his breath, he said, "Woman, I love you."

I grinned at him and placed a quick kiss on his lips. "Good because I love you too. Now, I'm pretty sure you of all people would want to say goodbye to Ariel."

"And you would be right about that."

I watched him scoot out of the room quickly. He didn't alert anyone else though. He wanted a private moment, and I could respect that. Even though I would miss Ariel, I was so glad she was part of my family now. I fought hard for this. And I wasn't going to take any of it for granted.

---

### Ariel

"SO, you weren't going to say goodbye?"

I paused in the middle of the south hallway. I could try running faster, but he would likely catch me. So instead, I paused and turned around. Roone was coming from one of the secret tunnels. I'd taken three to get to this hallway, hoping to avoid anyone. But still he'd known exactly where I was going.

"Goodbyes make me crazy, so I figured I'd leave on a high note."

He shook his head. "That's bullshit. You don't think there is a whole team of people in there who wouldn't want to hug you and say goodbye?"

I blinked away the tears threatening to well in my eyes. "Don't you get it? Those guys in there, they are my family. I don't want to have to say goodbye to them. I just wanted to slip into the darkness and start a new chapter in my life."

He dug his hands into the front pockets of his jeans and rocked back on his heels. "I get it. It sucks, but I get it." It was only then that I realized he had a folder tucked under his arm. "What's that?"

"It's a present."

I frowned. "What do you mean a present? It looks like a folder."

He nodded and handed it over. I wasn't sure if I was supposed to open it or not. He spoke quickly. "So, I know that there's no chance of you staying. It was hard to accept. Even though in the early days of this assignment I didn't exactly want you in charge. But you're good at your job. Excellent, actually. And you've been there for me in a way that I don't think anybody else would have been."

I choked back the little sob threatening to escape my throat. "Shit, Ainsley, you're going to make a girl break into tears."

He suspiciously cleared his throat too. "Let's not have any of that. No uncharacteristic displays of emotion needed. But, um, that folder. That's someone who could use your help."

"Oh yeah?"

He nodded. "Jax Reynolds. He was a guard. He was a year behind Sebastian and me when we joined the military. Good guy. Strong. Smart. Works hard. His fiancée wasn't real thrilled about him being a guard. Not prestigious enough for her, even though he was on King Cassius's detail. So after Cassius died, he left. I guess they were good for a bit, but she had someone else and left him, dumped him out of the blue. As a rule, if you leave the guard, that's it, you're out. I think he's been drifting, a little lost, so since you're starting your own outfit and you'll need a team, I figured I'd help you get started."

I fingered the edge of the folder. "You didn't have to do this."

He shook his head. "I haven't done anything yet. He might not be too keen on working with you. He's a little distrustful after what happened. So anyway, you need a team, he needs a family. I think you two could help each other."

I nodded and opened the folder. Jesus Christ, the guy had awards and commendations up the ying-yang. His guard photo was tucked in the file. Good looking asshole. That was the last thing I needed, but if Roone was giving his name to me, it meant he was really good at his job. And Roone was right. I did need a team. "Thank you for this."

He shrugged. "You know, just looking out. You don't be a stranger, yeah?"

I nodded. "Yeah. It's not like I'm far. I'm basically just down the shore. Not even a half mile away."

"I know. It still won't feel the same though, so I want to make sure we don't lose track of you."

"I'll be here next week for game night."

"You better be. I have plans of kicking your ass."

My lips twitched. "Aw, I guess by now you're used to disappointment."

His chuckle was low when he stepped forward, and I knew immediately I was going to be hugged. I braced myself for it because hugging was not something I was usually down for. But somehow when Roone's big body wrapped around mine and he squeezed me tight, I felt happy. *Safe.*

And goddammit, one of those tears leaked out. I gave him a

tight squeeze back and then shoved at his chest. He didn't budge. I shoved again, ducked my head and swiped at the tear that had escaped. "Yeah, I'm out. Thank you for this."

He sniffed and then abruptly turned his head. "Don't be a stranger, yeah?"

"Never. I'll see you around, Ainsley."

"See you around, Ariel."

# EPILOGUE

*Ariel*

I WAS GOING to kill Roone if he'd sent me on a wild goose chase. I needed a team and I'd take any help I could get in building one. But I had my doubts.

Jax Reynolds was my best lead, and so far I found him... lacking. I'd been watching him for a week. So far all he had done was drank, skulk around, pretend to be some kind of investigator bodyguard type of person. How was this guy supposed to help me?

*Do you really have a choice?*

No. I didn't. Besides, Roone would never steer me wrong. Maybe he knew something about this guy that I didn't.

In the week I'd watched, Jax, so far he'd been tracking someone called Max Teller. I didn't know what Max Teller had done, or who wanted him tailed. But, at least I knew from watching, that Jax didn't suck at tailing people.

What I did know about Jax, was that he drank too much. It was one thing to be undercover, but he was taking undercover work to new heights. Max Teller had been at The Porkbelly pub every night. Which means Jax had been here. But instead of just sitting down and watching the guy, quietly skulking in a corner like every other normal PI, he posted up at the bar, and took drink after drink.

I rolled my eyes. What had I gotten myself into?

*You have no choice. Make your move.*

The fall from Royal Guard grace had been a steep one.

*Doesn't that apply to you, too?*

Indeed it did. Right now, I had backing to start my own shop. Thanks to Sebastian, and Penny, and Roone. Basically everyone I ever loved had put in all kinds of support, friend equity and contacts. I refused to take their money. I had money saved up, from working with the guard so long. I hadn't had to spend much of it. And I'd made good investments. So I had enough to invest in the perfect location.

And before I could even blink, I had a roster dozens of clients. All clamoring for my services. Some were easy enough that I could take care of myself, basic network security kind of things. I could manage all those clients. But, also on that list waiting for me, were clients that required actual physical presence. Which meant I needed to hire.

And Jax Reynolds was at the top of my list. Also on that list were Zia Barnes, a referral from Ethan, Tamsin Jacobs, a referral from Lucas, and Theo Denton, a referral from my bestie. With five, I could get started. Most jobs didn't require around the clock service, so I could do this. I would be fine.

I just prayed to god I didn't let everyone down. Ever since joining the guard, I never imagined that I would have to leave. That the palace would no longer be my home. But thanks to dear old dad, it wasn't my home, not anymore. So, I had to make the best of it. Which meant getting my ass in gear.

I followed Jax out of the pub. The guy he was tailing was some public school educated guy. Money running out of his nose. From my light look under the hood, Maxwell Teller had been a naughty boy, stealing corporate secrets. The company had hired Jax to get the proof, and catch Teller in the act. I didn't know why they didn't just fire him after they suspected him. But there might be more to it than I knew.

Chiswick at night was still quite pretty in the main part of the village. But as I drove away from the high street, it became more industrial. Warehouses, dark alleys, chain-link fences. Signs that practically screamed "Keep the fuck out, dodgy as hell in here."

Sure enough, Teller walked right on into dodge city. And Jax wasn't far behind him. Which meant ... double check my weapons time. I zipped up my leather jacket, pulled up the hoodie attachment, to cover my hair. And I kept to the shadows.

From behind a dumpster, I watched as Reynolds made his approach on Teller, who had been talking to someone else. I couldn't hear everything they were saying. But there was an exchange of words. And Reynolds' tone said everything. Pure sarcasm, derision. He loathed him. Or maybe it wasn't personal and that was just how he talked.

There was a minor scuffle where the man talking to Teller tried to run. When that didn't pan out. He attempted to hit Jax...which really didn't work. Next thing I knew,

Jax had the first guy patted down and tied to a chain-link fence. He was patting down Teller when trouble showed its face.

There had been another man. And currently he had the nozzle fo his gun pressed against Jax's neck.

I cursed under my breath. What, he didn't check to see if Teller had any friends or if the guy Teller was meeting with came with anyone? Rookie mistake.

"Roone, are you sure about this guy?" I muttered to myself. Either way, I couldn't let him get shot in the back of the head. I made my calculations on what it would take to disarm the new guy, in time with my problem. The barrel was at Jax' neck. Slowly I approached, staying in the shadows. Surprise would have to work for me and I hoped Jax was good at talking himself out of shit. I couldn't move my new team member before he was *actually* even on my team.

My heart hammered in my chest as I watched Jax turn slowly. And he was talking. I could hear him better now. "What's the matter? Performance anxiety? You don't want to do it now?"

What the hell was he doing?

The assailant muttered something under his breath that I couldn't hear. And then I stepped out of the shadows. My own gun at the shorter man's neck. I whipped my hoodie off. "Tsk, tsk. Don't you boys know how to play nice?"

Jax' gaze flickered to me. And then back to the guy between us. "Thanks for the assist, Red, but I'm good."

"Oh yeah? You call this good? He was about to blow your head off."

"I promise, Red, I had it completely under control."

"Oh, sure you did."

The guy between us whipped his head back and forth. "Oi, if you two wankers can stop bickering, that would be great."

"Oh, you're in a hurry for me to shoot you?" I asked.

Jax chuckled. "If I were you, I'd put your hands behind your back. Let the pretty lady zip tie you, leave you here. And wait patiently for the nick. I get the impression Red's handling some heavy weaponry there. She shoots, you're going to get blood all over my nice jacket. And I love this jacket."

I glowered at him. "You'll have to do the zip tying if you don't mind."

He rolled his eyes. "Sure, sure, leave me to do all the work."

"You know what? Next time, I will let the guy blow your head off."

Jax flashed a grin at me. And I could tell that like Roone, he had that charming, roguish kind of swagger that women probably loved. Just not *this* woman. "You know, I'm still waiting for you to say thank you."

He had his friend zip tied, and then secured him to a nearby pole. He slapped the guy on the cheek and grinned. "Don't move."

And then he turned his attention back to me. "Thank you. Now, do you mind me asking who the fuck you are?"

"I'm Ariel Scott. Roone Ainsley sent me. He's under the impression we could help each other."

Jax' brows lifted. And his gaze swept over me. I could see it, even in the dark. Mild interest. Curiosity. The hint of attraction. "Red, if you wanted a date, you probably should have approached me at the pub. But instead you tail me over here. You interrupt my business."

"Please, you were so busy drinking at the bar, you didn't even see me."

"Oh, you've been on my tail for a week. Of course I saw you."

"No way you saw me. You're making some educated guesses right now. And P.S., you shouldn't drink on a job."

"Ginger ale, love. You think I don't know any better?"

"God, I will kill Roone. Why did he send me to you?"

"I don't know, love. But whatever his reason, it's not happening. I don't need any help."

"Are you insane? Your life is in the shitter."

"Huh, says the redhead skulking in the shadows. Something tells me if you're looking for me to help you, your life's not much better off either."

He had a point there. "Roone said we could help each other, so I'm here."

"Yeah, Roone, good mate. But, even good mates make mistakes. I'm not interested in whatever you're selling."

He brushed past me. "Where are you going?"

He dug through the pocket of Max Teller. Who was coming to, and moaning. Jax fished out a flash drive. Then muttered, "Thanks, Max. Pleasure doing business with you. Do try and stay out of trouble now, won't you?"

And then he stood. Heading back towards the alley exit. "Wait. You haven't even heard my proposal."

"I don't need to hear it. I'm not interested."

What the hell? I followed after him. "You haven't even heard it yet. And, let's face it, you owe me now."

"No, I don't owe you."

"I didn't ask you to follow me. Like I said, you're not that good at it."

"Oh, I'm excellent at it."

He laughed. "I've seen you at the pub every day this week. Your hair. Either cover it, or dye it. I saw you outside my flat too."

"Oh really? Just at the pub and outside your flat? Where else did you see me?"

His brows furrowed. "Does it matter?"

I grinned. "Oh, you didn't see me everywhere. Interesting."

"Where else were you?" He crossed his arms.

"Teller's office. I was one of the security guards. I also managed to get in as a day temp. I guess you missed that one. I knew you were tailing him, so I figured to tail you, it'd be easier to get in closer to Teller."

He lifted one brow then. Assessed me again more shrewdly. "What day?"

I shrugged. "Tuesday last week."

"I knew it. I saw you with the sandwich cart."

I grinned at him. "Yeah, but you didn't *recognize* me, did you?"

"You looked familiar."

"Did I? Or did you just want to bang me. Don't think I didn't notice you staring at my ass."

He shrugged. "I'm a bloke. I'm born to look. Besides, redheads aren't my type."

"Oh, overbearing roguish assholes, not my type either. I need your help. And you're going to give it to me."

He chuckled low then, the sound was rich, deep, mellow. "Oh yeah? What makes you say that?"

"Because you help me, I can get you the one thing that you want?"

The glower turned more into a sneer then. "You don't know what I want."

"Oh, but I do. You want back in the Royal Guard. And I can give that to you."

WANT MORE? Find out what happens next...Read Accidental Heiress NOW!

# THANK YOU

Thank you for reading TEASING THE PRINCESS! I hope you enjoyed this installment from the Royals United Series.

Find out what happens in the next book...Read Accidental Heiress...

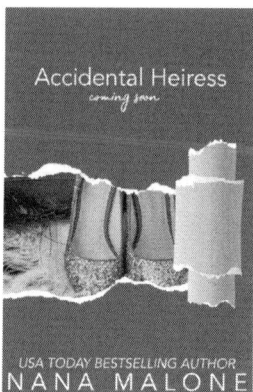

All I ever wanted was **family**. But one mistake **cost me everything** I've ever worked for.

To get it all back, I'll have to return home and **protect the most stubborn woman** on the face of the planet. To do that effectively, I'll need to go **undercover** as...**a Manny**.

I didn't mean to **fall for her or the kid**. I really should have known better. When you get this close, it's easy to get burned. But **I'll do anything to protect them**, even if it costs me everything...again.

Pre-Order ACCIDENTAL HEIRESS Now>

Sign up for my newsletter to get new release alerts, exclusive bonus scenes and more: http://nanamaloneromance.net/newsletterlanding

# NANA MALONE READING LIST

Looking for a few Good Books? Look no Further

### *FREE*
*Sexy in Stilettos*
*Game Set Match*
Bryce
*Shameless*

### *Royals*
### *Royals Undercover*

*Cheeky Royal*
*Cheeky King*

### *Royals Undone*
*Royal Bastard*
*Bastard Prince*

### *Royals United*

*Royal Tease*
*Teasing the Princess*

### *Royal Elite*
*Accidental Heiress*
*Royal Protection*
*The Bodyguard Dilema*

### *The Donovans Series*
*Come Home Again (Nate & Delilah)*
*Love Reality (Ryan & Mia)*
*Race For Love (Derek & Kisima)*
*Love in Plain Sight (Dylan and Serafina)*
*Eye of the Beholder – (Logan & Jezzie)*
*Love Struck (Zephyr & Malia)*

### *London Billionaires Standalones*
*Mr. Trouble (Jarred & Kinsley)*
*Mr. Big (Zach & Emma)*
*Mr. Dirty(Nathan & Sophie)*

### *The Shameless World*

### *Shameless*
*Shameless*
*Shameful*
*Unashamed*

*Force*
*Enforce*

*Deep*

*Deeper*

*Before Sin*
*Sin*
*Sinful*

## *The Player*
Bryce

Dax

Echo

Fox

Ransom

Gage

## *The In Stilettos Series*
*Sexy in Stilettos (Alec & Jaya)*
*Sultry in Stilettos (Beckett & Ricca)*
*Sassy in Stilettos (Caleb & Micha)*
*Strollers & Stilettos (Alec & Jaya & Alexa)*
*Seductive in Stilettos (Shane & Tristia)*
*Stunning in Stilettos (Bryan & Kyra)*

~~~

## *In Stilettos Spin off*
*Tempting in Stilettos (Serena & Tyson)*
*Teasing in Stilettos (Cara & Tate)*
*Tantalizing in Stilettos (Jaggar & Griffin)*

## *The Chase Brothers Series*
*London Bound (Alexi & Abbie)*
*London Calling (Xander & Imani)*

## *Love Match Series*

*Game Set Match (Jason & Izzy)
Mismatch (Eli & Jessica)

### Temptation Series
Corporate Affairs
Exposed
The Flirtation

### The Protectors Series (Superhero Romance)
*Betrayed a Reluctant Protector Prequel
Reluctant Protector (Cassie & Seth)
Forsaken Protector (Symone & Garrett)
Wounded Protector (Jansen & Lisa)

### The Hit & Run Bride Contemporary Romance Series
Hit & Run Bride (Liam & Becca)
Hit & Miss Groom (Alex & Vanessa)
Hit the Billionaire Jackpot (Jenna & Jacob)

**Don't want to miss a single release? Click here!**

## ABOUT NANA MALONE

USA Today Best Seller, Nana Malone's love of all things romance and adventure started with a tattered romantic suspense she "borrowed" from her cousin.

It was a sultry summer afternoon in Ghana, and Nana was a precocious thirteen. She's been in love with kick butt heroines ever since. With her overactive imagination, and channeling her inner Buffy, it was only a matter a time before she started creating her own characters.

Now she writes about sexy royals and smokin' hot bodyguards when she's not hiding her tiara from Kidlet, chasing a puppy who refuses to shake without a treat, or begging her husband to listen to her latest hair-brained idea.

Printed in Poland
by Amazon Fulfillment
Poland Sp. z o.o., Wrocław